The Unexpected Consequences of Iron Overload

EDITION 2

An awareness raiser for
Haemochromatosis

James Minter

MINTER PUBLISHING LIMITED

MINTER PUBLISHING LIMITED

Minter Publishing Limited (MPL)
4 Lauradale, Bracknell RG12 7DT

Edition 1 - Copyright © James Minter 2011-2014
Edition 2 - Copyright © James Minter 2016

James Minter has asserted his rights under the Copyright,
Design and Patents Act, 1988 to be the author of this work

Edition 1 – ISBN-13:1479392421
Edition 2 – ISBN 9781910727416

Cover Illustrations copyright © Paul Shinn

Printed and bound in Great Britain by Ingram Spark,
Milton Keynes

Over 40 four and five star reviews:

Minter manages to do it again, blending simple everyday life with the most extreme and incredulous events, all combined to produce another piece of humoristic brilliance.
J.J Collins

An unexpectedly good read... Although ... aimed at us with the condition, I'd highly recommend it to anyone who likes their spy thrillers with their tongue firmly in their cheek.
Peter Morgan

I love James Minter's sense of humour and his choice of characters in this fast London based comedy. Hilarious spy thriller with a serious edge.
June Finnigan

Light-hearted, gripping, and all for a good cause!!
L. Riddell

... vintage Minter in the combination of the catastrophic with the everyday. The humour of the characters and the situations keeps the whole thing frothing.
Tony Sims

You don't have to have Haemochromatosis to enjoy this book..., it's witty and gives the funny ups and downs to having Hereditary Haemochromatosis.
A. Valentine

This is a novel full of humour with a fascinating storyline of romance, spies and totally crazy events.
Nails

DEDICATION

To everyone diagnosed with the Haemochromatosis condition, and for all those who have the condition but are yet to know. There is always a smile in every situation, no matter how bad it seems at the time. I hope this book brings you that smile.

FOREWORD

In her foreword to the first edition of this book, the founder of The Haemochromatosis Society Janet Fernau, MBE, wrote " … When James told me about writing this book I was pleased, excited and curious. Pleased in that it will generate funds for the society; excited because promoting the book will promote GH; and curious as to how he was going to approach it. James chose humour as his approach which particularly appeals to me. Unlike other ways to wind down at the end of the day, it's free, has no side effects and does you the power of good. His spoof thriller I believe hits the spot from all angles."

I could not agree more.

The novel has raised funds for The Haemochromatosis Society and awareness of iron overload. Iron overload does kill, and awareness of the condition can prevent that. By purchasing the book you are contributing to that awareness. I encourage you to tell your friends and family about iron overload — and about this entertaining author. You can learn more about the seriousness of iron overload at www.haemochromatosis.org.uk.

David Head MBA
Chief Executive
The Haemochromatosis Society; Charity No. 1001307

PREFACE

For those of you who don't know *Iron Overload* or, more correctly, Haemochromatosis, it is usually an hereditary genetic condition where the body continues to absorb iron from one's diet even though it has sufficient stores to meet the body's needs. Normally the absorption of iron is a good thing. We need around 18 milligrams per day (this varies a lot by age and gender). Actually iron absorption is an essential function of the body. Without these very small amounts of iron our blood wouldn't be blood and we wouldn't be … Quite literally, we wouldn't be; we couldn't live. Iron is found in all cells and, more importantly, is used in the production of red blood cells. And of course, red blood cells carry oxygenated blood to muscles, so enabling us to move, and much more besides.

The iron absorption process is regulated by a gene, but for around 1 in 300 people the regulating gene fails. The iron extracted from our diet—from foods like liver, greens, red meat, shell fish, sardines etc.—is processed by our amazingly clever body and stored in our liver and bone marrow for later use in the production of red blood cells. Since red blood cells last on average 120 days we have a continuous need for new red blood cells, and so for iron. All sounds great. However, as a population we tend to eat more iron rich foods than we require. For those whose absorption ceasing gene fails, they continue to store more iron than they might averagely use. Most of us don't bleed too often—a nick when shaving hardly counts. Women, on the other hand, do regularly have a need to replace blood following their monthly menstruation, which is why iron overload is less of an issue in the female population. But for men and older women they just keep accumulating more and more iron in the body. Being so extremely clever the body finds more and more places to hide the excess iron in—for example, the liver, heart, and pancreas. Our bodies become iron rich.

It's only in the last few years we have become aware of this condition as medical science, in particular the understanding of genes and their role in human development, has progressed. Additionally the fact that humans are living longer and are better fed means the accumulation of iron is greater than ever before. However, this is not a new phenomenon but only one that is coming to our attention more and more.

Iron in the body is measured by ferritin levels in the blood. Ferritin is a protein found inside cells that stores iron for later use by your body. A ferritin test indirectly measures the amount of iron in your blood. The amount of ferritin in your blood (serum ferritin level) is directly related to the amount of iron stored in your body. The target range for normal healthy adults varies from 20 to 200, but generally 50 is thought to be ideal.

I was diagnosed in 2004 at which time I had a ferritin level in excess of 1390. High yes; unexpectedly high yes; a danger to my health yes; a long term problem to my health if left untreated—yes, very much so. However, I am thankful for the fact that since the age of 21 I'd been a regular blood donor, giving a total of 25 pints over the years. Although I wasn't aware of it at the time it was this act of generosity which kept me from experiencing any (to date) long term damage as a result of Haemochromatosis. Without the voluntary donations my ferritin level would have been closer to 3000 prior to discovery. An eye watering and without doubt very serious, if not deadly, amount.

My initial treatment was to give 26 pints of blood in as many weeks. Understandably the effect on my ferritin level was dramatic, reducing it down to the 50 ng/ml as desired. Since then I've regularly had bloodletting—around 3 sessions per year—to maintain that level. It's something that will continue for the foreseeable future. Getting to where I am today—I'm 64 years of age—has been an interesting, eventful, startling, surprising, funny, extraordinary and adverb rich journey.

An explanation of iron overload is not the purpose of this book. Nor is the purpose to help those with the condition understand what has been or is happening to them over their lifetime. For Jimmy, the main character, living with iron overload has had many unexpected consequences. The purpose of this book is to share his fictional journey with you, to make you chuckle and, most importantly, to raise much needed funds to help with awareness raising and research into this condition so it can be better understood, diagnosed, treated and even corrected. Both my parents and a sister succumbed to the condition. They died through ignorance – I want to help stop this.

If you are a medically trained person reading this please don't shout at the pages or say what an idiot this guy is, or what rubbish he is talking. Okay, it may not be a sophisticated explanation but as my dad used to say *it's good enough for colliery work*.

Before we embark on the journey I need to remind

you of some school-boy science. This is stuff you've learnt and no doubt forgotten. Maybe I speak for myself and perhaps you are better able to retain this material than me but it won't hurt to reiterate it here. The subject is iron: the properties of iron and in particular magnetism and electricity.

A major property of iron is it's very hard. If in doubt try hitting a friend or colleague with an iron bar. They won't remain a friend or colleague for long! Where iron is present it makes the item it is found in, very hard also. A second property is that iron, exposed to moist airy conditions, will rust. Rust is the colloquial name for a very common compound, iron oxide. Iron oxide is visible on old, unkempt cars as the brownie red colour often seen around wheel arches and sills. Third, iron is an extremely good conductor of electricity. And fourth, iron can be magnetised very easily. Iron is magnetised by using an existing magnet to influence the non-magnetised iron until the groups of atoms or domains line up in the same direction to form a magnet. Magnetism is an invisible force which can push and pull through air and some materials such as paper and plastic. Once magnetised, iron retains this condition, and with very little persuasion will remain so indefinitely. Magnets are numerous and widespread in the home, including anything with an electric motor like a vacuum cleaner, electric drill or food processor, door entry systems, hi-fi speakers, older television sets and the like.

Magnets themselves are characterised by a north pole and south pole—a lot like the earth. A characteristic property of the area around the magnet is its force field, radiating out from the poles. Another distinguishing feature is that when two magnets attract, they only attract when the north pole of one magnet is beside the south pole of another, or vice versa. Similarly, when two magnets are placed north to north, or south to south, they repel each other.

Furthermore, if a magnet is moved inside a few turns of copper wire it will generate an electrical current in the copper wire. Anything joined to the copper wire, like a light bulb, will glow. Alternatively if a magnet is placed inside a copper coil and a voltage is applied to the coil, an unrestrained magnet will shoot out at high velocity. By restraining the magnet within the coil so it's free to rotate the magnet will be set in motion. This is the principle upon which electrical motors are based.

Now that wasn't too difficult. These properties are worth remembering when reading the book and will aid your understanding and enjoyment.

Of course I'm a fiction writer – I make stuff up, but the underlying symptoms Jimmy experiences are true, just maybe their manifestation is slightly exaggerated. I'll let you be the judge.

And finally, please tell family and friends about the condition. Use this book as an ice-breaker. Don't let what happened to my family happen to yours. Haemochromatosis is deadly, and induces a lot of unnecessary suffering on route to the grave.

CONTENTS

ACKNOWLEDGMENTS

Like all projects of this type there are always a number of indispensable people involved. Maggie, my wife is definitely one. I always write my first draft long hand. She types my script from dictation—I read it aloud to her, otherwise she would have no chance of deciphering my scrawl. Of course Marmite toast plays a big part in keeping us sustained, with coffee and the odd glass of wine to boot—to them I owe a debt of gratitude.

Paul and Louise, my children, offer their critical opinions—but that's what children do. It helps keep me on track.

Lisa, my daughter-in-law, is an excellent beta reader with a great eye for detail. And finally Paul Shinn for his cover illustration. The old adage *never judge a book by its cover* doesn't, in my opinion, hold true. The cover is the first thing people see — even for an eBook—and prompts the browser to pick it up for closer inspection. I believe Paul captures the spirit of the story to the letter. www.paulshinndraws.com

CHAPTER 1

32 RED

Sparks flew as the lighting tower buckled. The mains electricity cable pulled taut, acting as a temporary stay until capitulating under the strain. The tower gained momentum, falling in the direction of a table of seated delegates. Up to that point everyone was focused on the presentation—a simultaneous worldwide launch of Microsoft's Windows™ computer operating system software. Bill Gates and Steve Bulmer in the US were doing a double-act via satellite to 50 major venues worldwide.

Jimmy, sat at a second table reserved for Zylog staff and adjacent to the one directly in the path of the falling tower, was alerted by the first burst of sparks as a trailing cable came into contact with the steel structure. He jumped to his feet, yelling.

Like many software launch parties of the 1980's loud music, laser lights, tracking spots and copious amounts of animated graphics and video footage punctuated proceedings. Indoor fireworks were common, and the shower of sparks could easily have passed for some. Jimmy sensed this was different. The sudden high voltage discharge went through him like a kick in the chest. He reeled around as he tried to work out what had happened.

Drawn towards the falling tower, something needed doing. He didn't have a plan, he just knew that "his" Barbara—she didn't know yet of his love intentions—was in danger; in the direct line of descent, and that he must do something. The act of him jumping up alerted others around his table to what was happening. Panic set in; soon pushing and shoving followed as they tried to make good their escape. His eyes were fixed on the tower.

The noise and razzmatazz of the event didn't abate. The stack of blaring loudspeakers close by, drowned out the cracking and shouting. The table of people sitting in the tower's path failed to hear. Focused on the presentation, they appeared totally unaware of the impending disaster. Jimmy had no time for thinking; he was desperate. By now he'd arrived at the structure's base. In a reflex action he lifted his arms aloft, hoping to somehow steady it, much like a child grasping for a pile of falling wooden bricks. He never made actual contact with the steel tubing, but in raising his arms he felt a surge; a connection between himself and the metal. It wasn't an electrical shock, nor did it hurt or burn, he was just attracted to it. The force he emitted was strong enough to change the tower's trajectory away from the table of unsuspecting event goers. The tower completed its journey to the ground, and now lay safe in a heap of tangled debris.

The main ballroom of The Grosvenor House Hotel, Park Lane, London was filled to capacity for this significant occasion. Microsoft didn't do things by half and the launch budget was well serviced. At this time the emerging Personal Computer commanded huge attention from the IT industry, trade press and even national media. Microsoft pulled out all the stops, aware of how significant Windows would become. Their PR machine worked overtime across the world. The satellite links of the live TV broadcast gave it high visibility, generating interest and viewers from many diverse groups. Local camera crews were present, capturing reactions to product demonstrations, and looking for sound bites from well-known industry pundits.

News reporters and camera operators seem to have a sixth sense. All eyes and cameras were on the main 70 foot wide screen where Gates and Bulmer's performance was in full flight. The flash of the sparks off to the left went unnoticed by many but caught the attention of one BBC cameraman. From his position high in the gallery at the rear of the ballroom he had an uninterrupted view. Without hesitation he panned left and zoomed in to capture the unfolding drama. Training his camera onto the collapsing tower, even with a long focal length lens, in the dark it was difficult to see what was happening. He could make out movement; delegates scattering, and one person heading towards the tower, contrary to everyone else. Zooming compresses the depth of field so the absolute distance between objects is difficult to calculate. In the near darkness this is even tougher. It wasn't clear if the figure, seen raising his arms, actually connected with the tower or not. The net effect, caught on film, was of the tower shifting violently from its initial line of descent, ending up instead crashing to the ground out of harm's way.

Many of the event goers were unaware of what had happened. The immediate vicinity was made safe while the show continued. The noise, distraction and confusion made it difficult to say what actually happened. It was all over in a few seconds. Jimmy was left, like everyone else, not really knowing what had occurred or what he'd done. The only thing for certain was he'd saved eight people, and in particular his Barbara, from serious injury or worse.

Several journalists tracked him down, all wanting to get his take on what happened. He was subject to a barrage of questions but had no real answers. He didn't know the details himself. It was one of those spontaneous moments where actions come before thoughts; when stopping to think before doing would lead to untold tragedy.

He struggled to make sense of what occurred. He wasn't being evasive, misleading or obtuse, he just didn't know what to say. Personally he reflected on events but failed to make head nor tail of them. He knew what he'd felt—the surge of energy in response to the electrical cables snapping, followed by a strong attraction, sufficient for him to displace the tower of steel.

This wasn't the first time he'd experienced something like this. All through his youth he'd felt it, but more recently the sensations appeared stronger. He wasn't sure if he was more aware now or if the force was more powerful. But after this incident it seemed he could control it by some means. Intrigued, he wanted to know how his ability to control objects worked.

4

* * * * *

At the time Jimmy was living in Maidenhead. After the formal part of the Windows launch, Microsoft held the inevitable party. 3,000 geeks, journalists, industry bosses, their PA's and marketing sorts from major corporates, software vendors and public sector bodies were all determined to make the most of the free bar, food and entertainment in the name of hospitality. Microsoft lavished their generosity. Jimmy was sure the booze would be his downfall.

'Jimmy—another pint?'

'Pace …'

'Pace off yourself, get this Guinness down you before it gets warm.' Rob wasn't taking no for an answer.

'Look, it's only half five. I'll be ratted by six if I'm not careful.' He took the pint.

'Where are you staying tonight?' Rob took a large swig of his beer.

'Compared to this,' Jimmy swung his arm in an inclusive gesture, 'some dive not far from Paddington, the Crown, at Lancaster Gate. The Grosvenor's full, and anyway Mike wouldn't sign off my expenses for here.'

'You never know, you might get lucky. Your Barbara's here from sales.' Rob looked directly into Jimmy's eyes, 'I've seen you watching her in the office. You remember last week, when she dropped her coffee and had to bend down to wipe it up.'

Bugger, busted, he thought. 'You saw me!' He felt his cheeks redden. 'You can hardly blame me. She's all woman.' Jimmy drank at his pint to try and hide his

5

embarrassment.

'And a very fine one too.' Rob's face was unequivocal.

'Rob, you're a married man. Leave the lechery to me.'

'Look, there's no harm in window shopping,' Rob took a mouthful of Guinness,' provided it's just looking.' He drained his glass, wiping the froth off his top lip. 'Gosh, that's good. I need another.' Pivoting on his heels, Rob set off across the crowded room towards the free bar where it was at least four people deep waiting to be served.

Jimmy sat pondering the events of earlier, trying to make sense of what had happened. Lost in his thoughts, he was oblivious to the person standing beside him.

'Uhumm …'

He didn't react.

'Uhumm …' Barbara raised her voice. Still nothing. 'What does a girl have to do to get noticed?' She tapped his ankle with her foot.

'Oh, what? He looked up. 'Sorry.' Jimmy responded without really seeing who it was. After a couple of seconds the penny dropped. 'Barbara, oh hi it's you! Yeah, sorry, miles away. What are you doing here?'

She tilted he head to one side.

'No, I know what you're doing here, but what I meant … oh nothing. Have you got a drink?'

She rattled the ice in her glass as she stooped to sit down. In doing so her hand brushed his knee. He turned towards her. She considered him; his dark brown pools for eyes, his sallow Mediterranean skin, his abundant almost black hair, and his obvious muscular physique. She was besotted, and had been for a long time, but chose not to show it. After all, she didn't want to appear too eager. *Men make the running, women like to be chased. Old fashioned maybe—but it works for me,* she thought.

Jimmy's thoughts still preoccupied him, and he failed to notice she'd held her gaze longer than was ladylike.

* * * * *

'Hey you two.' Rob was back. 'Fancy losing some money on roulette? Look in your welcome packs—there's a voucher for £50 of chips. I'll meet you at the table.' No sooner had he arrived than he was gone with Jimmy and Barbara in pursuit.

'I've never done this before,' Barbara giggled, placing a red chip on the seven. The ball bounced from pocket to pocket of the roulette wheel, eventually landing on fifteen. 'Oh well—next time.'

Jimmy fared no better; his lucky three wasn't so lucky after all. The table was crowded, and to place their bets they had to stretch. At the end of each spin there was a swap around of people; those who lost moved away while budding hopefuls moved closer.

'What number are you going for this time?' Jimmy asked.

'I'm going to stick to seven. You?' Barb had to shout over the noise of the crowd.

'Quick, get your chips down,' Jimmy pointed to the table,' she's about to spin the wheel.'

Barbara bent forward to place her chips. In the crush her elbow was knocked and she dropped two onto the seven square.

Jimmy saw. 'Go on, get it back …'

'Too late. Anyway it's only pretend money; it's just for a bit of fun.'

'You think so? Look there.' Jimmy pointed to a large poster of a Caribbean cruise ship. 'You cannot win money but the person with the most chips by the end of the evening wins a two week cruise.'

Barb looked back at the roulette table. Everyone was jostling and pushing around her. Caught up in the swirl, she ended up facing Jimmy. Her ample bosom squashed against his chest; her face was within an inch of his. His nostrils were filled with her perfume, and combined with the closeness and warmth of her body he reacted with an anatomical change she felt against her thigh. Neither said a thing. It was an awkward moment. He was in turmoil; should he lean in to kiss her—he so wanted to—or should he do the gentlemanly thing of moving away and apologising? He needed to do something quickly, however his dilemma was short lived. Rob appeared behind them.

'How's it going? You won anything yet?'

'Oh, hi Rob. Barb's had a couple of goes but nothing. What about you?'

'I want that cruise. My misses would love it. Her mum would take the kids and we could have a romantic holiday, like a kind of second honeymoon.'

Barb took his comment as a challenge. 'Right Rob, you're on.' I want it, and I'm going to get it. Jimmy, give me your chips, I'm feeling lucky.'

She had no idea what she was doing but played eight chips on a variety of numbers, colours and lines. The croupier cleared them away in one brisk movement.

'If it's that easy we'd all be millionaires.' Jimmy offered. He was keen for her to win since they were his chips so she'd have to take him with her.

'Okay Barb—not so rash. Just put one chip on your lucky seven. It must come up sooner or later.'

'Let's hope it's not later. I've only nine chips left.' Barb held out her palm.

'Go on, play, she's about to spin.' Jimmy moved towards the table to get closer to the roulette wheel. It occurred to him, if he managed to deflect a falling steel lighting tower, getting the ball to stop in pocket seven— or any other pocket—would be a doddle. He concentrated hard, watching the ball interact with the spinning wheel, and the way it bounced from pocket to pocket with each counter revolution. Knowing the mahogany wheel pivoted on a steel pin running in metal bearings, he reasoned by altering the spin speed, he could control the outcome.

Moving tight in, he lifted his arms to see the effects it had. He hoped by changing the shape of his limbs he'd alter the strength of his magnetic field or whatever this force was; and the energy would allow him to stop the ball where he wanted.

The guy next to him was very animated and pushed him accidentally. Jimmy fell forwards. He had no choice but to steady himself by grabbing for the table. The croupier stared at him.

'No more bets please.' Her glare cut into him.

He regained his balance, and without warning Barb planted him a big kiss.

'We won,' she shouted, beaming and pointing to the roulette wheel. In the confusion the ball had stopped on seven. She collected her winnings. 'Okay, what next?' She was keen to bet again.

Jimmy lifted his hand to his mouth and spoke in hushed tones, 'Look, I'm not sure what happened then. Let's just watch the next spin. I need to understand how or even if I did that.'

'What do you mean, if you did that?' Her brow creased.

'You know.' He hesitated. 'My powers, remember, this afternoon, the tower. Do I have to spell it out?

'Yes you do, I've no idea what you're talking about.' She raised an eyebrow. 'Do you think you can somehow control the ball? Jimmy Kavanagh, are you serious?' She tried to read his face. 'But that's cheating.' She curled her lip and broke into a broad smile. 'Go on then, show me.'

'Okay keep it down. Now don't play—just watch. What pocket do you want the ball to stop in?'

'Seven, of course.'

'No, not seven. If it keeps going into the same pocket the croupier will get suspicious.'

'Okay—fifteen then.'

The wheel was set spinning and the ball set loose. Jimmy focused on the wheel, counting the number of times the ball bounced between pockets before it stopped. It landed in 28.

'That's not fifteen.' Barb sounded disappointed.

'Look, I'm just trying to understand how it works. Right—just watch again.'

'Come on, just one chip. My last win paid out 35. We've loads now.'

Jimmy liked the sound of *we've loads*. 'Go on then, but put it on black, not fifteen. You'll still win but not anywhere near as much.'

The croupier set the wheel in motion, followed by the ball counter clockwise. Jimmy counted the bounces. Suddenly he leant right in, throwing his arms forward. The wheel slowed dramatically as the drag on the bearing intensified. Other punters close by stared at him in a *what the hell are you doing?* sort of way. Worst of all, the croupier noticed and glared at him once more as if to say *I'm watching you*.

Barbara was oblivious to all this, focused only on her winnings. 'What, only a measly two chips for black? How are we going to win our cruise like that?'

Jimmy didn't pick up on her remarks. He was too busy pretending to be drunk. He slung his arms around Barb's neck.

'Oi, what's wrong with you?'

'Show me the way to go home … I'm tired and I want to go to bed.' His singing faded as he leant hard onto Barb.

'Jimmy Kavanagh, all you men are useless, just when we were winning.' Barb grabbed his arm, scooped up her chips and dragged him back towards the seating area in the bar.

* * * * *

She was both annoyed and concerned. 'You've only had a couple of drinks.'

'Shush … there's nothing wrong with me. Look, these croupiers are trained to spot cheating. Okay it might only be for fun but she's watching me like a hawk. I've been clocked twice at least. You should have seen her. I pretended to be drunk to throw her off the scent. We'll give it half an hour and go back again.'

'Well you had me fooled.' Her face softened. She took his arm and placed it around her shoulder, bringing her face up to meet his. Their lips touched. He moved his other arm onto her back and pulled her towards him. They locked in an embrace, oblivious to where they were.

'Come on you two, get a room.' Rob slipped onto the seat beside them. 'I thought you were going to win a cruise. Lost the lot, have you?'

'Not you again.' They both stared at him. 'Look mate, can't you see we're a bit busy?' Jimmy nodded at him to go away.

'So you've lost the lot then?' Rob didn't take the hint.

'No, we're up actually. We just needed a break.' Barb tapped at her chips. 'We're going to win. You just watch us. Jimmy's got this plan. He can …'

'No, Barb, don't tell him. He's the competition, don't forget. … So how's it going for you, Rob?'

'Won a couple on the black and a three way so I'm up. Just needed a fag and beer. I'll be back at the table later.' He wandered off.

'We need a plan,' Jimmy said, turning to Barb.

Her eyes was transfixed on him. 'What is it?'

'I've waited for this moment for so long. Jimmy, I think I love ...'

He raised his fingers to her mouth. 'Not now, we need to win a cruise first.'

'But Jimmy.'

'Shhh darling,' he said without thinking. 'Look, we need a plan if we're going to beat the croupier.'

They both sat back, lost in thought. Jimmy was first to speak.

'I've got to get close enough to the wheel to be able to slow it down without having to make exaggerated movements. Nor can you keep betting on the same numbers. Also we'd better vary the amount of winnings. Sometimes single numbers, other times black or red, others a three-way.'

'A three way?'

'Yeah, you, me and Rob.'

Her eyebrows shot up into her hairline.

'Just joking. Take a look when you go back to the table. The numbers are divided into groups of rows and columns. A three way is when you bet on a group. And I think we ought to split up. You go to the far end of the table and I'll be around the wheel. I've no idea how close I need to be. I'll just have to practise; a bit of trial and error. So for the first half dozen spins just do colours and three-ways with single chips. Then we'll take a break and meet back here.'

She grabbed his arm. 'I've never done anything like this. It's so exciting.' She leant up and kissed him hard. He stroked her hair.

'We need to concentrate on the prize right now or there'll be no cruise.' He walked away to be swallowed up by the sea of people.

'You'll be a winner tonight, JK. Trust me.' Her face changed to a broad smile, but her words were lost in the commotion. They never reached his ears.

*　*　*　*　*

Jimmy made it to the table first. He stood behind the croupier, one person deep. He had no idea if he could influence the wheel from where he was, but he concentrated on 28. The croupier spun the wheel and released the ball. It did two revolutions before bouncing into the first cup.

Now concentrate, he told himself. '28, 28, 28,' he kept repeating under his breath.

Barb wormed her way to the front to bet and so Jimmy could see which numbers she'd placed her chips on. Scanning the faces across from her, he wasn't visible. All the while she was being jostled by other players betting, losing, winning, coming and going. She placed a single chip on red. Crossing her fingers, she was anxious. She still couldn't see him.

For him the crowds were just as boisterous. The free bar was taking its toll. Jimmy tried to keep behind the croupier while maintaining his line of sight on the table, the wheel, and Barbara. He struggled to keep his balance as the crowd heaved around him.

'No more bets please.'

'Concentrate. Come on 28. You can do it.'

'It's only a bit of fun, mate. Don't take it so serious.' The guy standing next to him heard his mutterings. 'You sound like your life depends on it.'

Jimmy smiled. 'No, you're right. I just hate to lose.' The chap never heard as he was pushed on by the churning revellers.

'28, black,' called out the croupier.

'Yes.' Jimmy punched the air. Standing on tiptoe, he scanned the faces opposite. Barb spotted him and smiled.

'We won,' he mouthed in her direction.

She cocked her ear. Frown lines appeared on her brow. He said it again.

'Place your bets please.'

'We didn't … did we?' She was confused.

'Quick, quick, put a chip down.'

She could see he lips moving but had no idea what he was saying. She strained to hear. He gesticulated while mouthing, 'Put a bet on.'

She shrugged. 'I've no idea.' Muttering to herself, she placed a chip on red. He saw. The ball was now starting to bounce from pocket to pocket. He had little time.

'Focus, focus, focus. Yes.' It landed on 7 red.

Barb saw and was now ecstatic. She left her winning chip and stake on the red. Jimmy concentrated, this time stopping the ball on 5.

The croupier pushed 4 chips in her direction. She placed all four back on red.

'No more bets please.'

Jimmy did his thing and stopped the ball in 30

red. Barb took her eight chips, put seven on red and one on 16 red. He saw. The ball was set spinning. She bit at her bottom lip as she watched the ball bounce randomly around the wheel.

'16 red,' the croupier confirmed.

Barb couldn't contain herself—almost hysterical she squeaked, 'I've won,' to nobody in particular. As there were so many people at the table it took the croupier several minutes to sort out winnings. Barb stacked her chips into neat piles of ten. She piled up three stacks and dropped two of them into her handbag. This time she was betting on black and 20, placing ten and two chips respectively.

'No more bets please.'

She looked up to check in on Jimmy. He wasn't visible. She had a twinge of panic.

Hearing *20 black* from the croupier, she soon forgot her angst.

What the heck? She thought, and took her 90 chips plus the twenty from her handbag and placed the lot on her age. *After all, my thirty second year has been a good one for me,* she thought. The number was obscured by her stacks of chips. The croupier gawped, checking her out as if to say *what's your game?* Barb just smiled back, trying to look innocent.

The ball was set in motion. Others around the table noticed the large bet. Jimmy's head reappeared opposite. He saw the table and did a double take. His face registered fear. Ashen, his concentration was now in overdrive. The ball bounced, its familiar *ting* audible despite the noise of the raucous partygoers.

Some bloke muscled in in front of Barbara, obscuring her view. Without hesitation she elbowed him aside.

'Hey blondie, what's your game?' In his drunken state he leant on her, trying to grope her bum.

She didn't hear nor care. She got back to the front just in time.

'32 red.'

All decorum went out of the window as Barb's shrieks penetrated the air. She couldn't nor didn't contain herself; her joy was overwhelming. The croupier started the long job of working out her winnings, before handing over three one thousand pound chips, a five hundred pound chip and an assortment of hundreds and tens; a total of 3,960's worth. Close to four grand! Excitement prevailed; she couldn't play anymore. She had to find Jimmy.

'Well who's a lucky girl then?' The drunk asked.

'I was blondie just now. You've changed your tune. Just sod off, won't you!' Turning to leave, she managed to place a stiletto on his foot, bringing her full weight to bear. In her wake she left a very hurt, angry young man. She returned to the bar area; Jimmy appeared carrying champagne.

'We did it.' She took a glass. Before she had time to raise it to her lips he planted a kiss on them. Wrapping her arms around him, she responding with her own. The kiss ceased being a playful embrace and became a passionate prelude to lovemaking. Lost in the moment they held position, unaware of the rest of the revellers. Surfacing, a few minutes later they came back into the room.

'Oh Jimmy.' She couldn't manage any more, her feelings were so heightened. Their eyes locked.

'So how did we do?' He broke the spell.

She said nothing; the faraway look in her eyes said it all. She'd gone to where love takes you; while he was being more pragmatic.

'Are we going on that cruise or not?' Jimmy needed to know.

*   *   *   *   *

'Hi guys. How'd you two get on?' Rob held out his hands. 'Look at this lot.' He dove into his pockets to retrieve more chips.

'How much have you got?' Barb was interested now.

'No idea. I've been playing all evening. Different games, roulette, blackjack, poker and the slots. I'm just going to count up. What about you?' He looked at Jimmy.

'Don't ask me, Barb's banker.'

'Three thousand, nine hundred and sixty,' she beamed.

Rob's pile of chips seemed impressive but were mainly low value.

'Two thousand, seven hundred and thirty five...' His voice trailed off. His obvious disappointment was clear. 'Claire won't be happy. She's been a bit down recently. A cruise would have done her the power of good.' He dropped his head into his hands.

Barb caught Jimmy's eye. Returning her look, he wasn't sure what she had in mind. She mouthed to him

'Let him have ours,' while cocking her head to one side as if to say *what do you think?*

Before Jimmy had time to answer the MC organising the evening boomed over the speakers.

'Ladies and gentlemen, your attention please.' The noise in the room remained unchanged. The house lights dropped, a spotlight was brought up picking out the MC standing on the stage apron. He tried again.

'Our evening's entertainment will continue with the UK's number one band ... Wham!' A massive cheer went up. 'But first we must clear the room so the gaming tables are now closed. And of course we need to find a winner for the cruise.' His voice was at fever pitch. The noise abated. 'So is there anyone with ten thousand chips?' No one came forward. 'Okay, nine thousand.' He waited. Nothing. 'Eight ..., seven ..., six?' The spotlight panned over the crowd, trying to find a winner. Everyone looked around to see if anyone nearby was the lucky one. 'Surely someone must have five thousand?' He sounded incredulous. A hand went up, and a chap started making his way towards the stage. People around him pushed him forward. The spotlight caught him up.

'Ahh, Okay we have a winner, come and join me on stage.'

'Barb, what did you say we had? Quick ...'

'Oh umm three thousand, nine hundred and sixty.'

'And you Rob?'

'Two thousand, seven hundred and thirty five. Why?'

'Cos we have a winner here! Go on Barb, give him

our chips.'

Before Rob had time to argue, Jimmy was shouting at the MC. 'Over here. We have a winner.' Jimmy patted Rob on the back, 'Go on, mate. You take your missus cruising.' He pushed him forward. Barb sidled up to Jimmy, slipped her arm around his waist and moved her mouth close to his ear.

'Hey big boy, you're a winner too ...' She took her room key from her handbag and placed it into his hand.

He glanced at the room number. 'George Michael's Okay but hey, I can listen to him any day.' Jimmy led her from the ballroom, arm in arm. 'See you up there; I've something I must do first. Here.' He handed her back the key before disappearing in the direction of the gents toilet. No luck there. Panicking, he went in search of the hotel bellboy.

'Is there an all-night chemist around here?' Urgency was written across his face.

'No problem sir. Straight up Park Lane, virtually next door to the tube station.' Jimmy was already moving towards the exit, 'You can't miss it, sir.' The bellboy finished his sentence but doubted he heard. *Lucky bleeder,* he thought, *I'm on duty for another five hours.*

Jimmy ran most of the way. He had one thing on his mind. 'Excuse me,' he muttered, managing to dodge the old lady walking her dog, but not its toilet.

Finally he was back and standing outside room 207, gasping rather than panting. Running up two flights of stairs, two at a time was the last straw. He kicked his shoes off; trying the door, it was unlocked. He hung the *Do Not Disturb* sign on the outside before shutting it behind him.

* * * * *

'Oleg, pick up phone.' The telephone continued to ring. 'Come on, my friend, where you are?'

'Please leave your message after the tone.' If Vladimir had been listening hard he would have heard a faint click—the sound of someone eavesdropping—following the automated voice.

'Damn machines. Oleg, it is me. Did you see news on TV?'

Vladimir put the phone down, disappointed he wasn't able to speak to him. His watch showed 10:30. *I wonder where he is?* He mused. *He's not often out on a Wednesday.* He poured the milk into his mug and stirred in the cocoa powder, followed by three spoons of sugar. *We don't get same cold nights in London as Moscow,* he thought. *I do miss home.* He drifted off into his memories. His front door knocker rattled; three taps, followed by a pause, followed by three more.

'Oleg, I am coming,' he shouted, approaching the closed door. He opened it, leaving the security chain in place. 'You cannot ever be certain.' He peered out the crack, expecting to see Oleg's face staring back. He was speaking to no one. Leaving the door ajar, he waited. After a few minutes—still nothing. 'I think I get too old for zis job,' he muttered, wandering back to find his cocoa.

* * * * *

Born in a Moscow suburb in 1925, Vladimir Pankov was co-opted into the KGB just after the Second World War. His father, a long term serving officer, first in the Cheka, later renamed KGB, he worked under the control of Lenin following the Russian Revolution. At home he often talked of Rasputin and his influence over Czar Nicholas. In particular, how Rasputin was able to mentally control the Czar for his own ends. And how for many, the murder of Rasputin confirmed his powers, and provided a springboard for the investigation into paranormal phenomenon. Vladimir's father and later Vladimir himself, sought to make the paranormal his specialism.

In Russia psychic weapons development took many forms, as did anything that might tip the balance of power in favour of the Soviets during the Cold War. Not until Operation StarGate did the USA offer any credible paranormal research programme of their own. By the 1980's this type of research was well established with a variety of successes and failures. Unlike the USA, the Soviets had no compunction about experimenting on their own, so gained significant headway in this area.

The door knocker went again using the same coded signal. Vladimir rose to his feet and hurried down the corridor. Light on his toes, he was mindful to keep as quiet as possible. He kept low to avoid being seen through the glass in the door. He pressed his ear against the wood, listening for any movement outside. Holding his breath, he strained. The sound of breathing came from the far side. He wasn't taking any chances.

'Vladimir, open door. I know you zere.'

Although he recognised comrade Oleg's voice he left the chain on just in case.

'Zere you are, silly man. Come on, it freezing.' Oleg pushed at the door.

You are going soft, Oleg. You would not put coat on if you were in Moscow.' Vladimir slipped the chain. 'Were you at door before?'

'Aah, so I have not lost my magic. Walking here from Queensway tube I knocked using mind only.' Oleg smiled to himself. 'I heard phone go, was not able to get zere quick enough. After I listened your message I watched news and came straight here.'

'So what you make of it?' Vladimir continued to stir his cocoa.

'We must get copy of video. I want to watch it slow down, but know what I zink I saw.'

'So you zink it telekinesis also?' The excitement in Vladimir's voice was apparent.

'Well, seem he did not to touch anything yet he moved tower across room.'

'Have you got contact at BBC, Oleg?'

'Not very easy. Zat is why I come over. Zis big, I zink. If zis man can move such big size, it will cause difficulties. Every person will want him. If we saw it you can bet our rubles, Americans saw, and British too.'

'By morning all newspapers will carry pictures. Look, nearly midnight now, if we go Fleet Street we can get first editions.'

'Underground is closed. Is your joke of motorbike working?' Oleg mocked.

'You never like Japanese engineering.'

'It is like sewing machine. I wait for you here, you go buy paper. Two fat Russians on moped at midnight will bring too much interest. While you zere, get takeaway. I zink we going to be here for late night.'

Vladimir wheeled his Honda 90 out of the garage onto the cobbled mews. All appeared clear though he could see the glint of streetlights reflected on the first floor windows diagonally opposite.

'You obsessed,' he grunted to himself. 'You zink everywhere is full of spies.' He buckled up his helmet and coat against the cold night air. Not Moscow cold but still chilly. Dropping the bike into gear, the engine sounded strained as the clutch began to bite. By paddling his feet, he was soon moving. From the Mews he drove down Lancaster Gate to join the steady flow of traffic on the Bayswater Road.

The door to the house number 12—across the mews from theirs—opened. The interior was in darkness. No sooner had it opened than it was shut. A figure slipped into the shadows, disappearing into the night. If they had noticed, they would have known they were being watched.

While Vladimir was gone Oleg kept himself amused moving objects around the occasional table Vladimir used as a dumping ground. By concentrating hard he found he could get a cigarette butt to jump out of the ashtray and onto the floor without touching it. 'Oh power of mind; I always am impressed,' he chuckled to himself.

* * * * *

Vladimir returned: 'Oleg, you talking yourself again? You will make our American cousins crazy.' He appeared back in the room carrying two plates of Tandoori chicken and rice. 'Here, put inside you. It is very chilly outside.'

'Well, what zey say? Have more details? Have pictures?'

'No time to look. I must eat before it cold. Here, you look too.' Vladimir had half a dozen first editions. 'I take one. You take others.' Both men busied themselves flicking through the pages searching for pictures.

'Well zat no good. We must get into BBC and get copy of video.'

'The Financial Times has article on importance of Microsoft Windows™ and how it going to change world; looks like start party was very spectacular.'

Oleg wasn't listening. He'd finished his curry and was now stretched out on the sofa snoring his head off.

'You younger ones have no stamina. See you in morning.' Vladimir switched out the lights and took himself off to bed.

* * * * *

'Well?'

'Well all I know is it's darn cold out there.'

'Look, we're the CIA, not some nursery for over pampered kids. What do the papers say?'

'Okay, okay, I was just saying it's cold. Nothing more.'

'Well—papers, what do they say?'

'Only what we already know—which is nothing.'

'Langley are on my back. We need to do better.

We've got to get this guy before the Ruskies do. Any ideas?'

'I'll go to the Grosvenor hotel first thing. They'll still be clearing up. Maybe we can get a guest list and find out who he is and where he works.' Brad took off his coat and scarf and stood in front of the one-bar electric fire, rubbing his hands in a vain attempt to get warm.

'Why's London always so cold? I thought this spying game was meant to be glamorous. It always is in the movies. I'd never have joined if I'd known what it's really like. Look at this shit hole.' Brad pictured himself on some white sandy beach with a blond hanging off his arm. '007 does alright.'

'You think 12 Lancaster Mews is a shit hole? You want to see some of the real dumps I've stayed in. Quit moaning. You take the couch; I'll have the chair. Let's see if we can get a few hours in. I'll treat you down at Sheila's. She does a great breakfast, and is open from 6. Not a real diner, I grant you, but the best we can do, and it's close by.'

Matt slumped into the arm chair and pulled his overcoat up to his chin in an attempt to keep out the cold. Brad flopped onto the couch. Being so tall he was really a three-seater guy so a two-seater was worse than an armchair. He thought, *it's not always advantageous to be tall, and this was one of them.*

'Do you really think this guy has some special powers? I mean it looks like it on TV but what you think you see is not always what actually is.'

At this Matt sighed, 'I can see why you were recruited into the Service.'

The irony was lost on Brad. 'I was just saying.'

'Yeah, I was just saying get some sleep, we need to be out of here in a few hours.'

The listening device attached to the window relayed a cough, or snore, or an expulsion of wind coming from the Russians. Matt noted the sounds. He soon realised they weren't going out again tonight, and he too, was off to the land of dreams.

CHAPTER 2

MY HERO

Oleg stirred at the sound of the nearby church bell chiming six. *This work is not me,* he thought. He hauled himself up onto his elbows, catching his reflection in the mirror hung over the mantelpiece. His hair, always so neat slicked back by generous helpings of Brylcreem, had in the night rearranged itself. He was more reminiscent of a Gonk, and not the hot shot Russian spy he saw himself as. He dove his hand into his inside suit jacket pocket. He was a creature of habit and knew his black plastic comb would be there. Tugging at his tousled mane, some semblance of order returned. He needed Brylcreem to ensure it was maintained. Stumbling off the sofa, he headed towards Vladimir's bathroom. Pulling open the cabinet door, he wasn't prepared for what happened next. The contents, plus glass shelves, cascaded into the awaiting sink. Instinctively, Oleg jumped back to avoid being hit by the mass of detritus and glass shards as the shelves surrendered under the force of gravity.

The noise woke Vladimir. His response was automatic. Before the falling contents had time to complete their journey he had the cold steel of his Gyurza pistol nestled into the nape of Oleg's neck.

'Слава Иисусу, ты боишься меня почти мертв. And for our American cousins who I know are listening

…'

'Glory be to Jesus, you scared me nearly dead! It is not funny.' Vladimir held his chest to try and calm his heart.

Oleg pulled away, wanting to put some distance between the two of them.

Vladimir put away his gun. 'You must be more careful. You get yourself shot.'

Oleg picked away at the mess until he found what he was looking for. Smoothing and combing his hair in place, he felt much better.

'Right, happy trigger, we get some breakfast before we go to Grosvenor.'

Opening the front door, Vladimir peered up and down the street to check all was clear. He needn't have bothered. It was a cold dark November morning. Rain threatened. The wind gusted around the mews, scattering leaves in little eddies. He gestured to Oleg. Dressed against the cold, their coats fastened tight, collars pulled up and trilbies over their eyes, they appeared suspicious even if they weren't. Without a word they processed across the cobbles, keeping to the shadows and away from the pools of light cast by the street lamps. Sheila's Café came into view. The light from within cascaded out via the large window running along one side. Not salubrious, it had appeal; an oasis for all and sundry, for anyone foolish enough to be up at this time. Empty, apart from the eponymous owner and the milkman doing a delivery, the two Russians took the table nearest the radiator. It was not their first visit, but to Sheila they weren't regulars. She didn't know their orders off by heart, or how they liked their tea, but their faces seemed familiar.

'Gentlemen, wot can I do for you today? Full English or just tea and toast?' Sheila held her wide-eyed smile she greeted every customer with despite how she was feeling. And at six in the morning she didn't feel like smiling.

Vladimir and Oleg perused the plastic coated menu. From years of experience, Sheila had pared the number of items to the bare bones. She knew if you presented too wide a choice it created hassle in the kitchen, and if the choice was too limited she wouldn't meet with everyone's approval and lose customers. She reasoned losing a few customers was worth the ease of preparation and reduced wastage.

'So wot will it be?' It was difficult to keep smiling at six in the morning when your shoes pinch and your skirt rides up every time you move. She battled on in the name of earning a living. Her customers appreciated her efforts; she had great legs, as the skirt testified. She noticed the older man taking a sly peek. She smiled at him. *I could write a book,* she thought to herself. *Men are all the same the world over; sex or food is all they think about — and not necessarily in that order.*

'Aah my dear, you are very beautiful. I have travelled from far distance and seen many zings. Often seeing zings men should not, but you extraordinary. A pleasure on eye; dream come true; vision, poetry in human, no, in female shape. Seeing you make my day and it is only quarter past six!' Vladimir waxed lyrical.

She raised her eyes to heaven. 'So wot will it be

then?'

'In your fair hands I am sure you could turn plainest eggs or fattest bacon into feast fit for king. It be full English for me with white toast and tea.'

She scribbled in her pad FE, WT and T, leaving enough room between her letter groups so she could write an "X" plus a number if necessary.

She turned to Oleg but didn't speak. Her body language was sufficient. Without looking up he muttered, 'Same, but coffee.'

'Please,' added Vladimir.

She added two Xs, two 2's and a C to her pad.

'Anyfing else, gentlemen?' Her smile stayed put as she faced Vladimir. He noticed and smiled back.

'A little civility means very much. No, zat is all, my dear. Zank you.'

She passed through the plastic beaded curtain used to separate the kitchen from the café, to disappear from sight. The old fashioned shop doorbell clinked as the front door opened and closed. Neither Russian looked up. They didn't need to. Outside it was still dark and the large window acted as a mirror. They both saw the two Americans walk in, acknowledge them, and move to the far side of the café where they were half hidden by a display cabinet.

Sheila reappeared carrying two cups and a wide smile.

'Five minutes, gentlemen. Just need the sausages to cook through,' she said, placing the cups on the table before pivoting on her heels and heading off in the direction of her new clientele.

'Hey Missy, we're starving. Got something to keep out the cold?' Brad placed his arm around her waist and pulled her towards him.

'That's more than you can afford,' she wriggled free. 'Now wot will it be?'

'Oh come on, don't be like that. Anyway we're pretty well paid at Langley.'

'Shush, keep your voice down.' Matt sounded annoyed. 'You never know who's listening ...'

Right, scrambled eggs, ham and hash browns plus coffee for us both.' Brad gazed up at her.

'Where did you see 'ash browns?' Sheila thrust the menu under his nose.

'Everyone does hash browns. What's with this darn country, some third world backwater?'

'This is England, we are English. We offer a full English breakfast.' She smiled all the while.

'Okay you made your point. Two full English,' he emphasised the words, 'but make sure it's coffee, not that tea—I need to wake up.'

She scribbled on her pad. 'Any toast?' She directed her question at Matt, not wanting to encourage Brad.

He nodded.

'Brown or white?'

'Has wholemeal made it to your shores yet?' Brad smiled at his comment.

'Yes but you can't have any.'

'Why in heavens not? I suppose it's not the correct time of day to eat wholemeal. You Brits are weird.' Brad shook his head.

'Actually it's 'cos we've not 'ad our delivery today, and wot I've got is stale. Is that all, gentlemen?' Before they answered she left for the kitchen.

'I'll never understand these Limeys,' Matt called after her.

Neither group of men said much. Each aware of the other and both knowing who the others were. Spying is one thing, but everyone has to eat. Sheila was right about the needs of men. The silence was broken by the click clack of her heels as she traipsed back and forth carrying plates of food, racks of toast and pots of tea and coffee.

Conversations remained stilted. All were aware of the need for discretion. A problem was looming, apparent to both—who was going to leave first?

'What we can do, Vladimir?' Oleg cast his eyes in the direction of the Americans. 'We do not want zem to know what we are doing.' He raised his hand to his mouth. 'Possibly ...' he went on, 'we can slip through back before zey notice. Many streets and alleys we could disappear into.'

'Shush, I am zinking.' Vladimir checked his watch. 'It is twenty minute walk to Grosvenor going across Hyde Park or thirty minutes going through back streets. We must leave.' He checked his watch again. 'Ok, act as usual. We pay and when outside go back in direction of house for benefit of zem watching through window. Actually, we hide behind pillars of next door's façade. It still dark enough to hide but we can watch zem from there.' He finished speaking and walked over to Sheila, who was standing by the till.

'Is everyfink okay?' she said, through her smile. Her eyes twinkled and a cute curl appeared on her top lip. She knew how to get a bigger tip.

'Fine, my dear.' He pressed a £10 note into her hand. 'Keep change.'

She thought about protesting but thought better of it. 'See ya again soon ... I 'ope.' She studied the note. *I knew this skirt and these shoes would pay for themselves,* she thought. What she didn't notice were the Americans slipping out without paying. She saw the empty table and cursed. 'Ya can't trust no bugger these days,' She muttered, but her disappointment was shorted lived. Under a saucer was another £10 note. 'Okay this is turning out to be a good day after all.' Her smile was back.

* * * * *

'Hey, sleepy head, we need to make a move. It's seven thirty.'

Jimmy stretched and yawned. 'I need some breakfast. I'm famished.' He swung his legs out of bed.

'Not so fast, big boy. I need a little something to wake me up.' Barb grabbed his trailing leg and stopped him in his tracks. Turning back towards her, he leant down, bringing his lips to hers. They kissed long and hard. He encircled her with his arms. Their naked bodies entwined. All thoughts of work, or food, or anything vaporised. Their focus was on nothing but satiating lust.

The bedside phone rang. They ignored it. It continued to ring. A hand emerged from the ruckus, flapping about blind, determined to knock the handset from its cradle; it didn't. Insistent, the phone continued. Jimmy surfaced.

'Yeah.' He listened. 'No, you haven't got the wrong room, she's here.' Barb's head emerged from under the covers. He held his hand over the mouth piece. 'It's for you.'

'Who is it?' she mouthed back.

'Your boss.' He passed her the receiver.

'Oh hi, Mike.' She oozed professionalism, 'No Jimmy Kavanagh. He just came by on his way to breakfast. We'd arranged to meet up with a few people to discuss yesterday's launch. You know, one of those breakfast meetings. Get a few ideas going before the day starts. How can I help?'

While she listened she rummaged around for her clothes. One way or another, talking to her boss naked didn't seem right.

'Yeah, everyone's very excited. There was a real buzz in the room. Pity you couldn't make it back. Was the funeral okay? Shame you didn't make it to the launch.' She paid scant attention to his responses as she fought with the phone, her bra fastening and Jimmy taking advantage of her vulnerable state.

'Right, Mike. Great idea; your office at two for a debrief.' She put the phone down.

Jimmy, standing at the end of the bed, waved her knickers around.

'Are dees de briefs ya waz on aboot?' His Jamaican accent, wasn't.

'Jimmy Kavanagh, give me those right now. I'm not joking.'

'Or what?'

'I'll give you *or what*.' She snatched at his waving hand. 'I'll ... I'll ... you just wait and see.' Peeved, she grabbed for her handbag to retrieve her emergency pair. 'You can keep them. Have them as a trophy. Hang them on your bedpost ..., cause you ain't getting near mine ever again.' The bathroom door slammed and was soon followed by the sound of showering. The running water masked her laughter. *I'll show him*, she thought. *My chance will come.*

Jimmy did as he was told and shoved the knickers into the top pocket of his suit jacket hanging on the back of a chair. Scavenging around the floor he recovered the rest of his own clothes, including his lucky boxer shorts with hearts on. *They never fail*, he mused. He dressed and readied himself as best he could, given all his overnight stuff was at his hotel in Lancaster Gate. Finally, he rescued his shoes from outside the hotel room door. It didn't escape him that he smelt of stale beer, cigarettes, and far worse. He looked about himself trying to find the source.

The bathroom door opened, and Barb emerged wrapped in towels. Her disdainful look fooled no one.

'You're not really mad with me ... are you?' Jimmy moved towards her, his arms outstretched. She backed off pretty sharpish.

'Cor, you stink. You're not coming near me!' She pushed him away.

'Look I'd better get back to my hotel and get cleaned up. Anyway, it's probably not a bad idea I don't join you for breakfast. Otherwise all the tongues will be wagging. See you at Mike's debrief.' He stepped towards her again.

'That's far enough. That suit will have to go to the cleaners. You sure you've not got a dead rat in the pocket? Go on, get out of here.' Barb squeezed her nostrils shut with one hand and waved him away with the other.

'A chap knows when he's not wanted.' Jimmy closed the room door and left.

*   *   *   *   *

The lift door opened on the second floor. Jimmy got in. As the doors shut there was a visible shift as everyone stepped aside to give him as much space as possible. Even the two Russians standing against the back wall tried to move further away. They'd been in some pretty gruesome places in their time but this smell was even getting to them.

On the ground floor the doors opened. Within seconds the lift was empty, leaving Jimmy alone, confused and wondering what was going on.

The bellboy, standing close by, sidled up to him.

'I think sir may need to check the underside of his shoes.'

Jimmy raised his left leg up to his right knee.

'Shit.'

'Exactly, sir.'

Realising what the problem was he sped off towards the front door, hopping as he went. He wanted to get as far from the hotel as possible to save further embarrassment.

*   *   *   *   *

'Zere is no point standing in corridors or going in lift, how are we going to see who is zis man?' Although Vladimir spoke aloud it was a rhetorical question.

'Perhaps we ask some guests if zey know him. You know, point him to us. Zey will be at breakfast now. If we go to restaurant, we will pretend we are foreign journalists.' Oleg looked for any signs to a restaurant.

'Okay Oleg, but which way? Grosvenor has more restaurants zan …'

'Look, zere, he will know.' Oleg pointed to the bellboy.

'Pardon me.' Vladimir approached him.

'How may I be of service sir?'

'Where guests take breakfast?'

'Are you wanting breakfast, sir?' The bellboy eyed them up and down.

'Da.'

'Are you guests?'

'Nyet.'

'Then sir, may I suggest you and your companion find one of the many cafés here about. The Grosvenor House Hotel doesn't provide breakfast for non-guests.'

'But we look to find someone.'

'And whom might that be, sir? Maybe I can help. Is he or she a guest?'

'I am not sure. I zink so perhaps.'

'Think so? What makes you think so?'

'Well he was here at Microsoft computer party

yesterday. So I believe he stayed.'

'His name sir, do you know that?'

Vladimir shot Oleg a look. He shrugged.

'Sorry, we do not. Just forget it.' Vladimir turned to walk away.

'One moment, sir. Are you gentlemen from the press?'

'Why you ask?' The two Russians exchanged glances.

'We've had a lot around after the excitement of yesterday. By any chance are you looking for the gentleman who saved the table of guests from the falling tower?'

'Da, zat is him'. Vladimir's face lit up.

'I may be able to help but ...,' the bellboy sensed an opportunity,' my mind's a little blank right now.'

Vladimir twigged, and pulled out his wallet. 'Would zis help your hole in memory?' He tucked a five pound note into the bellboy's jacket pocket.

'You're very fortunate. The gentleman in question shouldn't be difficult to find. You'll smell him before you see him. Actually, you travelled in the lift with him just a few minutes ago. He went outside ...'

Before he'd finished both Russians set off at full tilt towards the street exit onto Park Lane. They looked left and right in quick succession. 'Zere, Vladimir, look — by railings.' Oleg was less than subtle as he pointed and waved.

Early in the morning there are plenty of people rushing to and fro on their way to work. The Russians didn't look conspicuous. In London no one seems to notice anymore. Quite the contrary, people make it their business not to notice in case they are drawn into conversation, or worse. The Russians moved closer to Jimmy. He wasn't aware, being preoccupied cleaning dog crap from his shoes.

'We follow him for now. Not too close, we do not want make him suspicious.'

'Zen what?' Oleg wanted more decisive action. 'How will following him help us? Why we not just tell him we want to talk about tower. We can say we are journalists interested in zings unusual. You know, zings not ordinary. We could say we write for scientific paper, like Journal of Mystical and Paranormal Experience.' Oleg beamed.

'Sounds good ..., quick, he is moving.' The two men followed. They wanted to keep under cover until it was appropriate to stop Jimmy.

At the top of Park Lane he crossed over Oxford Street, turning left towards the Bayswater Road. The air was chilly. Jimmy moved quickly to keep warm. Oleg and Vladimir remained at a discreet distance, mindful of losing sight of him. After a couple of hundred yards he came to Lancaster Gate tube station.

'Where he going, you zink?' Oleg was enjoying this spying carry-on. 'No, look ..., not on tube, he has gone straight past. The Crown Hotel is close on corner of Lancaster Gate. Let us follow him to see.'

'Zat is around corner from where we are. Perhaps we can get him to come to Lancaster Mews. We can talk with him without interruption there'

'What, kidnap him!' Oleg didn't sound sure.

'No, not KGB tactics. If we make him suspicious he will not co-operate. We need to bring him carefully. Make him offer he cannot refuse.'

'Zere, did you see him?' Oleg pointed like an excited child as he watched Jimmy pass through the revolving door into the Crown Hotel.

'Da, let him get key and we will speak to receptionist.' By now both men were in the foyer, trying not to look too obvious but keeping a close eye on their target.

The Crown was alright as hotels go: nothing fancy. All the room keys had large metal fobs designed to stop guests walking off with them. Jimmy spun his fob around his fingers as he walked towards the lift. He fumbled and dropped it. It never touched the floor. In a trice he shot his arm forward, palm outstretched and sort of scooped it up, not by getting his hand under it but by getting the fob to jump back up into his open hand. Both Russians saw.

'Did ... did ... you see that?' Oleg was beside himself. 'He is really special. We must get him alone.'

Jimmy continued nonchalantly. Smiling to himself he thought, *I like this, I can have some real fun with these powers.*

Once he was out of sight Vladimir spoke to the receptionist.

'Aah my dear, can you help me? Zat young man who just collect his key.' He was over ingratiating.

'Mr Kavanagh, what about him?'

'Da, Mr Kavanagh, we need talk with him. Did he perhaps say if he was staying in or going out?'

'Well he's only booked in for last night so has to vacate his room by eleven.'

'Zank you. My colleague and I shall wait for him here.' He pointed to the easy seating arrangement next to the revolving door.

'Would you like me to call his room? It's no trouble.'

'Zat is so kind but no. Zank you.'

Vladimir and Oleg spent the time watching guests pass by, some struggling with luggage, others struggling with language. London is so cosmopolitan and nowhere was this more obvious than in a hotel foyer. Their line of sight to the lift was unbroken. Every time the doors opened their heads turned to check out who was coming and going.

Jimmy was soon shaved, showered, suited and booted. He took a last look around his room before heading to reception.

'Is breakfast still being served?'

The receptionist checked her watch. 'Sorry sir, I'm afraid you've missed it. Since you've checked out you can't use room service either.'

He checked the time. 'Do you know anywhere around here I might get something?'

That was the cue for the Russians. Vladimir jumped up. 'Excuse, Mr Kavanagh.'

Jimmy spun around, his face contorted. 'Sorry, are you talking to me?'

'Yes, you not know us,' he looked at Oleg, 'we know you only by reputation, but we be most happy if you join us for breakfast—we pay, of course. We have questions we like to ask.'

'Questions? What questions?'

'It is about yesterday and what happened at Grosvenor.'

He eyed them suspiciously. 'You're journalists.' His ego rose. 'Why didn't you say so? And you'll buy me breakfast. Lead on.' Jimmy bounced as he walked enjoying his celebrity status.

All three men passed through the revolving door onto the street. Vladimir was first. He shepherded Jimmy right, and then up Lancaster Gate.

'It is only 100 metres.' He pointed to a row of seventeenth century city terraced houses. 'Here in Lancaster Mews. Sheila's, on corner. She does very special *all day full English*. How sound it?'

'Yeah great … You're obviously not English—which paper are you from?'

'You will not know it. It is scientific journal.'

'Try me.'

Vladimir glanced at Oleg, who came to his rescue. 'Journal of Mystical and Paranormal Events.' Oleg sounded far more foreign than Vladimir.

'So where are you two from?' Jimmy spoke slowly and deliberately.

'Ahh we are here.' Vladimir pushed open the café door. He guided Jimmy through. It was busier now and the only free table was where the Americans sat earlier.

'How come you know this place? It's a bit off the beaten track.' Jimmy looked around and noticed Sheila.

'We stay nearby and found it. London is so expensive, Sheila's so much good value.' Vladimir tried to catch her eye. 'And she is very helpful girl.'

'What he says is he is dirty old man who would like his chances with her although he is old as her father.' Oleg laughed at his own comment. Sheila appeared at the table wearing her usual smile. Jimmy took in the sight, nodding in agreement.

'I wasn't expecting to see ya so soon. Wot will it be, gents?' She had her pen poised.

'I hear you do a mean full English. That'll do me.' Jimmy put his menu down.

'Tea and toast?'

'Yeah fine.'

'And for you gentlemen, the same?'

'I would love to my dear, but I must remember my shape.' Vladimir patted his paunch. 'I afraid I must say nyet this time, just white coffee.'

'And for me, but please make strong.' Oleg gathered up the menus and stood them between the sauce bottles.

All three men were silent.

'So how …' Jimmy was cut off.

'We did not see what happened and only saw on TV news. Can you tell us what happened?' Oleg took a notebook and pen from his jacket pocket.

Jimmy took a deep breath before launching into an explanation of the events of the afternoon. He never mentioned anything about the roulette wheel, figuring that should remain a secret between him and Barbara. Oleg wrote copiously as both men questioned him in detail. The more he spoke the more excited the Russians became, believing they were onto something big, something very important, and something that would make them notorious back home. With each new detail they glanced at each other like excited children who couldn't believe their luck.

Using the bread crust Jimmy wiped the last of the egg yolk from the plate before draining his mug of tea. 'Well thank you for breakfast.' He stood: 'Must go, I've a train to catch.'

'Really? Nyet, please stay.' Vladimir stood in an attempt to stop him.

'Sorry guys, I've a meeting with my boss. Must dash.'

'But we have not finished …'

'Would love to stay,' he glanced at his watch, 'but my train goes in 15 minutes from Paddington.' He headed for the door.

'How can we make contact wiz you?' Vladimir sounded desperate. 'You know, if we have need for more questions. You would not like us to print wrong information, I am sure.'

Jimmy dug his hand into his breast pocket to find a business card. Barb's knickers fell out. 'Ooops,' he said, scooping them up, 'give me a ring.' The ping of the café doorbell complemented his words as he left.

Both Russians sat and stared in silence.

'Nyet, we are good, zank you,' Vladimir said, brought back to the here and now by Sheila's voice. He took a £10 note and pushed it into her hand. 'Sorry my dear, we cannot stay. Important work to do.'

Sheila bent over to clear the table. Her skirt rode up but Vladimir wasn't in sight.

'Cor blimey, it must be important. I wonder wot they do?' No one heard her comments although several other diners noticed the show of legs.

* * * * *

'They're back. Listen …' Matt and Brad stood still, waiting for another confirmatory noise from their eavesdropping device. 'Quick, turn on the recorder.' Both strained to hear every sound coming from the Russians.

'What you think?' came from the speaker.

Matt and Brad exchanged looks as if to say *I wonder what he's talking about*?

'Do we write what he told us, or wait until more proof?'

'They must be onto something,' whispered Matt.

'I zink we wait. We only have his story. I would like to see him doing action.'

'What you suggesting?'

'We take train to …' Vladimir pulled out Jimmy's card. Matt and Brad just heard a rustling sound. 'Maidenhead.' He went on. 'Let us go see him.'

'We can't afford to lose them this time,' Matt said. From their bedroom window the Americans had an uninterrupted view of the Russians' safe house. 'We'll wait for them to leave. They're off to Paddington so we don't have to follow too close.'

* * * * *

On cue, Vladimir and Oleg appeared at their front door.

Checking all was clear, they set off at a brisk pace up the Mews. Passing Sheila's, they noticed she was busy as usual. The large picture window afforded an uninterrupted view of the café interior and of her bending over, clearing a table. From the back her rising short skirt showed off her shapely legs; from the front her low cut neckline did an equally pleasing job. Vladimir nudged Oleg just in case he hadn't noticed.

'Keep your mind on work or you will get in trouble.' They kept walking. Sheila saw them and waved. Vladimir returned a broad smile.

'Are we being followed?'

Oleg took a quick glance over his shoulder. 'Nyet.'

'I have not seen Americans since Sheila's. I am certain zey have not given us up.' Vladimir looked across the street at shop windows to see if he could see them following in the reflection.

Paddington station came into view. They went down the ramp onto the concourse and waited, hidden behind one of the many pillars supporting the vast domed roof.

After several minutes Vladimir said, 'I zink it is all clear. You wait here; I go to ticket office.' He disappeared into the crowd.

Oleg waited — in a state of heightened alert, he scanned the faces of the travellers to-ing and fro-ing.

'We want platform 1. Train goes in 10 minutes.'

On hearing Vladimir's voice Oleg spun around. 'Have you seen zem?'

'Nyet.' He took a furtive glance, to be on the safe

side. Vladimir pushed a ticket into Oleg's hand, 'Here. Take it. I zink we must separate. We will meet at taxis at Maidenhead station. Keep your eyes open.' He was gone.

Again Oleg was alone, or so he thought.

Matt and Brad slipped onto the concourse via the station porter's entrance. It was busy, with people milling around. The CIA operatives went unnoticed, although they caught sight of Oleg.

'There, by the pillar, third along from the left.' Brad cast an eye over the crowd and spotted him. 'I wonder where his buddy is.'

Matt shrugged. 'Bet he's not too far away.'

'There …' Brad pointed in the direction of Oleg. 'He's making a move.' Following, both men were watchful, moving in unison across the concourse towards Platform 1, keeping a safe distance behind him. 'We haven't got tickets,' Brad said in a whisper.

'Just show your Government ID. We've got Diplomatic Status so don't have to pay.'

They saw Oleg walk down the platform to the far end of the train where the passengers were few and far between. The Americans waited until he'd climbed aboard before doing the same. They got on at the concourse end thinking it would be safer. Vladimir, sitting in the first carriage with his nose buried in a newspaper, saw everything.

Lurching, the train moved forward. Anyone standing was thrown off balance.

'Darn Brits, can't they do anything right?' Matt recovered his composure. He continued walking the corridors looking for an empty compartment. In First

Class it was easy to find one. Safely ensconced, swaying to the motion of the train, they listened to the rhythm of the wheels. Maidenhead, only a short commute with a stop at Slough, soon came into view.

Oleg was ready. He opened the door and leapt onto the platform while the train was still moving. Before anyone else saw, he was down the stairs leading to the ticket barrier and out into the car park looking for the taxi rank. Matt and Brad wanted to lose themselves in the crowd of other passengers alighting. They waited until the platform was busy before joining the throng. Swept along by the tide of travellers all intent on getting to the barriers before disgorging from the station, they had their ID's to hand. The automatic barriers stayed shut.

'Excuse me, sirs, would you wait over there please?' A ticket inspector appeared from nowhere and pointed. 'Charlie,' he called without looking up, 'can you take these gentlemen to my office? There's a good chap.' The two Americans looked panic-stricken. If they stayed they risked losing the Russians, but if they ran there would be a chase, the police, a diplomatic incident. They stayed.

'Can we make this quick? We're here on sensitive business where time is of the essence.' Matt tried to sound important without undermining the ticket inspector.

'I need to make a phone call, sir. You know it's a serious offence to travel unless you hold a valid ticket. It's more than my job's worth to let you go without checking first.' The ticket inspector picked up the phone and dialled. They waited expectantly.

'Ah John, Jack here. I've a couple of Herberts who claim to have Diplomatic Passes. Don't we usually get notified first?' He never finished his sentence. The reddening of his face, the loosening of his collar and his change in demeanour all indicated John was less than an ally, and Jack had overstepped his authority. He put the phone down. His grin fooled no one as he dismissed them both: 'Charlie, show these gentlemen the door.'

Vladimir, had tagged onto the end of the crowd of passengers, and witnessed the Americans being challenged. Seeing the door to Station Master's office close, he couldn't help smiling to himself. Right, zat is problem solved, he thought. Emerging from the station, he saw Oleg leaning against the wall looking for all the world like a tourist on a day's outing. He was unaware that the Americans had been on the train or of what had just occurred.

Climbing into a taxi Vladimir took Jimmy's card from his pocket. 'Moorbridge Road please.' They sat back watching the sights of Maidenhead slip by.

'Any particular part, Gov?'

'Is it long road?' Vladimir could see the taxi driver looking at him in the rear view mirror.

'No, just a few businesses. Who are you after, mate?'

Vladimir checked the card: 'Zylog Systems.'

'Why didn't you say? I go there all the time.'

To the taxi driver it was obvious his fare had no idea where they were going. Taking advantage, he took them in a circle via Bray Village, adding extra time to the journey and another few quid to his bill.

'Want a receipt mate, you know, for your expenses?'

'Nyet zank you. Oh, and keep change.' He left the two Russians at the front entrance to Zylog Systems.

'Now what?' Oleg didn't have much faith in their plan.

'We wait, unless you have better idea?'

'We can't wait here, we look too in open.'

As he said it rain drops hit his face, 'That is not good,' he said. In unison both men pulled up their coat collars, tugged down their trilbies and fastened all the buttons on their trench coats.

The weather didn't disappoint. Within seconds the skies opened, water bounced off the pavement and puddles appeared from nowhere. People who had been mindlessly walking suddenly had a new purpose. The stroll back to the office after lunch was now an Olympic dash. The suit jacket was no match for the torrent now falling on Maidenhead. Office workers shoved past, knocking the Russians every which way, desperate to get out of the rain. No one stopped to question who they were or what they were doing there. Keeping dry, or rather not getting wetter, was their only priority. The volumes of water overwhelmed the gutters. These too now added to the cascade, proving the final straw for Vladimir and Oleg. They pushed into Zylog's reception.

'Can I help you, sir?' A voice called from behind the large desk. Given so many people had packed into the reception area at once, the agency temp had little chance of being heard. Neither Vladimir nor Oleg answered. The sound of the rain beating off the window added to the cacophony. She tried again but achieved the same result. The phone rang and distracted her. Vladimir nodded in the direction of a corridor leading off the reception area. Oleg saw, and moved without anything more being said. Each door was labelled. At Meeting Room 1 they stopped and listened. Talking came from within. Meeting Room 2 was the same. Meeting Room 3 proved luckier. Vladimir tried the handle. It was locked. Starting to panic, he moved onto the next door: Training Room 1. The door handle succumbed to his pressure. Quickly they passed through, shutting it behind them.

'Okay, what we do now?' Oleg sought guidance from Vladimir.

*   *   *   *   *

'You took your time.' Rob was at his desk as Jimmy strolled over to him. He looked like the cat who got the cream. 'No, don't tell me details; the look on your face says it all. But Barb's been back here for ages. Where have you been till now?'

Jimmy was aware open plan offices don't afford much privacy: 'Look, I don't want to broadcast what happened last night. Early days and all that, you know.'

'Mum's the word.' Rob patted the side of his nose with his index finger. 'Oh and by the way, thanks for what you two did. The Missus is really grateful. She's out right now getting a few things she'll need for the cruise, and we haven't even booked it yet.'

'Great, our pleasure. Where's Barb, by the way?' Jimmy surveyed the office, hoping to see her.

'She said she was going up town to get a

sandwich. We've got that debrief meeting with Mike at two.' Rob noticed the time. 'If you want lunch you better look sharpish.'

'I'm fine, had a full English at an excellent café near the hotel, and it was free.'

'How come it was free?' Rob was curious.

'I was treated by a couple of journalists, foreign guys. Sounded Eastern European or even Russian. They were from some science journal, Paranormal Events, or some such thing. They're very interested in me, kept asking loads of questions. Said they saw it on the news and knew they had to talk to me. You should have seen them. I think they've been watching too many old films. They reminded me of Bogart or Maigret, with their trilbies and trench coats.'

The sound of the rain beating off the windows drew the attention of Rob and Jimmy. They wandered over to look.

'Look at that. I'm here just in time.' Jimmy saw Barb running towards the building for all she was worth. 'She'll be soaked through.' He pointed to a rather pathetic figure more reminiscent of a drowned rat than his beautiful Barb. Her blonde hair clung to her head and shoulders, her smart Armani suit was soaked and her red patent leather opened toed three-inch heel sandals, so much her trademark around the office, were of no use against the deluge.

Both men watched helplessly; they said nothing.

'What the ...' Jimmy pointed. For a brief second he thought he caught sight of Bogart and Maigret. Rob followed his finger. They'd long gone, having been pushed into reception by everyone ducking for cover.

'What was it?'

'Oh nothing, I'm imagining things. Where's this meeting, in Mike's office?'

'No, there's too many so he's moved it to Meeting Room 3.'

Jimmy checked the wall clock. 'I'm going down to see if I can help Barb.'

'Out of her wet clothes, no doubt.' Rob winked at him.

*   *   *   *   *

As they were on the first floor Jimmy ran down the stairs. It was quicker than waiting for the lift, but still not quick enough. Barb was nowhere to be seen. He milled around for a few moments hoping she'd come out of the Ladies, but no such luck. Wandering down the corridor to Meeting Room 3 he was first to arrive. Trying the handle, he found it locked. *I wonder*, he thought. Taking hold of the handle and concentrating hard, he sensed a connection with the metal. After a series of clicks, the handle freed and the door swung open. He was so intent on opening the door he failed to notice Barb arrive. She'd taken off her shoes and jacket and was now standing beside him. Her bedraggled blonde hair clung to her white blouse, turning it transparent. She looked ravishing. Actually, she looked more ravaged. Jimmy jumped back in surprise.

'Barb I didn't know you were there.'

'I was getting the key but it looks like I don't need it.'

He scanned the corridor, checking the coast was clear before planting a kiss.

'Jimmy, not here!'

'I couldn't help it, you look so ...' His words dried up.

'So what?' She waited. 'Wet is what you're trying to say.'

'No, well, yes. Beautiful.'

She blushed and pushed past him into the room. Soon there were half a dozen people sitting around the large table, including Rob. Mike walked in last.

'Does anyone know how to use the VHS player?' He waited for a response. 'Come on, we're a technical computer software company. Someone must be able to use it. My daughter's only five and she plays her Disney films all the time.'

'Well maybe you ought to get your daughter in then!'

'Thanks Jimmy, very helpful. Since you're being so lippy, here.' Mike slid the cassette across the table to him. 'Anyway, it's you in action.'

'What do you mean?'

'It's an edited copy of the Windows launch. It was couriered this morning. Come on, we're waiting.'

He placed the cassette into the player as Rob shut the blinds and Mike switched out the lights. The screen came to life. Cue numbers used by professional filmmakers played. In unison, everyone, apart from Mike, counted down.

'Five, four, three, two, one ...'

'You lot are worse than sodding school kids.'

Mike sounded genuinely hacked off. From there on everyone was focussed.

The music was loud, passing through the partition wall with ease. It got the Russians' attention.

'Here, quick.' Vladimir passed Oleg a glass tumbler from the hospitality tray. Both men placed them against the wall and listened intently.

'It is recording of computer software launch at Grosvenor.'

'Are you sure?' Oleg needed convincing.

'Pay attention, zere is only one Bill Gates.' They listened some more. 'I wonder if the tower falling is on there.' No sooner had Vladimir finished speaking than a gasp came from the next room.

'Zere, did you hear that?'

In the meeting room, Mike stopped the cassette and replayed the section again. It was clear to everyone Jimmy was a hero. Most of the delegates sitting around the table in the direct path of the tower were Zylog staff or major customers. Barbara was plainly visible seated next to Rob. Being Account Manager for Land Registry and National Audit Office, two major Government customers, she had senior IT Civil Servants sitting with her.

Mike hit the slow motion button for everyone to see Jimmy leaping from his seat in response to the cracking and flashing as the tower collapsed.

'What on earth did you think you could do?' Mike sounded sceptical.

'I didn't think. I just knew Barbara—I mean, the whole table—were in danger and I had to do something.'

In the dark of the meeting room no one saw her blush.

'So what are you doing now?' Mike paused the video at the point where Jimmy was holding out his arms. He moved on, frame by frame. It was clear the tower shifted off to the right, away from the table and out of harm's way. What was not clear was Jimmy's role. Did he move or influence its trajectory or did one of the many leads attached to it pull the tower?

Mike saw the sales potential of Jimmy's action and was happy to believe the former.

'We owe you, Jimmy Kavanagh, all of us. If you hadn't done ...' he paused for words, 'whatever you did, we'd be several staff down, never mind a few major customers light.' His gratitude was evident. As Mike finished speaking a general buzz of excitement filled the room as everyone talked ten to the dozen. It was still dark. Jimmy felt a hand under the table slide across his lap and give him a squeeze. He sensed Barb next to him.

She leant in, her mouth almost touching his ear. 'Hey, big boy.' He could feel her warm breath. It sent shivers down his spine. 'I've not finished with you yet.'

'Lights.' Mike had taken back control. The meeting rumbled on, discussing the sales strategy for Microsoft Windows, availability, technical support and so forth. Jimmy tried to look interested and stay focussed. In truth, his mind was making passionate love to Barb on some distant Bahaman island, just the two of them. He now realised she was the one for him.

* * * * *

'We got to get copy.' Vladimir paced around the training room. 'It is close; I almost feel it.'

The sound of chairs moving followed by no noise from the meeting room suggested it was now empty.

'Quick, let us hope zey not locked door.' Vladimir held the training room door open enough to look down the corridor. It was all clear. He tiptoed his way to the meeting room and tried the handle. It turned. Within seconds he was inside, searching for the video player. Right at the table's centre, tantalisingly, it waited for him. Power on, it hummed into life. 'Eject, where eject button?' he said, frantically trying to make sense of the controls.

'Here Vladimir.' Oleg was holding the remote control. He pressed the eject button. The cassette holder popped up. It was empty.

'Damn. Okay, we need plan.'

Oleg pulled the door shut. He heard noises coming from the room they had just vacated. 'Ok, maybe we not have all luck but we got out from next door in time.'

'It is nearly five, zey soon go home. We stay here zen can search building once zey are gone.' Vladimir relaxed.

* * * * *

Matt and Brad were soaked, hungry and frustrated. An afternoon of wandering aimlessly around Maidenhead hoping to get a glimpse of two Russian spies doing the same, had come to nothing.

'Where could they be? Who is this guy? Why was

he so uncooperative, I'll show him,' Matt seethed. 'We'll head back to London and Grosvenor Square. At least at our Embassy our ID's work. We can get a change of clothes and a shower. God, I need a shower, I'm soaked.'

Brad couldn't help smiling.

'What are you laughing at?' Matt didn't see the funny side. 'Go and get a couple of tickets back to Paddington. The last thing I need is another person who goes by the book. The sooner I'm out of this godforsaken place the better.'

'Actually I was getting to like Maidenhead.'

'Well we've seen enough of it this afternoon.'

'Down by the River Tams, is that how they say it? I thought it was particularly nice, the bridge and Boulter's Lock.'

'Yeah okay, this is not some geography field trip, just get those god-dammed tickets and let's get the hell out of here.'

The early evening train stopped at every station between Reading and Paddington. By the time it reached Maidenhead it was full of people returning from work. There were no vacant seats.

'Holy crap! Have we got to stand all the way to Paddington?' For Matt this was the last straw. 'I hate this job.' They travelled in silence.

The US Embassy delivered on its promises; in addition, they served proper American food.

'Give Sheila her due, she tries but you can't beat good old home cooking.' Matt was more his old self again. 'While we're here we'll have a listen to the wire and see if those Ruskies have found anything.'

They spent a couple of hours searching through faxes and other intercepts, all mundane stuff but nothing on their man.

'The wireless listening post in Caversham Park, Reading usually throws up some good stuff, or GCHQ Cheltenham. I guess the Ruskies have had about as much success as us, otherwise they'd be shouting about it.'

'Back to the Mews then?'

'Yeah, I guess so.'

* * * * *

'You saved me. My hero!' Barb cooed in Jimmy's ear.

'Not here, wait till after work.'

'Look, I got soaked through. Mike won't mind if I head off now. You come to my flat when you're ready. See you there.' Barb breezed out of the office and was gone before he had time to answer.

He sat at his desk with an inane grin on his face.

'You're on a promise, Jimmy boy,' Rob was standing beside him. 'I'm off now. Long night last night. I need my beauty sleep.'

'You planning on going to bed for a month then?'

'Yeah, yeah, very funny. See you in the morning, *my hero*.'

Jimmy screwed up a sheet of paper into a ball, hitting Rob as he disappeared down the stairs. The place was deserted; even the lights in Mike's office were out. Right, Jimmy boy, he thought, time to get freshened up. Important night tonight, mustn't keep Barb waiting. He stood and waved his hands across his desk. All the metal objects—pens, steel ruler, stapler, hole punch—all moved to form neat lines. He smiled, turning off the lights as he left. At the front door he set the alarm and dropped the latch. Reception lighting was on a movement sensor and after a short while it switched itself off, leaving the building in darkness.

*   *   *   *   *

Vladimir and Oleg sat listening to the sounds of the office, not daring to move in case they were discovered. The phones stopped ringing—night service was on—and no voices or other sounds of activity could be heard, suggesting they were alone in the building.

'Wait few more minutes, we must make certain.' Even Vladimir's whisper sounded loud in the silence.

The blinds in the meeting room remained closed. Anyone passing couldn't see in. With the room in total darkness moving about wasn't easy.

'Ok we go,' Vladimir hissed. No sooner had he said it than he stumbled into one of the many chairs around the table. 'Ouch, damn, I bang knee.'

'Shhh Vladimir! We are silent operators. Where is map in your mind of room you made when we walked in?'

'In my head, but it seems it is wrong!' He didn't appreciate Oleg's sarcasm.

They found the door. The corridor, lit only by streetlights, showed there were no objects to fall over. They quickly moved its length to the reception end and waited before proceeding. Oleg, in front, listened. He heard nothing.

'I zink it clear, so what now?'

'We must search offices for tape. We will look for Kavanagh's desk too. See if we can find more about him. We will take it from top. Look, stairs are zere. No lift, it makes too much noise, you do not know, someone perhaps working late.' Vladimir finished speaking; he pushed past Oleg into Reception. All the lights came on. He froze, caught like a rabbit in the headlights; Oleg retreated back into the corridor. No alarm sounded, but Vladimir, complete with trench coat and trilby, was illuminated like a mannequin in a Burberry shop window modelling the latest fashion in rainwear. Outside the weather was still appalling. No one was in Moorbridge Road to see, or if they did, they were too preoccupied with their own journey home to care.

He dashed for the stairs and soon the lights went out.

'Vladimir.' Oleg's whisper wasn't loud enough. 'Vladimir.' He tried again, this time with more volume.

'Keep voice quiet.'

'What do you want me to do?'

'Keep still. The office has only one floor, it is open plan; I will search quick.'

Systematically, he visited each desk in turn. They were all different, reflecting the personalities of the occupants. Photographs of loved ones, piles of papers, copies of Computer Weekly and other trade magazines, all the usual stuff you'd expect to find. He passed by Jimmy's without even stopping to look. His mind was set on one thing and one thing only: the video cassette. After completing a brief scan, frustrated by the fact it hadn't just jumped into his hand, he knew a more thorough search was necessary. He'd wanted to leave without a trace but now he'd given up caring. The cassette was all that mattered. Returning to the top of the stairs, he called for Oleg.

'Here, now.' The urgency was evident.

Oleg appeared out of the corridor, assessed his target, and bolted across reception for all he was worth. With a couple of bounds he was up the stairs and standing next to Vladimir.

'Did you find?' He sounded puffed. Oleg stood resting against the door of the only office on the floor. The door's sign was clear. 'Look here, Mike Wiley, Sales Manager. He was man showing video. Have you tried here?'

Oleg leant on the handle. Before Vladimir answered he was back brandishing the cassette like a victor holding his trophy following a prized fight. Vladimir snatched it off him, none too amused.

'Right, back to Mews.'

'What about Kavanagh desk?' Oleg had wandered off.

'I not see it.'

'So what is this?'

Vladimir rushed over to where he was. 'What?'

'Here.' Oleg pointed to the neat rows of objects.

'I not understand, what you showing me?'

'I not know, zis person very neat or zey have used telekinetic powers to make zem straight. From what we are doing, I zink zis his desk.'

'Very good, Oleg, but one thing you have not seen is all zese things are metal, or have something metal in.'

'What this means?'

'Kavanagh special ability only works wiz metal, I zink he is ...' Vladimir paused. 'He is ...' He stopped again, unsure of his conclusion.

'Made of magnet.' Oleg completed his sentence.

They exchanged glances, trying to understand the implications of their findings. Vladimir was even more excited.

'Wait til we tell zem back home. If it is so, we be heroes.'

'More slow, we need make sure.' Oleg put the brakes on Vladimir's dream. 'We need him back in Mews to test him, see what he really do. If we give him to KGB we never see him again. Our prize will go. You have worked for years in paranormal, why let him disappear through your fingers like sand?'

Vladimir considered Oleg's words. 'You are right, we must make ourselves all important so zey take us back to Russia wiz him.'

With a renewed sense of purpose, both men set about Jimmy's desk opening every drawer, file, letter, and document to learn as much as possible about him.

Oleg found a sheet of paper in readiness to make notes. After a few minutes it was still blank. 'So now what?' Oleg's mood swung from elation to despondency.

'Hey look here.' Vladimir lifted a pile of papers; under them was Jimmy's passport. 'We have found gold.' He slipped it into his inside jacket pocket.

'No we cannot take it, we need copy.' Oleg once

again put the brakes on Vladimir's enthusiasm. 'Here.' He pointed to the Xerox copier. The dark of the office was temporarily replaced by the eerie light as each page was scanned. 'Anything else?'

'Look! Is his diary on his desk.' Vladimir waved a large A4 sized hardback book.

'We do not have time to copy all zat. What are interesting entries?'

'Not much, only work appointments. Looks like he travels in Europe often, seems to be France and Switzerland. One name always same, someone called Barb. He keeps record of everywhere zey are. Here, see. Barb in London, Barb on holiday, Barb ill and for yesterday, Barb at Windows launch. Perhaps Barb is his woman?' Vladimir carried on flicking through. 'Ah, a page of telephone numbers and addresses. Quick, copy zese, and his appointments for next few weeks. Perhaps zey are of interest.' Oleg read the pages emerging from the copier. 'Barb is Barbara Cooke. I have seen this name on one desk.' He scurried off, peering at each one in turn. 'Look,' he said, waving a photo around. 'Most beautiful.'

'Copy it.' Vladimir didn't look up as he was still working his way through the diary. 'It seems like she lives in town centre, 32 High Street, Flat 2. Sounds nice.'

'Do not want to say but we have no idea where we are or how we can find railway station. Come on Vladimir, we must leave. We do not know how long it will take to get back to the Mews.'

'Zat is easy to say but we cannot leave from front entrance, it will be locked and have alarm. Did you see any other way?'

'I saw corridor wiz meeting rooms had exit for emergency.' Oleg came to the rescue again. 'Perhaps zat will be alarmed.'

'But it will not be so public when we leave. It is wet; not many people will be here. We just push it open and run.'

It was alarmed but no one was around. The door led into an alleyway and on to a multi-storey car park. Nonchalantly the two men walked out of the pedestrian exit, following the signs to the town centre. It made sense the station would be nearby. Soon they joined the High Street. With the exception of their trilbies and trench coats, they appeared quite at home. In their wake, the Zylog building alarm was doing its best to let everyone in the vicinity know there was a problem. The direct link to the Police Station worked and several squad cars were mobilised. At eight in the evening the police had little else to do. Not wishing to miss an opportunity to broadcast to the tax paying residents of Maidenhead they were doing their duty, sirens were deployed with the obligatory blue flashing lights. For the police, advertising their pending arrival had the added benefit of scaring off most criminals, so reducing the threat to life and limb and the inevitable paperwork.

Oleg and Vladimir heard, and guessed it was their doing.

CHAPTER 3

TRIUMPH WONDERBRA

In Flat 2, 32 High Street, Maidenhead, Barb was busy, ever so busy; showering, restyling her hair, plucking her eyebrows, lengthening her lashes, and trying on outfits. She tried sexy ones, demure ones, and brightly coloured ones. With such horrendous weather she thought it would cheer up their evening. She settled for her little black number. It came just above her knees, and the plunging neckline revealed sufficient cleavage to send out the right message rather than *take me, I'm yours*. Her makeup was equally subtle; just enough to make her appealing but not so much to appear tarty. After all, she wasn't, and didn't need to behave so. Her ensemble was complemented by diamond drop earrings and a thin gold necklace with an ammonite pendant with diamond inlay. She finished off with a generous splash of Opium by Yves Saint Laurent.

She'd gone all out with dinner, preparing mussels to start, and lamb's liver with mash and French beans to follow. Men, she thought, are so predictable—except for her Jimmy. He was so special. Aiming for seven, she was ready; all she needed was her man. The hall mirror afforded her one last look to check all was perfect. An errant hair had escaped its French plait. *Lucky I checked,* she thought. She set about making good. Focussed on her coiffure, she didn't hear the front door open, or close. It was only as Jimmy slipped his arms around her waist she knew he was there. She let out a gasp.

'God, how did you do that? I never heard the bell.'

'I never rang the bell. I thought I'd surprise you.'

She rotated in his arms to face him. Her face, her beautiful face, filled his vision. Her perfume assailed his nostrils as she melted into his arms. He couldn't help but bring his mouth to hers. He drank her in, a long lingering deeply intense kiss.

Normality returned in the form of a question on how he'd let himself in. 'You haven't got a key! Come on, tell me. How'd you do that?' Pausing to wait for an answer she looked deep into his eyes; he held her gaze. She noticed a twinkle, one of those micro gestures, so fleeting yet so revealing. The penny dropped.

'I was right,' she said. Jimmy cocked his head. 'Like this afternoon, in the corridor, you didn't have a key for the meeting room either, did you?'

He smiled a deep, telling smile but still said nothing.

'Come on, tell me.' She beat his chest with both her fists.

'Okay, okay enough. Yes, no, you're right. I didn't—don't—have keys for either.'

'Are you telling me, Jimmy Kavanagh, you can walk into any locked building anywhere?'

'Well, put like that, I guess so. Today's the first time I've tried it and it's worked on two occasions.'

'And this is the same skill, power, whatever you

want to call it, you used on the tower and roulette wheel?'

'I guess so. I'm still experimenting myself.'

'But Jimmy, this is big, amazing. Just think what you can do.' They fell silent reflecting on the possibilities.

'That's what the two Russians said.' Barb looked curious. 'Yes, this morning they were at my hotel. I assumed they'd followed me there from the Grosvenor; they even bought me breakfast at some café, Susie's or Sheila's or some such name.'

'And?'

'And what?'

'I'll give you and what? You can't leave me hanging. What did they want, who are they, how long did you chat? Come on, I want answers, details, more!' Barb led Jimmy into the lounge.

'They said they were journalists from a scientific magazine, Paranormal Events maybe, I'm not sure. We talked for about an hour. They wanted a blow by blow account of yesterday's happenings.'

'You didn't tell them about roulette did you?'

'No course not, that's our secret.'

'You say they were foreign.'

'Russian, I guess. I didn't ask, I was too busy with my full English breakfast. Much better than any hotel, and I should know, I've stayed in a few.'

'Yes, enough of food. Oh that reminds me — dinner. Tell me more while we're eating.'

'There's not much more really ...'

'Course there is. It's like getting blood from a stone. Why do you think they're Russian?'

'Their accents—they didn't use a's, an's or the's. Quite comical really. And their clothes, more like second-rate ham actors left over from the 50s; sort of Bogart ...'

'And Maigret. Yes I saw them today, here.'

'What, in your flat?'

'No, silly, Maidenhead. Well, actually at our offices, in reception, when it was chucking it down.'

'That's funny. During the rain I was trying to talk to Rob. We couldn't hear ourselves think. In fact, we went to the window. That's when I saw you.' His voice softened. 'Poor you. Absolutely soaked and I could do nothing about it. Actually I came down to reception to try and find you but I'm guessing you were in the Ladies.'

'Yeah, I had my head under the hand blower trying to dry my hair.'

'Really!'

'Never mind that. What were you saying about looking out the window?'

He never answered; a police car, sirens blaring, raced down the High Street. Jimmy wandered over to the balcony and slid back the patio windows to see what the commotion was about.

'Barb, here, quick, look.' He pointed to the bottom of the High Street where it turns into Moorbridge Road. 'There's half a dozen police cars down there.'

'Maybe it's our offices. They could have burned down or been burgled.' She let out an involuntary laugh.

'Barb, it's not funny.'

'Hey, lighten up. I'm only joking. Anyway, dinner will be spoilt. Come here we've some unfinished business to attend to.'

He turned back towards the door, as he did he spotted the two Russians passing under a street lamp. He caught the movement out of the corner of his eye.

'Barb, quick, quick.'

'What now?' She ran to where he was standing.

'Shhh, look.' This time he pointed up the High Street towards the town centre. 'There, look, by Lloyds Bank. Who does that look like to you?'

She peered into the darkness. 'Bogart and Maigret!' She clamped her hand to her mouth. 'Oh my God, what's going on Jimmy? Who are they, really?'

The evening took a new direction as their talk became speculative.

'Come on, you spent an hour with them this morning. You must have picked up some clues as to who they are.' Barb was in terrier mode and wouldn't let it drop.

'How many more times? They approached me in the foyer of the Crown. I'd just checked out and was asking about breakfast, remember I hadn't had any, when this chap said my name. Naturally, I was surprised. He said he had some questions about the falling tower …'

'My hero.' Barb, reminded of the real purpose of the evening, leant across the table to give him a kiss. 'You are so brave.' She lingered on her words, considering their meaning. A warmth spread through her whole being—that feeling you get when you know everything will be okay, safe, secure.

Jimmy sensed a change in her behaviour; she'd softened, and was more loving. He stood, taking her hand, he led her to the next course—for consumption not at the table but in the bedroom.

'No.' She pulled away. The moment had passed. He was confused. 'No, I mean we've pudding yet and I still want to hear about this morning.'

He sat down and took a mouthful of wine, savouring the taste before swallowing. Barb cleared away the dinner plates. She disappeared into the kitchen, returning with a lemon meringue pie.

'How did you know?' His face lit up like a child with a birthday surprise. She cut a piece, drizzling it with cream. He reached for the plate.

'Ah ha, not so fast.' She moved it away from him.

'Baaarb.'

'Jimmyyy ... I need more detail about our friends. Fair exchange is no robbery. You give me info, I'll let you have your lemon meringue.'

'Okay. Where were we?'

'They called out your name. How did they know it in the first place? Actually, how come they were at the Crown and not at the Grosvenor?' She wafted the plate under his nose.

'You remember last night ...'

'How could I forget?' she looked all doe eyed and cooey. 'Why would I forget?'

'Yeah, okay, I meant more this morning in your hotel room.'

'Before or after the phone call.' She winked at him.

'Look, how's a man supposed to stay focussed when you keep doing things like that?'

'Right, my hotel room—and then?'

'I don't know. What was the question?'

'Goldfish.'

'That's not fair, I'm trying to tell you stuff and you keep distracting me. What's it going to be, us or them?'

'Them first. My lips are sealed.' Barb did a zipper movement across her mouth.

'If you remember, my suit smelt of beer and fags.'

'And a lot worse.'

'Well, unbeknownst to me, I'd stood in some dog crap. When I left your room, I got the lift. It was nearly full but everyone cleared away from me because of the smell. Embarrassed, I tried not to look at anyone, sort of pretending it wasn't me. But now you ask, in the back of the lift were a couple of guys who were obviously not revellers from the night before. Everyone was bleary eyed, hung over, dishevelled. Except for them, in their trench coats and trilbies.' The realisation of what he'd said showed in his face. 'They were at the Grosvenor.'

'Why didn't they speak to you there?'

'When the lift doors opened, everyone rushed past me to get away from the smell. I was left standing, confused, until the bellboy sidled up to me and told me of my problem.'

'Then what did you do?' Barb couldn't hide her intrigue.

'Went straight out the exit onto Park Lane. I needed to clean off my shoes. Once outside I started wandering back towards my hotel till I found some railings and a patch of grass.'

'Yeah, I don't need those details.'

'I guess they tailed me back to the Crown.'

'So now we know how they found you, but what are they doing here in Maidenhead?'

'Following me, I suppose.' He shrugged.

'Didn't they get everything over breakfast?'

'Well, I cut them short. I had to be back for Mike's meeting, so I excused myself.'

'Anything else?'

He thought for a few seconds. 'Well, I did give them a business card. They wanted to know how to contact me so I could fill in any holes in the article they're writing.'

'Article?'

'Yeah, as I said, they're journalists for some magazine.'

'That's a cover story, more likely.' Barb pulled her furtive face. 'I bet they're Russian spies really.' She laughed at her own conclusion.

'I think that's enough of them.' Jimmy smiled. Standing, he took her hand. She saw the twinkle in his eye and didn't pull back. He led her into her bedroom.

'It's us now, I hope.' He squeezed his hand.

* * * * *

'Did you note numbers on buildings as we come in High Street?' Vladimir looked around to see if there were any close by. 'Zere,' he pointed to Lloyds Bank. 'Look, 45 High Street. She must live near.'

'Who?'

'His woman, Barb.'

'Barbara Cooke, you mean. Why we want to know

where she lives?'

'Oleg, we are spies, every information, big or small, may be useful. Did zey not teach you anything at spy school?' Vladimir set off back down the High Street.

Oleg stayed put. 'Can we go back to London?' He sounded like a whinging child. 'I have not eaten for hours and it late.'

Vladimir stopped outside a Chinese Restaurant to look across the road. 'Zere, look, up zere, those flats over Blockbuster shop. It is one of zem.' He pointed.

'Da, good, can we go now?'

Vladimir considered Oleg and rolled his eyes. With the brim of his trilby pulled down, Oleg didn't see. 'So where is station?' Both men set off back up the High Street. Lloyds Bank is on the junction with Queens Road. Outside, the council-erected signs pointed to local amenities: toilets, library, shopping centre and station, amongst others.

'Look, Vladimir,' Oleg spotted it first. 'It must be near.'

'What I cannot understand is why taxi took so long.'

'Vladimir, you must see, zere are thieves all the world over, not just in Moscow. We were taken for ride, as English would say.'

*   *   *   *   *

The train journey back to London was uneventful. They found a compartment to themselves and used the time to study the documents they'd copied. From Paddington they walked back to Lancaster Mews.

'What about food? I am very hungry.' Oleg patted his stomach. 'You can hear rumbling?'

'Would you like takeaway, Indian, Chinese?' Vladimir was feeling hungry too.

'No, I think drink as well.'

'Well The Mitre does food.'

'The Mitre?'

'Da, opposite Sheila café.'

'I seen pub zere but did not know name.'

Passing through the doors of the pub they were met by a barrage of piano music and song. The Russians removed their hats and coats and found an empty table.

'Vodka? And what you want to eat?' Vladimir shouted. Oleg pointed to the blackboard over the bar listing the specials. Communicating with the bar staff wasn't much easier.

'Four double vodkas and two specials,' Vladimir said it loud and slow.

'Smirnoff or Absolut?'

'What you zink?'

'We'll bring it to your table. That's sixteen pounds, mate.'

Vladimir handed over two tenners before returning to Oleg.

'Look, zere.' Oleg gestured at the crowd standing around the piano.

'What?'

'Not what, who! Zere, she has her back to us. I thought you would know zose legs anywhere, you spend time enough looking at zem.'

'Ah, Sheila, my lovely Sheila.' Now it was Vladimir's turn to look happy. 'What a lovely picture, especially after today.' He sat back in his chair, lost in his thoughts. He'd gone to his fantasy world where he and Sheila were one. His dream was interrupted by a laden tray landing on the table.

'Here you are mate, your tucker and grog. You boys had a rough day then?' The waiter unloaded the four double vodkas. 'Lost on the gee gees or celebrating?'

By the time they'd worked out what he was saying, he'd gone.

'Here, waiter,' Vladimir shouted after him just as the music stopped. His accent was so strong that everyone turned in his direction. 'I mean you to keep change. A tip.'

'Thanks mate.' He was gone. Before he returned to the bar all four vodkas were sunk.

'That's some drinking. Do you normally drink like that?'

Vladimir looked up to see Sheila standing by their table. 'You are beautiful sight to see,' he said.

'Ain't you gonna ask a gal to sit down?'

'Oh sorry.' Vladimir jumped up, pulling out a chair.

'Ow come you're 'ere then?'

'We were going home and needed food ...'

'And a shed load of booze, by the look of fings.'

'Back home in Moscow zat is nothing. What you English call a tipple I think.'

'Well tipple or not, if I did that I'd be good for nuffink.'

'What you mean, *good for nothing*?'

'Ammered, plastered, drunk as a skunk, you know.'

'Oh no, in Russia mothers have vodka in zeir breast milk. We start very early.'

'So you live close by then?'

'In Mews, and you?'

'In the flat over the café. Pretty 'andy for work, none of that commuting lark for me.' She giggled.

'Oh I love to hear you laugh, it is best of human attributes. It shows how a person is free. I zink you are free.'

'Well if you mean do I have a fella, well you're right, not now I don't. He was a bloody free-loader, 'ad to kick him out.'

'Free-loader? You English have funny expressions.'

'Yeah, you know, I did all the work, earned the money while he lazed around in bed or lost it down the betting shop.'

'It seems you did right to push him out door.'

'Well yes and no. Good riddance to bad rubbish, I says. The bastard—excuse my French—made off with my savings. It was over a grand.'

'Grand?'

'Yeah. God, you know nuffink; a fousand pounds. Don't they teach you nuffink in Russia?'

'I zink I was not at school zat day.'

Oleg who was happily eating his pie and mash special, nearly choked at that.

'Sorry, didn't mean to make you laugh. Anyway,

so where were we? Oh yes, I kicked 'im out about a month ago and the bugger ran off with my savings. That's it really. Bloody men, don't trust 'em as far as I can frow 'em ... well, present company excepted.' Sheila gave them one of her best customer smiles.

'So you require money?' Vladimir was tentative.

'Well yeah, I should say so. Why, wot's it to do with you?'

'So sorry, I do not mean to ask questions. I thought you could do some work for us. We would pay much.'

Oleg screwed up his eyes wondering what Vladimir was on about.

'Wot sort of job? Nuffink illegal, is it?'

'No, no, not illegal ..., not really.'

'Not really, wot's that mean?' Sheila leant in.

Oleg followed suit, he still had no idea what Vladimir was talking about or what the job might be. Vladimir scanned the pub; he was looking for the Americans in particular. And anyway it was too crowded for his liking.

'Not here. Come back to our house. We can talk without fear.' He sought confirmation; Oleg shrugged.

'Oy, wot'd you fink I am, some sort of tart?'

'Hey, keep voice soft. Of course not. It is proposition; is little bit delicate; not for ears of public.'

'Wot'd you mean?' Sheila moved back in her seat.

'Remember young man from zis morning.'

'Too right, he was gorgeous, a right 'unk, and those eyes, 'is tan. Yeah, wot about 'im?' Her eyes widened.

Vladimir lifted his hand to his mouth. 'We need to talk to him privately, alone, but he may need a bit persuading.' He swivelled his head left and right to check no one outside there group heard.

'Err, you ain't queers, are you?' She stood to leave.

'Oh no, my dear, not at all. In fact quite opposite. Nyet, matter we want to discuss,' he drew quote marks with his fingers, 'is absolutely nothing to do wiz sex, I promise.'

Sitting down, Sheila considered what he'd said. 'So 'ow much are we talking about?'

Vladimir looked to Oleg hoping he would provide some guidance but instead he shrugged his shoulders again. 'What do you zink about grand?'

Sheila fell back in her seat. 'A grand! Do you really mean that? It can't be legal if you're prepared to spend that amount of dosh. Anyway, wot do you two do? I can't work it out.'

'Shhh my dear, all in good time. Will you do zis for us?'

'Well I'm not a 'undred percent certain but I'd like to 'ear more.'

'What about now?' Vladimir gave her a puppy dog look.

'I can't be too late, up at five thirty.'

'Look, we will leave now, and you follow in ten minutes. Nobody will suspect zen.' Vladimir stood up.

'Where am I going?'

'Straight down Mews, last door on right, number 44. It is dark green. I will leave it unlocked. Walk in.' By the time he'd finished both men had their coats and hats on. 'See you soon. Oh and by way—as you English say, *Mum is word*.'

'I'll not tell a soul, promise.'

* * * * *

Matt and Brad returned from the US Embassy much happier, replete, cleaner, and with the latest info.

'Look, there's no lights on over there.' Matt dropped the net curtain and sat down. 'Anything on the recorder?'

Brad rewound the tape and hit play. 'Hiss, nothing else.'

'I guess they're still in Maidenhead. That damn station attendant.'

All the rest and recuperation of the evening disappeared. Matt seethed again about the ticket collector. 'Shoot, I forgot to put a word into command about getting that bloody turkey fired. Remind me when we're at the Embassy again.'

'He was only doing his job, fair's fair. Actually that was the problem, we hadn't paid a fare.' Brad laughed at his own joke. 'Fair's fair!'

'Yeah well, cause of him we've wasted a whole day.'

The sound of walking came from the speaker of the listening device.

'Shhh, they're back.' Both men leant in to hear more clearly.

'Put the recorder on,' Matt mouthed to Brad. The

clunk of the record and play buttons being pressed was clear to both.

'Когда Шейла прибывает мы возьмем ее на кухню, те, янки не может здесь нам есть.'

'What did they say? Brad stared at Matt in disbelief.

'You mean you're on a Russian watch and you can't speak Russian?'

'I'm here because of my knowledge of paranormal research; my Russian's a little rusty.'

'Well, they obviously know they're bugged. They're expecting someone and they're taking them into the kitchen where we can't hear.'

'Quick, get to the window, see if you can see who it is.'

Brad duly obeyed. He pulled back the net curtain an inch or two to get a clear view.

'There, look, coming down the Mews.'

Matt joined him. 'Well she's youngish, wears a short skirt—how do the Brits do that? It's nearly winter and these girls run around with virtually nothing on.'

'The dirty bastards. I bet she's a hooker. Those damn Russians either drink or screw.'

'You sound a teensy bit jealous, Matt.'

'No, look closely. It's the café owner, Sheila!'

'Maybe she's taking them a late night snack, you know, a take-out.'

'Yeah, what do the Brits say? Pull the other one, it's got bells on.' Matt rolled his eyes.

'So what do you think they want with her?' Brad sounded more professional.

'We can't hear, so maybe we'll have to call on her tomorrow.' Brad noted the time she entered the building. He settled down, focusing on the door; he waited for her to leave.

*   *   *   *   *

Sheila stood by the green door, listening. She wasn't sure what for, but hoped to hear something to reassure her it was the right door and safe to enter. She pushed—it swung open. The corridor was dark. She hesitated, concerned she was doing the right thing. The thought of a grand came to mind; she took a step in. A thin line of light was visible from beneath the closed door at the far end of the corridor. Now completely inside, she closed the front door. Shutting out the street light it felt more scary.

'ello …' she was tentative.

'Shhh, say nothing,' came from the other side of the closed door. It opened a few inches; the corridor was once again illuminated. 'Here my dear,' Vladimir whispered. He made a come hither gesture. She squeezed through the limited space. The door shut behind her, and Oleg stepped out from behind it pointing to a chair set beside a large wooden table.

'Please, make yourself comfortable.' He was matter of fact.

She looked around, wanting to make certain it was safe. The two men moved to the opposite side and sat. The un-shaded bulb, hanging by a single wire, was old; the dim yellow light hardly penetrated beyond the table. Drab and uncared for, the room looked as if it hadn't been decorated for years.

'You lived 'ere long? If I was 'ere I'd give it a damn good coat of paint, you know, cheer it up a bit.' Her remarks went unanswered.

'Now my dear, I expect you are wondering why we invite you.' Vladimir leant forward and lowered his voice, 'As I say in pub, we have proposition for you.'

'Yeah I know, but wot is it?'

'Shhh, please speak little quieter, you never know who may be listening.'

'Wot do you ...' she realised she hadn't moderated her voice, 'mean, you never know who's listening?' She was whispering now.

'Well zere are people who would like to know our business, and let us say, we would rather zey did not.'

'What is your business? Who are zey?' She realised she was mimicking his accent.

'What is our business is no concern to you.'

'Okay, 'old your 'orses, if I'm gonna work for you I fink I should know wot I'm getting into.'

'Zere are no horses involved. We just want you to be yourself—beautiful, sexy, alluring. Like French say, femme fatale.'

'A femme wot? Wot's one of those then?'

'You, my dear, wiz all your feminine charms. You drive men crazy wiz desire. For you, man is putty in your hands. He will do whatever you ask him.' *I'd be one of those men given half chance.* Vladimir thought.

Sheila sat upright and pushed out her chest. Her very ample bosom hadn't gone unnoticed and her action only sought to emphasise it. Vladimir loosened his collar and blushed.

'Is that wot you mean?' To emphasis her point she placed a hand either side of her breasts and pushed them together.

'Remember he is old man, you will give him heart attack,' Oleg joked.

'Hey, less of old. I am in my prime.'

'You will be in your grave if she continues like zat.'

'Yes, very good my dear, you can let zem go now.' Vladimir took a handkerchief from his jacket pocket and wiped his brow.

'Is that it? Is that all you want me to do and you'll give me a fousand nicker?'

'Nicker? What is nicker?' Vladimir was confused.

'It's another English expression. She means pounds,' Oleg said, coming to the rescue.

'Right, so you want me to be one of those fem fettles, or wotever you said, with that bloke you were with this morning?' She asked, her eyes darted between them looking for confirmation.

'Da, Mr Kavanagh.'

'So 'ow's that gonna work then? Remember I ain't no prossie. A gal 'as some pride. Mind you, he's very 'andsome and well built. I suppose I wouldn't mind.' She hesitated whilst she considered the idea. 'Actually, I fink I'd quite like it.'

'I not sure zat will be necessary,' Vladimir's voice had a hint of jealously. 'We want you to bring him here, we do rest.'

'Wot you gonna do to 'im? Not 'urt 'im or nuffink

like that! I 'ate violence. I don't want no part in that.'

'My dear, what do you take us for? KGB?'

'Who are they then?'

'Oh, not to worry. Nyet, we want to ask him some questions and try a few experiments.'

'Experiments? You don't mean torture?' She peered into Vladimir's eyes.

'I think you have been watching too many James Bond films. Of course not. Nyet, Mr Kavanagh has certain gifts, talents; we would like to see how far his powers can go.'

'You make 'im sound like Batman. Mind you, he could save me any day. So these powers, exactly wot do you mean?' She was intrigued.

'Zat is problem. We know what we saw on television but we do not know how good he is.'

'TV, I knew it. He's far too 'andsome to be an ordinary bloke. A star! And you want me to go with 'im.' She was lost in some fantasy world of television personalities, red carpets and glittering gowns. Vladimir didn't want to disillusion her; it was only a small bending of the truth and would do no harm.

'Okay I'll do it. Now wot?' She beamed a look at each in turn.

'Oleg, please.' Vladimir held out his hand. Oleg passed him a sheet of paper from the pile in front of him. Vladimir laid it out on the table facing Sheila. 'This is a page from his diary. Look here.' He pointed to Thursday 28th November. 'Are you free zat day?'

'Humm. Let me see. Monday I'm in the café working. Tuesday, working. Wednesday, humm, no working. Fursday … Wot do you fink? Every bleeding day, six till three thirty except Sundays, I work in that café.'

'No zat is good.' Vladimir smiled at her. 'So you can do Thursdays. Fantastic.'

'Didn't you 'ear wot I just said? Fursday is like any other friggin' day, I'm working in the café.'

'Okay, okay. As you English say, your hair is kept on!'

'Keep your 'air on, not … Oh it doesn't matter.'

'See I sorry, we, need you from five o'clock. So you finish three thirty, zat gives you time to get ready and get to hotel.'

'Otel? I fought you said you want 'im 'ere?'

'Zat is correct, you meet him at hotel and use your womanly charms,' he shot a look at her cleavage just to remind himself, 'to get him to return here. Once he is in house we take over.'

'And wot do I do then?'

'Whatever you like. Your job will be done. You can go to pub maybe and sing cockney songs. What is it? Roll out Barrel, roll out Barrel of fun! Such a happy tune. We do not sing in pubs in Moscow; zey just shoot pianist.' Both he and Oleg laughed. 'No, we joke wiz you. Actually we do not have pubs.' They both chuckled again.

'So, wot 'otel, no sorry, which 'otel?'

'Grosvenor House Hotel in Park Lane, of course. Do you know it?'

'Yeah mate, course, go there every weekend, when I'm not singing in the pub that is.' It was Sheila's turn to laugh. 'No seriously, I know where it is but I've never been inside. I'm not posh enough.' Her attempt at a refined accent was lost on them. 'Ow do you know he's gonna be there?'

'Look, here, his diary for next Thursday and Friday. Windows Deployment and Support Conference, Grosvenor.'

'Wot's that then?'

'I have no idea. Oleg, do you know?' Oleg shook his head. 'It does not matter. Mr Kavanagh works wiz computers. Anyway, important zing is you are zere when he finishes for day. You speak wiz him and persuade him to come here.'

Sheila checked her watch. 'I've got to go; up at five thirty to give all you fellas your breakfast, if I'm late …'

'We understand. Are zere more questions?' Vladimir wanted to make sure she was clear about her role.

'Umm, yeah, just one. If you want me alluring and that, I'll need a few fings.'

'Like what?' Oleg picked up a pen.

'No, you don't need to make a list. I'll get 'em. It's just, you know, going to the Grosvenor, I'll need to look my best.'

'But you look so beautiful, go like zis.'

'Look, we're talking Grosvenor 'ere, not The Mitre.'

'So what you want?'

'Well let's see. A new dress, shoes, underwear …'

'Underwear!'

'You know, one of those Triumph Wonderbras. The sort that lifts you up and pushes you out.' She used her hands again to demonstrate the effect. Beads of sweat formed on Vladimir's brow.

'Yes I see, but I thought zis was motorbike.'

'Wot you going on about?' She let her boobs go. 'Anyway, you can't have a bra without matching knickers. And of course, every bloke's favourite, stockings with suspender belt. They're a gal's best friend. Guaranteed to get his attention, they are.'

'Is zat all?' Vladimir hoped so, although he was having trouble losing the picture in his head of Sheila dressed in her stockings.

'Well, there's me 'air. That'll need colouring, cutting and styling. Some make-up; lipstick, blusher, eye shadow, oh, and some falsies.'

'Falsies? What are zey?'

'Eyelashes.' She opened her eyes wide and stared directly into Vladimir's while fluttering her eyelids. She knew how to play the game. Sure enough, he agreed.

'Zat is it?'

'Nearly.' She realised she was on a roll. 'In for a penny ...' she said aloud, not really meaning to.

'In for a ruble—or several, it may seem.' Oleg checked down his list.

'Yeah well, a gal's got standards.' She thought some more and counted off four items on her fingers, thinking if she said them quick enough they wouldn't notice. 'Andbag, coat, jewellery, perfume. Yeah that should do nicely.' She sat back, looking ever so pleased with herself.

Oleg scribbled down the additional items.

'Oh, and one more fing.' The two men exchanged *what now* glances.

'Do I get to keep this stuff after Fursday?'

'My dear, of course. Anyway, size 12 dress will not fit me.' Both men laughed.

'12? You cheeky git! I'm a 10, I'll have you know.'

'I think zat is it for tonight. We will let you go now.' They stood up.

'Woah, woah, not so fast, we haven't talked money yet. 'Ow do I get paid?'

'We agreed fee. What you call it, grand? Da, half now and half when finished.'

'And I want it in used notes. English pounds, none of those fings you have.'

'Rubles.'

'Yeah, them. They're not worth a light around 'ere.'

'Zat is good, yes?' Vladimir checked his watch.

'Nearly. All that clobber ...' she pointed to the list in front of Oleg. 'It ain't gonna come from fin air. It'll cost some serious spondoolicks.'

Neither Russian had a clue what a spondoolick was but guessed it meant they'd be paying out more money.

'Okay, how much?' Vladimir was resigned to his fate.

'I guess a monkey should cover it.'

'A monkey! What do you do with a monkey?' For Vladimir it was the last straw.

'A monkey, five 'undred quid.'

'We cannot pay zat!' They whispered together. 'Three hundred and zat is generous.'

'Okay, we'll split the difference—four 'undred.' She spat on her hand and put it out to shake on the deal.'

Vladimir took it and held it in his. Despite her job of running the café, she obviously cared for herself. Her hands were delicate and soft. He imagined them holding him, stroking him, massaging him after a hard day's spying. 'One condition, when you buy your new outfit, you bring it here. I do not want you wear it before Thursday. Zat okay?'

'Wotever you say gov, you're the boss.'

'Good. We will bring you money to café tomorrow. Zere is no time to lose.' Both men stood. 'Goodnight, Sheila.'

'Can I have my 'and back now?'

'Sorry, forgive me,' his fantasy evaporated.

'Goodnight then.' She looked at each in turn. 'Sorry I dunno your names.'

The Russians exchanged glances. 'Zat is no problem. I think it better you do not. Oh, and not one word to anyone else.'

Oleg held the kitchen door open. The light was sufficient for her to let herself out. The latch snapped shut.

The sound, picked up by the listening device, woke Brad with a start. 'Shit, she's leaving! What time is it?'

CHAPTER 4

MAGNO MAN

Sheila switched on the café lights and unbolted the front door. Her café clock showed ten minutes past six in the morning. A queue had formed.

'Wot time do you call this, darlin?' The milkman asked as he dropped off a crate of silver tops and collected the empties.

The bread delivery man was next. 'Just put it on the counter,' Sheila yawned, 'I'll sort it in a minute.'

As the bread van driver left Matt and Brad came in. Sheila went into customer mode.

'Morning gentlemen.' She smiled, though she felt anything but cheery.

'Hey Missy, you had a late night then?' Brad was as effusive as ever. 'Who's the lucky guy? I sure know it wasn't me.'

'There's no one guy.'

'More than one! Hey, that sounds pretty kinky. You can include me next time.'

She chose to ignore his comments. 'Look, you ready to order? I'm running a bit late and need to get the kitchen sorted.'

'Yup, I'd like two eggs over easy, ham, toast and coffee.'

She turned to Matt.

'Yup, fine, same for me.'

'Brown, white or 'olemeal?'

'Wholemeal! Wow, things are looking up. You know Sheila, you're a fine gal.' Brad slapped her bum. 'Now honey, get to that kitchen, you've two hungry fellas here.'

'Over bloody easy, I'll ram 'em up his arse, shells and all if he tries that again,' she muttered under her breath as she disappeared behind the plastic curtain.

'Right, so how are we going to play this?' Matt and Brad leant in so she couldn't hear. 'We need to know what went on last night, what she was doing for an hour with the Ruskies.' The plastic curtain rustled. 'Hey quick, she's coming.' They flopped back in their seats as she delivered the coffee.

'Everyfink all right, gents?' she said, before disappearing back behind the curtain.

'We can hardly say tell us what you talked about with the Russians, can we?' Matt sighed. 'What about ...' He paused and thought some more. 'What if we told her they were the bad guys and if she helps them she could get into serious trouble with the British police?'

'Yeah, but that's true isn't it?'

'Suppose so. Maybe you're right. She could've just been delivering a take-out. You know, some late night supper since they'd been in Maidenhead all day.'

'What, for over an hour? Looking at her long legs and tight butt I reckon she was seeing to some other needs.' Brad thought of her long legs and tight butt. 'I certainly would.'

'Yup, I'm with you there, buddy.'

The plastic curtain rustled as she came back from the kitchen. Both men stared as they watched her move her long legs and tight butt.

'You two look pleased with yourselves,' she commented, noticing their broad grins. ''Ere we are then.' She placed two plates of double eggs and bacon in front of them.

Brad noticed his, then Matt's, then her. She saw.

'It got lost in translation.' As she said it she smiled. Turning, she emphasised her wiggle. 'Toast's coming. Before they could say anything she'd disappeared from view.

'If she's friends with them, maybe she can be our person on the inside. You know, pillow talk and all that. They'll never suspect her.'

Matt pondered the idea. 'She'll want paying.'

'Who cares? It's not our money.'

Out of the corner of his eye Matt noticed the curtain move. 'Shhh, she's coming back.'

''Ere's your 'olemeal.' She placed a rack of toast on the table. 'Do you want more coffee?'

'Great idea. Had a bit of a late night ourselves. It takes a couple of cups to get the old brain firing again. You were late opening up, so what kept you up?' Matt was hoping she'd say *I was around the Russians' house servicing their needs*. But she didn't.

'We 'ad a knees up in The Mitre. I was enjoying myself too much to notice the time. You should come in sometime. Those other two gentlemen who were 'ere yesterday morning with you, they did.'

'Oh, you know them, do you?' Matt couldn't

believe his luck.

'Not really. They just came into the pub for sommat to eat.'

'Oh, okay.'

'Yeah, it was quite funny really. We were all singing away around the piano, it was real loud. We'd just finished a song when the older Russian shouted across the room to the Aussie waiter in a real strong accent. Everyone 'eard. Anyway, that's when I noticed them so I went over for a chat.'

'About the weather, no doubt?'

'Wot? Weather? Wot you on about?'

'Isn't that what you Brits do, talk about the weather?' Brad smiled at Matt's comment.

'No, don't be daft. Anyway he's Russian. He asked me about my boyfriend, or lack of one. I told him the bastard ran off with my savings, good riddance to bad rubbish I says, but shame about the money.'

'I'm sorry to hear that; was it much?' Matt sounded conciliatory.

'It was enough, over a grand. I'm skint now.'

'Grand, skint?' Brad cocked his head to one side while creasing his brow.

'Blimey, don't you Yanks know nuffink? You know, a fousand pounds and then nuffink.'

'So would you be interested in earning a few, what do you call them, quids? Is that right?'

'Ere, that's funny, that's exactly wot they said. You dunno that Kavanagh fella as well do you?'

Suddenly they were interested. 'Kavanagh?'

'Yeah, he's some sort of TV star. Anyway I can't

say no more, I promised them I'd keep schtum.'

'Schtum? For goodness sake, you're British. Just speak English!'

'Keeping your mouth shut,' she said in a mock posh accent. 'Is that alright?'

'Perfectly clear now. So what are you keeping schtum about?'

'Ahh, you can't trick me.'

'So how can we find out?'

Sheila thought for a moment. 'Well I need some new clothes and I'd like to get some savings back.'

'So what are we talking about here?' Matt flashed a look at Brad.

'About fifteen 'undred.' *If you don't ask you don't get,* she thought.

'What's that in dollars?' He directed his question to Brad.

'About two thousand.'

'No, like I told them, I don't want none of that foreign money; only pounds ... in cash,' she added as an afterthought.

'And what do we get for our sterling?'

'Weren't you listening? I said pounds, cash only.'

Both men raised their eyes skywards, wondering exactly what they were dealing with.

'Okay honey, you can have your pounds cash, but as Matt asked, what are you going to give us?' He slid his hand across her bum and squeezed.

'Hey, you're not getting that for a start!' She pulled away.

'Okay, just kidding you. But if you ever change

your mind ...'

Matt shot him a look to say back down, keep your mind on the job. 'So Missy?'

'Well wot'd you want to know?' *I an't gonna tell you the truth. I just want my own back you slimy Yank.*

'You know, names, dates, places. Any info that might be of interest.'

The café doorbell went as a group of dustmen came in. 'Hi Sheila darlin.'

'Hi Dave.'

'Give us the usual, with a couple of extra bangers all round, we're starving. Must be the bleeding cold.'

She turned back to the Americans, 'Sorry gents, must go, got some hungry mouths to feed. Come back when you've got the money ..., say three thirty. I shut then. We won't be disturbed.' She left them with her usual warm welcoming, *all is well with the world* smile, before disappearing into the kitchen. No one suspected a thing.

Matt and Brad watched her go. 'She does have fine legs and a great body, but not much between her ears.'

'Yeah but who cares.' Brad stared at the curtain, hoping she'd reappear.

As the Americans rose to leave they pushed a tenner under the sugar shaker.

Sheila noticed. She couldn't help herself, 'Ave a nice day y'all.'

*　*　*　*　*

Jimmy never made it home. He stayed the night—he

always planned to. From the inside pocket of his suit he took his toothbrush; Barb saw. She didn't know if she should be angry at his presumption or pleased at his resourcefulness. In truth, it was the latter.

'A boy scout, were we?'

He couldn't speak. From the reflection in the mirror in the en-suite she could see he had a mouthful of toothpaste. He spat and rinsed. 'Something like that. Isn't it time you got up?'

Barb checked the bedside clock. 'That's one of the great things about living so close to work—no commute, and I can pick up breakfast on the way. It takes all of five minutes.' She patted the bed. 'Which means that we have some time to spare.'

He came over to her and picked up his wallet from the bedside table. He peered inside. 'Sorry, no can do, I'm clean out of Durex.' He smiled. 'I'll have to pop down the cash and carry at this rate and get one of those mega packs, you know 144. Something for the weekend, sir, that ought to do it—even for you.'

'Jimmy Kavanagh, what are you saying? I'll have you know I'm a very respectable girl. Actually, I was thinking of getting an appointment with the clinic.'

'What, is there something wrong?'

'No you fool, to get fixed up with some contraception. I can't miss out on morning nookie because you're out of condoms.'

'Be my guest. I hate those things anyway.' His smile was so broad it almost hurt. 'You taken the pill before?'

'None of your business, that's private stuff.' Barb

looked at him from under her eyelids.

'You're trying to tell me you got to your age and never been pregnant and never been on the pill? You must be really lucky.'

'Well I did go on it when I was going steady but I felt terrible, quite ill. Swapped around a bit until I found one that was bearable. But as soon as I split from John ...'

'John, do I know him?'

'I doubt it. Anyway I'm not going to tell you about him, well not at the moment, maybe in the future.'

'Fine, suit yourself.' Jimmy pulled his socks on.

'Anyway I was saying, I came off the pill about two years ago and I don't fancy going back on.'

'Then what?' He slid his arms into his shirt sleeves.

'I read in Cosmopolitan about a new contraception method—the coil, I think they called it. I thought I'd try it.'

By now Jimmy was fully dressed and ready to leave. Barb had given up the idea of sex and wasn't far behind him. 'I just need to finish my make-up. Give us a couple of minutes, okay?'

He flicked on the TV while he waited.

'Now here's the news from where you are.' The picture changed to a reporter from an outside broadcast unit.

'Quick, Barb, here, quick ...'

She rushed into the lounge, mascara brush in hand. 'What is it?'

'Here, looks like our offices.'

'Are you sure?' She peered at the screen as she

didn't have her lenses in.

'Yes, look, that reporter chap, he's going to interview Mike.'

'So Mr Wiley, when was the burglary discovered?'

'Sometime late yesterday evening. The alarm was triggered and the police responded quickly by all accounts. I'm a key holder, so they phoned to say they'd discovered a fire exit open but no one was around. Because there was no sign of a forced entry, they assumed it was a faulty door, banged it shut and left.'

'Why are the police back here now?'

'When I got in this morning obviously I wanted to check. We have some expensive computer equipment here, never mind all the usual office things.'

'And was anything missing?'

'Well that's the odd thing, not really. There were signs of someone looking around, you know, stuff moved about, drawers open, but from what I can tell nothing of real value has gone. Apart from …' he hesitated.

'Apart from what, Mr Wiley?'

'A video cassette. It was on my desk. Now it's gone.'

'Was there something special on there?'

'Well, yes and no. It was from the launch of Microsoft Windows.'

'That's me, that's my tape. Come on, quick, let's get down there.' Jimmy stood, hit the off button and grabbed for Barb's hand.

'Hang on, I've only got one eye done.'

'That's okay, no one will notice.'

'Thank you, Jimmy Kavanagh, but everyone will notice. I can't walk around all day looking like half a panda.'

'Quick then.'

* * * * *

They ran down the High Street as far as the police cordon. Mike, had finished his interview, and saw them. He came over.

'You look great on TV, very eloquent and clear.' Barb knew where her bread was buttered.

'You saw it? So what do you think? Jimmy, it wasn't you who took the tape, was it? Wanting to show it to your mates how you saved Barbara and everyone else.' He gave him a heavy handed pat on the back.

Barb watched with her cooey, *my hero* eyes. Mike noticed.

'So how long has this been going on? You old rogue.' He fixed his usual salesman smile. *Bastard! I'd fancied her from the day I interviewed her.*

'No, I didn't take it, but I wouldn't mind a copy.'

'I'll get two more ordered from the software launch organiser. So I wonder who or why it was taken?' Mike maintained his grin.

'How long are they going to keep us out here, any idea?' Barb shivered as she spoke.

'The copper in charge said once they've dusted for prints we can go back in. They'll want to interview everyone at some point. Are you two around the office today?'

'Apart from going to get some breakfast ...'

Mike gave Jimmy a knowing grin. *You lucky bastard.*

'Yeah, we're both scheduled to be here.' Jimmy looked to Barb for confirmation.

'I'd give it at least half an hour.' Mike said as he left.

'Why didn't you say something?' Barb said as Mike went out of ear shot.

'What do you mean?'

'You know, about seeing Bogart and Maigret in the street last night. I bet it was them.'

'I never thought. Well done you, clever girl.'

'So what are we going to do now?'

'Get some breakfast, I'm famished.'

'You blokes and food. Come on then, your treat.'

* * * * *

'I have spoken wiz Moscow; said we must have emergency work done on Mews, and we need £1,500. Zey said zey would have it sent to my account by now. I will go to bank and take £900 out in cash. You wait till eleven. I will meet you at Sheila's zen. What does your watch say now?'

Oleg looked. '09.42.'

'Da, right, all set.' Vladimir pulled his trench coat belt tight and tugged his hat down hard. The wind was whipping down the Mews and rain was threatening. He got to Sheila's just before eleven. No one was in there. *Ah good,* he thought to himself, *we can chat without being disturbed.* The sound of the doorbell brought Sheila from the kitchen.

'Oh it's you. Where's your mate?'

'My mate?'

'Yeah, you know, the other one, your friend.'

'You mean Oleg. He will be here very soon.' He checked his watch. 'Perhaps in two minutes.'

'That's very precise. Is Oleg a bit of a punctual nut?'

Vladimir looked puzzled.

'You know, worried about time keeping. Some people are obsessed. I remember this teacher, a long time ago now, a Mr Stow. We called them all mister in those days, except for the women of course, they were misses as you'd expect. Anyway.' She was interrupted by the sound of the doorbell.

'Here he is now. Mr Stow must wait for another day.' Vladimir beckoned Oleg over. 'What would you like? Coffee?' Oleg nodded. 'Two coffees my dear, if you please.'

'Wot about a toasted tea cake or a Danish?'

'Just toast and jam would be perfect.' Oleg licked his lips at the thought.

'Jam? Don't you mean marmalade! Jam is for tea. It's still breakfast time now.'

'Da, whatever. You English have funny ways.'

'There's nuffink funny about that. Everyone knows—jam for tea and marmalade for breakfast.'

'I will know for next time.' Oleg glanced at Vladimir, who shook his head in disbelief. 'I think she is harmless.' They sat in silence waiting for her to return. She soon came back with a laden tray, including coffee and a round of Marmite toast for herself.

'What is zat?!' Vladimir pointed to her plate.

'Wot, this?' She held up her blackened slice of toast. 'It's Marmite.'

'Marmite? Here, I try please.' Vladimir took his knife and cut two small squares, one for him and one for Oleg. He sniffed it first. 'Okay, zat is different.' He licked it. 'It makes me think of worse things from home, eating salted fish all winter.' He popped it into his mouth, and as quickly spat it out. 'You eat zis voluntarily? Urrg, not for me!' He shuddered, taking a mouthful of coffee to clear away the taste.

Oleg finished his. 'Yes, I like zat. Do you eat for breakfast or tea?'

Sheila laughed—the Russians were quizzical. 'That's the thing with Marmite; you either love it or 'ate it. It's the same in England and you two have just proven it.'

'Anyway, we talk business.' Vladimir took an envelope from his inside pocket. He pushed it across the table towards her. He left his hand resting on it. Sheila tried to pick it up by one corner. He resisted her attempt to take it away.

'Isn't this for me?' Sheila's eyebrows met.

'Of course it is my dear, but you must know what we want before you take it. Once you accept money zere is no going backwards. We will expect you to keep your side of bargain. Like zey say in movies—or else. Oh also, we know where you live.' He sounded a bit scary.

'So wot do you mean, *or else.*' She let go of the envelope.

'We will worry about zat later. You do as you promise and all will be okay. Zere is no need to worry your pretty little head.'

'Ow much is 'ere?'

'Just as we agreed, half your fee, £500, plus money for outfit and of course your Triumph Wonderbra, stockings and suspenders.' Saying the words rekindled the picture he'd had the previous night. Vladimir's stern expression was replaced by a faraway look in his eyes as a broad grin filled his face from ear to ear. The tension around the table eased.

'So ...' She stopped herself.

'What is it, my dear?'

'So if I 'ad some other information,' she said, tentatively, 'would you pay me more money?'

'Zat depends on what information might be.' He thought they were already paying her too much, but as he liked her, he was prepared to let it go. 'Can you give example?' He flashed a look at Oleg, who looked blank.

'It's to do with the Americans.'

Both men sat bolt upright. Vladimir lowered his voice. 'Yes, but we cannot talk here. Can you come tonight, say seven in Mews?'

'Well I was washing my 'air ...'

'No please, seven.'

I've got them, she thought, 'Right, 'til seven.' She stood to clear away the crockery. 'Bye now, Oleg.'

Oleg was just taking the last mouthful of coffee and he nearly choked. 'How do you know my name?'

Vladimir put his arm around his shoulder and guided him towards the door. 'I tell you later.'

Sheila continued to tidy up. Through the picture window she saw them going down the Mews. 'Oi,' she called after them, 'you forgot to pay.' She picked up the envelope. 'Okay I guess I can stand the loss.' No one heard.

*　*　*　*　*

The police lifted their cordon, and all Zylog's staff drifted back to their desks. Gossip was rife, not so much about the robbery, but more about the new office romance: Jimmy the hero and Barbara the spectacularly beautiful sales person, loved by all men, her colleagues, customers and even visiting photocopy repair guys. Since her very public split from John some two years earlier, it was as if her light had dimmed. Yes, she was still fun to be around, yes still good for a laugh, everyone who knew her thought the same, but she wasn't her usual self. On the one hand they were disappointed they weren't the chosen one, but on the other hand they all hoped this was the beginning of a new lasting and fulfilling relationship.

'I feel violated. Damn Bogart. It's not nice to know someone's been fiddling around in your drawers.' Barb slammed her desk draw shut.

'Shhh.' Jimmy checked to see if anyone heard. 'You don't know it was them.'

'Look, there are too many coincidences: them following you from the Grosvenor, buying you breakfast, having your business card, turning up here at your place of work. And to cap it all, being outside my flat.' She hesitated. 'You do realise they know where I live? Jimmy, I'm scared. These guys might look like comic book figures, but they're after something or someone. I guess it's the latter, and it's …' she could hardly bring herself to say it, 'you!'

She stared into his eyes, his oh so come hither eyes, those dark brown pools of mystery and intrigue. She placed her hand on his cheek. 'What are we going to do? I couldn't bear anything happening to you. I need you. I want you.' She cooed.

'Wow, wow, steady on, less of the melodramatics. Like you say, these are coincidences. They seemed like okay guys—foreign, eccentric, but not dangerous. You know journalists, they'll do almost anything for a story. Spending a fiver on a breakfast is hardly the work of desperate criminals.' Jimmy removed her hand.

'Well all I can say is keep your eyes open—we both will. If you see anything suspicious, out of the ordinary, let me know, and vice versa.' She relaxed a bit. 'Oh by the way, have you seen the key to my filing cabinet? It's not in the lock where I left it.' She searched around her desk, moving stuff from one side to the other and back. 'Oh my God, it's not here.' Her voice shot up several octaves. 'It's them. That's how they know where I live.' She scooped everything off her desk onto the floor.

'Hey Barb, steady. Was your address in there?'

'Well no. It's just customer files.' Feeling silly, she looked at the mess on the floor.

'So there you are then.' He took her in his arms and pulled her close. 'No more of that stupid nonsense. I'll sort Bogart and Maigret out. Don't you worry.' He let her go.

'Yeah, but without that key I can't do anything.

All my working papers are locked in there.'

'Why didn't you say so? That's easy.' Jimmy placed the palm of his right hand flat on the cabinet, covering the lock. He took a cursory glance around to check no one was watching before rotating his palm in the same direction you would turn the key. He pulled open the top drawer. 'Your files, Madam.'

Smiling to himself, *once more the hero*, he headed towards his desk. Seeing her across the half height partitions, she mouthed a thank you and blew a kiss. At his desk he was confronted with a mess. The neat lines were no longer neat, piles of papers looked haphazard, and his usually tidy desk was far from it. Lying across the top of everything was his diary, open at the page of addresses. 'Shit, I better not let Barb see this,' Jimmy said, alarmed. 'Maybe she's right.' His phone rang. 'Jimmy Kavanagh, how can I help you?' Work had taken over again.

'It's only me.' Barb spoke softly. 'I'm worried about going home tonight. Will you come round again?'

He could hear a tremble in her voice, 'Of course my love, anything for you.'

'Ahh, how sweet.' Mike was stood by him.

'Must go.' Jimmy put the phone down. 'Hi Mike, what can I do for you?' he said shuffling in his seat. He felt embarrassed.

'Conference Creations, near Henley, well Hambleden, organised the Microsoft Launch. They've a stack of tapes, thought you might like to take my car and pop over to pick up a couple. No, make it three, we can use one for sales purposes. Take the Missus,' he looked in

Barbara's direction, 'it might cheer her up.'

'Yeah, great. Thanks. We'll go lunchtime.' He took the keys from Mike. 'Are they expecting me? Who's the contact?'

'Yes, a Maggie Childs. She's very helpful. Here's the address. Their offices are in a barn conversion. Maggie says the lanes leading there are pretty narrow, so remember whose car it is.'

With Mike gone Jimmy picked up the phone. 'Barb, you doing anything lunchtime?' He didn't wait for an answer. 'Mike's given me the keys to his car. Wants me to go to Hambleden to collect some videos. He suggested I take you, he thinks you could do with cheering up so ...' He checked his watch. 'In an hour, say.'

* * * * *

Mike's car, an Audi A6, was parked in the bay closest to reception reserved for Senior Management. Barb was standing by the passenger door.

'Come on, its spitting.'

'Just be patient, I want to try something.' Jimmy fiddled around the lock on the driver's door. A loud *clunk* signalled the release of the central locking. He held up the keys for her to see.

'Jimmy, you didn't! Oh my God.' Concerned, she checked to see if anyone was watching.

'Come on get in. Talk to me as we drive.' Jimmy put the car into reverse.

'So that's four locks you've opened without keys. The meeting room, my flat and filing cabinet and Mike's car. How do you do it?'

'I've no idea. It's easy though. I just twist my palm over the lock in the same direction as you'd turn the key, and hey presto.'

'Can you lock a lock too?'

'Not tried. We'll see once we're at Conference Creations.'

The winding lanes of the Oxfordshire countryside weren't easy to navigate in a large car designed for autobahns. Every turn held many opportunities for damaging the wings.

'Slow down Jimmy, Mike will go ballistic if you put so much as a scratch on his pride and joy.'

'Don't I know it?' Their *jolly* was missing the main ingredient, becoming stressful instead.

'Stop!' Barb screeched at the top of her voice.

Jimmy jumped on the brake pedal. The automatic, with disc brakes all round, stopped without hesitation.

'What was that for?'

'Look, up ahead.' She pointed.

His view was obscured by a sharp right-hand bend. A large metal gate, the sort used to block an entry into a field, had swung open, roadside.

'Shit, that's dangerous. What would have happened if it had been night?' Jimmy got out to inspect. 'Looks like the lock thing's broken. Probably clipped by a tractor as it came through.'

Barb had the window down. 'Can you move it?'

'Yeah, no problem.' He stood back. 'Just watch ...' He put both arms out in front at shoulder height. After standing like that for a few seconds, he walked behind the gate. At first nothing happened. As he got closer it started moving towards him as if he was pulling it shut — but without actually touching it.

'There, see. Easy.' He climbed back into the car and slipped the gear lever into *drive*. Reaching over, he used his fingers to shut her gaping mouth.

'Did I see what I thought I saw?'

'Well that depends,' he smirked.

'Which journal did you say these Russians were from?'

'I don't know, Paranormal something or other.'

'That's all that spooky stuff. What's his name, he's on TV doing the spoon bending thing. You know, Uri something or other.'

They both fell silent trying to think of his name. 'Uri … Uri … Ustinov.'

'No, that's Peter, silly, and he can't bend spoons.' She rolled her eyes.

'Okay smarty pants, who is it?'

'Mellor. Yes that's it, Uri Mellor.'

'Nope, Peter again.'

'What?' She was convinced she was right.

'Uri Geller!'

'Yeah, that's him. See, I told you so.'

Jimmy said nothing, letting her take the credit. Conference Creations came into view. 'Here we are.'

Being an old farmyard there was loads of parking.

'Stay here, I'll only be two minutes,' Jimmy informed her, jumping out of the driver's side and leaving the keys in the ignition. He shut the door, placing his hand over the lock and twisting it clockwise. The loud *clunk* confirmed he could lock locks too.

'Hey, I'm in here!'

The Audi's soundproofing meant he couldn't hear her protests as he walked into the building. A few minutes later he was back.

'What would have happened if there'd be a fire or something, locking me in like that?'

'Come on Barb, I was only gone two minutes. Anyway, we said I'd try locking without the key when we got here.'

'I suppose so. Give me a kiss to make up.' She turned towards him, closing her eyes and puckering her lips, making a face like a sucker fish.

'What do you expect me to do with that?' Jimmy laughed.

'Kuss me, kuss me,' she tried to say without un-puckering.

Jimmy was out of control with laughter, and she opened her eyes. Indignant, she hit him a playful thump.

'Ow,'

'Wuss.'

'Fish.'

'What?'

'You look like one of those sucker fish doing that.'

'That's no way to talk to a lady.' She sounded very hoity-toity. 'Home James, and don't spare the gas.'

'Will the office do, m'lady?' Jimmy doffed an imaginary chauffeur cap.

* * * * *

Sheila checked her watch. The café was empty and all the clearing up had been done. A crate of empty milk bottles stood by the front door. She flicked off the light. *I guess they're not interested after all,* she thought. At five foot four, even in her heels, it was a struggle to reach the latch securing the top of the door. She was standing on tiptoe, stretching and pushing to get it to move as Brad rushed in, knocking her flying. With his head down against the driving rain he hadn't seen her on the other side of the door. All he was thinking about was getting to the cafe before she closed.

'Gee Missy, I'm real sorry. I didn't see you there. Are you hurt?'

As she fell she'd caught a heel in the milk crate, pulling her shoe off. Empty bottles rolled around the floor. She lay on her back, legs waving in the air, her skirt almost up to her waist. Brad just stood and stared.

'Oi, stop looking at my nethers. Be a gentleman, look away. When a gal's in a predicament you should 'elp 'er out. Dirty old sod. Anyway, wot you doing bursting frough the door like that? Why don't you look where you're going? You could kill someone!' She managed to restore her dignity. Hobbling around on one shoe, the heel of the other hung by a thread, 'Ere, look wot you've done. Thirty quid they were, from down Camden Market. Wot you gonna do about it?'

Not wanting to inflame the situation, Brad thought it prudent to keep quiet while she ranted. From his jacket pocket he took a manila envelope. It was the second she'd seen that day.

Her focus shifted. 'So wot you got there then?'

'Are you sure you're alright? No bones broken? Any cuts? I'm really sorry. And your shoes ... I knew I was late, I didn't want to miss you.'

She checked herself out. 'Everyfing seems okay. My ankle 'urts a bit and I bet I'll have a great bruise on my bum by morning.'

'I could check it out.' Brad smiled at her. Her look of daggers said *not a good idea!* 'Maybe another time.' Brad slapped the envelope down on the counter. 'I'm really here to talk about this.'

'Where's your mate?'

'My mate ...?

'Yeah, the other bloke. You know the one you were with the other day.'

'Well that's what I wanted to say. My buddy and I have been talking and decided it would be better if we had our discussion back at our place. More private, discreet, away from prying eyes. He's there waiting for us now.' Brad put his arm out to take Sheila by the arm.

'I'm not so sure. Is it far?'

'No, just down the Mews. You'll need a coat, oh and some different shoes I guess.' He picked up the money, slipping it back into his pocket. 'Shall we go?'

'Yeah, I suppose so. I just need to pop up to my flat. You clear up these bottles while you're waiting.'

Special Agent Brad Mason busied himself collecting bottles scattered about the café floor. *If only I'd known what I was signing up to,* he thought. She reappeared, suitably dressed.

'We'll go out the back way. Slip the latch for me. I don't want to fall arse over tit again.'

'Another of your English expressions, hum.'

'Ere, follow me.' She led Brad through the kitchen out the back door and into a small yard. They left by the side gate that opened onto the Mews. 'After you.' She let him lead the way

He took her across the Mews, heading for the road opposite. 'Oi, I fought you said you lived down the Mews. Where are you taking me?'

'Look, the Russians live down there.' He pointed to the house with the dark green door.

'I know that, I was at their 'ouse last night.'

I know, Brad kept that information to himself. 'So I don't want to let them see you with me. The Mews is a triangle. If we go this way we can get to our place without them seeing. We need to be discreet, okay?'

'If you say so. Only I'd 'ave put my wellies on if I'd known we were going on a route march.'

'Wellies?' Brad creased his brow. 'Oh never mind.'

* * * * *

In Brad's absence Matt had done his best to make their safe-house feel more welcoming for Sheila. He'd cleared away old newspapers, hidden secret documents, removed food takeout containers, and dumped their dirty coffee mugs in the kitchen sink. He'd even gone to the trouble of preparing a tea tray with a plate of chocolate Digestives.

Sheila entered the lounge ahead of Brad. Matt offered her a seat on a rather tired looking leather sofa.

'Milk?' Matt was being the host.

'Okay, ta.' Sheila's eyes moved between the two men, she stayed sat forward, unsure of their motives.

'Sugar?' Matt was doing his best to put her at ease.

'Wot, with my figure? You must be joking. I watch wot I eat real close. It's easy to put it on, but a bugger to get it off.'

'So I guess you won't want a biscuit either.'

'I'm no saint! There are some things a gal cannot say no to, like chocolate Digestives.' She took two. 'So now wot?'

Brad placed the envelope beside her saucer on the tea tray. 'Now we talk.' Both men looked serious.

'Bloody terrible weather. I 'ate November. All wind and rain.' She bit into her Digestive.

'That's as may be but we're not paying you for a forecast. Have you got anything to tell us we don't already know?' Matt stared at her.

'I'm not a bleeding mind reader, 'ow would I know wot you know?'

The sound of a Russian accent came from the speaker of their listening device standing in the corner of the room. Sheila jumped in surprise.

''Ere, that's my Oleg. Are you spies or summat, listening to other people's conversations? That ain't allowed, is it?'

Neither man responded.

'With that listening thingy you probably know wot I know already. So that's the end of that then.' She put her cup down and rose to leave.

'Hey, not so quick Missy. We knew you were at

their house last night ...'

'Ow'd you know that?'

Brad pointed to the window. 'We saw you go in.'

'So you're watching their 'ouse.'

'That's what spies do.'

'Yeah alright, no need for sarky comments.

'You arrived at,' Brad checked his log sheet, '22.05, and left again at 23.26.'

'Wot's that in English time?'

They glanced at each other, shrugging in unison.

'So wot else did you spy on? If you're so clever you must know everyfing about me. Go on then, tell me summat secret, personal like.' She searched for inspiration. 'I know, I bet you dunno wot colour knickers I'm wearing?'

Without hesitation Brad said, 'Pink with white stripes.'

'Ow'd you know that? Cor blimey, you are good.'

'We have our ways.' Brad smiled, recalling her falling over the milk crate.

'Like I said, why'd you need me?'

'Well we know what time you came and left, but nothing of what went on in between.'

'That's cos we were in the kitchen, out back. I guess you can't 'ear wot goes on there.'

'So what did go on out there?' Matt sat beside her and brought his face close to hers.

'Well ...' She hesitated. 'Before I spill the beans, we need to sort out the dosh.'

'Are you sure you're English? I never understand a word you say. So what does that mean?' Matt had lost the will to live.

'Have I got to teach you everyfing? Spill the beans means tell me wot you know, and dosh is money. Easy really.' She slumped back on the sofa, feeling pleased with herself. Her skirt rode up, confirming Brad's earlier observation. She noticed.

'You dirty old letch. You been looking up my skirt, and I fought you were good at your job.' She wriggled her skirt down.

'Before I give you the *dosh*,' he wanted to make sure she understood him, 'I need to make myself clear. Once you take the money we expect you to deliver. That is, to keep your end of the bargain. We know the Russians are up to something but haven't any more detail. We believe you have. If you renege...' Matt noticed the look of confusion on her face. 'Okay, I don't want to confuse you. Just keep your end of the bargain, otherwise, as they say in the movies *or else.*'

'Oh, and by the way, we know where you live,' Brad added for good measure.

She smiled. 'Is that wot all you spies do when you're not spying, go to the pictures? I wish I had a job like yours. That's wot they said when they 'anded me the cash.'

Brad scribbled a note. *Sheila's on the Russian payroll.* 'So Missy, are you on board?'

They waited in silence. She took a bite of her biscuit and chewed. The two men looked at each other and then back to her. She swallowed.

'Can I count it first?' She leaned over to pick up the envelope.

'Sure, be our guest.'

'*Vladimir, get your coat.*' All eyes focussed on the speaker of the listening device. Brad leapt across the room to the window. Matt picked up his coat then tossed Brad his.

'We must go. Let yourself out. Wait until you can't see us before leaving.' Both men stood by the front door and looked through the spy hole. Sheila saw the Russians leave. They were nearly out of sight before the Americans opened the front door. As they passed through Brad called back, 'Don't forget, we know where you live!'

*　*　*　*　*

Sheila heard the clunk of the latch as Matt and Brad shut the front door behind them. Alone, her focus shifted to the piles of banknotes neatly laid out on the tea tray. Taking up a Digestive she licked at the chocolate coating. Letting her eyes close, her head filled with dreams of faraway places the money could take her to. In her mind's eye she and Mr Kavanagh were lying on a white sandy beach with warm turquoise blue water lapping at their feet. The sun embraced their naked bodies, their limbs intertwined, and he was running his tongue slowly over her expectant lips. She breathed in his smell—a mixture of coconut oil from the suntan lotion, Brut aftershave, and his testosterone driven pheromones. It all felt real to her. Lost in her imagination, her closed eyes rolled back into their sockets, and her hand slid slowly down her torso to caress her leg—she was there.

Rat a tat tat. The sound of the doorknocker broke

into her fantasy, and brought her back to the safe house.

'Oh cripes, wot's that?' Sheila froze, and hoped whoever it was would go away. *Rat a tat tat*. Sliding off the sofa and crouching, she moved, with the stealth of a hunting cat, into the hall. With her body pressed flat against the wall, she could see through the ornate glass panel of the front door, the top of two men's heads. Rigid with fear, she dared not move, not even to breathe. The clank of the letter box flap opening made her recoil. Something was pushed through, but she wasn't sure what. Watching with every part of her being, she saw the heads disappear, although she was convinced the sounds of breathing remained. Still too scared to move, a new distress troubled her—an overwhelming desire to pee.

Hesitantly she rotated her head away from the door so she could discover the whereabouts of the stairs, and hopefully a toilet. Once located, her focus snapped back to the front door; she didn't want to be caught out a second time. Inch by inch she edged her way along the corridor, feeling every emboss of the wallpaper as she progressed. Her eyes never strayed from the front door.

Finding the stairs, she kicked off her shoes, and with a single bound, reached several steps up the flight. Now out of sight of the door and in sight of the landing, she felt safe enough to take another breath. Bending low to the floor until she was all but crawling, she made her way to the first door. It was ajar. She pushed it—it moved. The legs of a bed came into sight. 'Where's the bog!' She moved further down the landing to the next door—it was wide open. The room was empty except for a camera mounted on a tripod. Its big lens faced the

Russians' house.

'Come on, I'm bursting, there must be a loo 'ere somewhere,' she gasped. The door at the end of the landing looked more hopeful. It was shut. She pushed the handle but it was stuck fast. 'Sod it.' One door remained. She leant on it. *Why is it you only find fings in the last place you look?* She thought.

Sat on the toilet with her pink and white striped knickers around her ankles she enjoyed the feeling afforded by her bladder emptying. 'Shit,' she heard the front door open. Believing she was alone, she'd not bothered to close the bathroom door. Now in mid-stream she couldn't stop. The sound of footsteps came nearer.

'Shit, shit ...' She searched desperately for a loo roll. The footsteps were getting closer. Immobilised by fear she went nowhere.

'Well, what have we got here? I've often heard the phrase *caught with your pants down*, but this is a first for me.' Brad appeared. She was expecting him to slap his thigh and shout *yeeha*.

'Hey Missy, want to hear the message from the Jehovah's Witnesses? Something to read while you're sat there.' Brad held out the leaflet that had been pushed through the letterbox.

'Go on, get out of it, give a gal some privacy. And I 'ate Izal. It's like wiping yourself with sandpaper.'

Brad retreated to the corridor. 'Sorry, we weren't expecting guests. Hey Matt—up here. Take a look at this.'

'What's up?' Matt called up the stairs.

'Missy's sat on the *can* with her pink and white panties around her ankles. Now that's not a sight I was expecting to see today.'

Sheila flushed the toilet. Brad was laughing as she emerged from the bathroom. She hit him repeatedly before pushing past him. He grabbed her arms, and brought his face in line with hers.

'What are you still doing here?' His eyes bore into her.

She could feel his breath on her face. He wasn't laughing now.

'Did you and those Commie bastards organise this little escapade?'

She struggled to free herself. 'Get off me.' She kicked at him with her bare feet.

'I bet you did. Well Missy, you're well and truly on our payroll, and working exclusively for us—get it? You're going to feed those halfwits bogus info. Make them run around in circles with their heads stuck up their butts. Is that clear?' He squeezed her arms more than she cared for.

'Clear.' The word came out as a whisper.

He pushed his face into hers. 'I didn't hear you. I said is that clear?' he shouted.

She cleared her throat. 'Yes, clear.'

'Right, now collect your stuff and scram. We'll contact you later.' As he let go of her arms she ran.

'Bastard,' she said under her breath. Almost tumbling down the stairs, she slipped her feet into her shoes and retrieved her coat from the sofa. Matt stood watching.

'He's not as bad as he sounds. It's just his father was killed in the Second World War by the Russians. He never really knew him, but he's hated them ever since.'

Sheila stood by the sitting room door with her coat on.

'Haven't you forgotten something?' Matt mocked.

She looked around, he was pointing at the bundles of notes. 'Go on, take it. You're gonna earn it.'

*   *   *   *   *

'Two fousand, three 'undred and sixty, seventy, eighty, ninety. Four 'undred quid.' Sheila beamed. Her bed was covered with neat piles of bank notes, 100 pounds in each. She revelled at the sight. *From nuffink this morning to two fousand, four 'undred pounds by tea-time, now that's wot I call a good day's work* The thought raced around her head. Still naked following a shower taken after her meeting with the Americans, she looked at the bed and the piles of cash.

'Oh sod it.' She flopped onto them and rolled back and forth in the money. It felt so good. 'Good riddance to bad rubbish. Who cares now I'm rich?' She laughed as she lay there contemplating what she'd agreed to do. 'Oleg and—wot's his name—Vladimir. Strange names, but I guess they're normal back in Russia. And the Americans.' She tried hard to remember their names, but since she'd not been told them she couldn't. *Smarmy git that younger one, and scary. Why is it the older ones are usually nicer? Vladimir's the same, just a bit of an old letch. Mind you, looking at Russian women, no wonder he can't take his eyes off me.*

Sheila stood up and looked at herself in the full

length wardrobe mirror. 'You've still got it, gal,' she said, pushing her boobs together and bending her knees while half twisting, finishing off the pose with her Marilyn pout. 'Grrr,' she purred at her reflection. 'Mr Kavanagh, you've no idea wot's gonna hit you.' A tingle of excitement ran through her body.

The church bells chimed six times. 'Okay gal, time to earn your money.' Sheila stuffed all the notes into a Tesco carrier bag, making sure she missed none, before pushing the whole lot into the gap between the back of the wardrobe and the wall. 'The Bank of England it ain't, but it'll do.'

'Right, where's my undies.' Scanning the floor she saw her pink knickers with white stripes and shuddered. 'No I can't put these back on, not after that awful man.' She picked them up, and the matching bra, dropping both into the Ali Baba washing basket.

Okay, wot to choose? She held her finger to her lips while she thought. Inspiration hit. *They're Russians, Communists, red. I'll wear as much red as I can, in sort of sympathy.* Rummaging in her underwear drawer she retrieved a pair of skimpy, see through, lacy, red, crutchless knickers her bastard boyfriend bought her as a Valentine's Day present. 'Blokes are so weird. Why would I wear anything like that?' she mused, tossing them into the rubbish basket next to the dressing table. Hesitating, she took them back. 'Maybe Mr Kavanagh—I must find out wot his first name is—enjoys such garments.' She continued rummaging. 'Red silk cami-knickers, not very business-like, though it depends on your profession.' She slipped them on. Catching sight of herself in the mirror she preened. 'Okay, bra.' The matching one was a front loader which emphasised her cleavage. Another preen confirmed it was a good choice.

'Skirt and blouse, dress, or shirt and trousers?' The rack in the wardrobe was packed tight. Most of her clothes were short skirts and blouses. It kept the café customers happy and the tips flowing. She took the advice of her mum — also a Sheila — who told her sex sells, and to make the most of your assets. It worked for her. She chose a skirt and blouse, both with a good proportion of red. The overall effect was one of red. Now for the big decision. How many buttons to leave undone? One was prudish, three was more like she should be in Praed Street with the other ladies of the night, two allowed men sufficient opportunity to get interested but doesn't say *I'm easy*. After all, the Russians were paying her for her charms to lure Mr Kavanagh back to the Mews. She needed to show them she was right for the job.

The quarter hour chimed. 'Wot time is it?' She scrabbled for her watch, 'I need to get a move on. Make-up, make-up, wot am I gonna do?' Seeing herself in the dressing table mirror, she thought, black eyeliner and red lipstick, a bit corny but they'll love it. Moving the curtains she peered out of the bedroom window. It wasn't raining and the cobbles were dry. She squatted down to retrieve a pair of red stilettos. Closing the wardrobe door she sat on the bed end facing the mirror to put them on.

'There, that looks okay — more than okay.' She twisted herself left and right, admiring the effect. The church clock struck seven. She took one last glance, 'Cor blimey, I can't go out like that!' She realised short skirts and cami-knickers didn't go together unless you want to advertise your wares. *Too late. Just remember to sit with your knees touching. Don't forget, or poor old Vlad will have a heart attack,* she smiled to herself. *I suppose there's worse ways to go.*

* * * * *

With her coat slung over her shoulders she clicked clacked down the Mews. Like before, the door was on the latch. With less trepidation, she entered. As she closed the door, she did a little wave to the house diagonally opposite.

'She's risking it a bit, that one,' Brad said, noting 19:07 in his log.

'Oleg, Vlad, it's me, cooey.' The hall was in darkness. The only illumination was from the light coming under the kitchen door.

'Shhh my dear, discretion. Always zink discretion.' Vladimir held the door open for her.

'Oh, it's bright in 'ere.'

'Da, we went out zis afternoon to get a new bulb.'

'I got it in the neck cos of you from them bloody Yanks.'

'Got it in neck? What is *got it in the neck?*'

'Ere we go. Yeah the Americans were pissed off, no sorry they were angry, yeah, you understand angry …'

'Of course my dear, so why were zey angry wiz you?'

'Cos they thought we'd arranged for you to go

out while I was in their 'ouse'

'What, here? Across Mews, you were in zat house?' Vladimir was genuinely surprised. 'What you do zere?'

'I'll come back to that in a minute …'

'No, now, it is important.' He thumped his fists on the table.

'Okay, keep your 'air on.' She waited for the inevitable.

'No, keep going, we know zat one.' Vladimir checked with Oleg. He nodded his agreement.

'When you went to get the bulb — and much better it is too — they followed you. I was left alone. There was a knock at the door. I was scared. It turned out they were Jehovah's Witnesses.'

'We have zem in Russia too, big nuisances. We shoot zem. Zey soon stop coming.' Vladimir and Oleg exchanged a smile.

'Well I didn't know who they were. I fought it could have been more of your lot, you know, spies or wotever. Anyway I needed a pee, desperate I was …'

'What, for little green vegetables? Zat is very strange.'

'No, no! A pee, a 'it and miss, Jimmy riddle, I dunno. Wot d'you lot call it?'

'I zink she means piss.' Oleg did the action to demonstrate.

'Oh, why you not say so?'

'Anyway, so I went upstairs, real quiet like, and eventually found the toilet. Toilet. Yes?'

'Yes, we know what zat is.'

'So I was sitting there doing my ...'

'Piss.'

'Yeah, thanks Vlad, when in walks the younger American. Bold as brass he stood there watching me with my knickers around my ankles. I couldn't stop, I was in mid flow so to speak, I 'ad to finish. Anyway, he comes on all 'eavy, saying we'd arranged it that you went out so I could snoop around their 'ouse.'

'Da, two questions, one, what were you doing zere and two, tell us about house, number of rooms, layout, equipment, and so on.'

'Look, you know they came into the café offering me money to spy on you. Well, like you, they asked me back to their place to discuss the terms, so nuffink to worry about.' She acted as if it was an everyday occurrence to be a double agent.

'What about layout of house?'

'Front door, 'allway, front room, stairs, back room with bed, front bedroom with no furniture except a camera with big lens, another room but the door was locked, and finally a bathroom, with avocado sink, bath and loo. Very trendy, but not to my taste.'

'Is zat it?'

'Well I guess there's a kitchen. I didn't go in there, but they brought me a cup of tea with chocolate Digestives.' She smiled, hoping they'd picked up the hint.

'Any equipment?'

'Well in the front room there's a leather sofa, comfy chair, electric fire and coffee table. On the floor in the corner is one of those big tape recorders, the ones with those big spools.' She drew two circles with her hands. 'Oh and a speaker thing, yeah, that's 'ow we knew you were going out. I 'eard Oleg 'ere say *Get your coat Vladimir*. That's 'ow I know your name. I fink that's it.'

'You have done very well, my dear. Here—I take your coat.'

'О боже мой.' Oleg's eyes nearly popped out.

'Wot's he saying?'

'You look beautiful, most ravishing. I must agree wiz him. As you English say, sight for sore eyes.'

'See, we'll make a Londoner of you yet.' Sheila chuckled.

'Sit, my dear.' Both men examined her every move, appreciating the effort she'd gone to.

'So wot'd you fink? Will I make a femme fatlee. Isn't that wot the French say?'

'Oh most definitely, my dear. Oleg, get camera. I zink it would be good idea to get picture for record. Our comrades back home ask about you since I told zem of our plans. Some pictures would be most helpful.'

Oleg reappeared with a Polaroid camera. 'Please stand by kitchen door, no smiling, and look straight at me.' He pressed the shutter release; the flash took her by surprise. The three minute processing time was more like an eternity. She just stood, unsure of what to do next.

'Here, look it's coming.' Gradually a very po-faced, even stern head and shoulder image came into view. 'I don't like that, that's not me. Can't you do another, please?'

'Of course my dear, how you like to stand?' Vladimir couldn't take his eyes off her.

She remembered how she'd posed after her

shower. 'Like this ... Okay?'

Oleg's finger trembled on the shutter release.

'Go on man, press the button ... now.' The flash fired.

'Oh my, zat is much better. Marilyn would be pleased.' Oleg and Vladimir stared at the picture.

'You know her?'

'Well, of her. In Russia she is famous. She did some work for us wiz zat Kennedy. Very helpful she was.'

'Oleg, can you take one for me? I've not 'ad my picture took in years.'

'My pleasure.'

Moving into her Marilyn pose, she undid the third button of her blouse.

'Yes, really my pleasure.'

Shelia was sure she could see Oleg's tongue lolling out of his mouth. *Poor bleeds.*

'Okay now, back to business. Sit please.' Vladimir twisted the two chairs so they faced each other. She and Vladimir sat down while Oleg disappeared with the camera and photos. *Knees together,* she thought, although Vladimir was too focussed on her third button to notice.

'I ain't got long, I've 'ad no tea and I'm going down The Mitre later.'

'Sorry, yes my dear, right, so you got money?'

'Yes fanks, it was all there, I counted it just to make sure. No 'ard feelings but ...'

'No of course, we would have done same. Now you are going shops?'

'Yeah, tomorrow, Oxford Street. Selfridges I

reckon, they should have most of wot I want.'

'Zen you'll bring it back here, remember, zat is what we agreed.'

'Yeah but I need to try it on, you know, to make sure it fits and co-ordinates.'

'Fine, I would expect no less. We have bedroom where you change. I tell Oleg to get some more film.'

'Wot! Pictures? Of me changing! You dirty old git.'

'No, you misunderstanding me, of the complete ensemble.'

'You're doing that French thing again, like your femmes fatlees. So wot's that mean?'

'Your complete look, so we know what you look like when we are Grosvenor.'

'So you're gonna follow me, watch me, with that Mr Kavanagh.'

'Jimmy—we found his first name.'

'Looking at 'im, I'm not sure I'd 'ave fought *Jimmy*.'

'Well his mother obviously did.' Vladimir smiled.

'Okay then, so same time tomorrow?' Shelia headed for the kitchen door.

Oleg came in. 'Here, I made copies for you.'

She glanced at them. 'I don't like that first one, I look like a criminal. The second's much better. Oh my gosh, wot was I finking! It's like wot you get in Playboy.'

'No, not quite—more Readers' Wives.' Oleg smacked his lips.

'Oleg, you seem very knowledgeable,' Vladimir winked at him.

He said nothing, just smiled.

'Right, must be off. See ya tomorrow.' Sheila picked up her coat.

The sound of her stilettos on linoleum and the front door closing were clearly audible on the Americans' listening device. Brad noted the time.

*　*　*　*　*

'God, you made me jump. I know you can open locks but please ring the bell on the way in. At least I know you're coming.' Barb was dressed only in a large bath towel.

'Sorry, my love.' Jimmy took her in his arms. 'I'm here to look after you, no worries now.'

She snuggled into his chest, relishing the feeling of his powerful arms holding her close. 'Drink?'

'Yeah great, got any Guinness?'

'Help yourself. You know where it is.'

'Glasses?'

'In the kitchen, second cupboard.' She went to finish dressing.

'What do you fancy doing?' Jimmy was flicking around the channels as he spoke.

'I don't mind, you choose, but can we keep it local?'

He wandered into her bedroom.

'Do you like ...?' She twirled as she spoke in a deep, slow, vampish voice.

'Yes! What's not to like?' He looked her up and down once, twice and as he did it for a third time she slowly moved closer to him. A lump formed in his throat.

'Don't bother with the dress, just stay as you are.'

'I see you're a stockings and suspender man ...'

'On women, yes.'

'Very funny.' She bent her knees, pushed her bum out and placed her index finger on her chin, 'So big boy, where are you taking me?'

'That's a leading question. Can I use your phone?' His eyes never left her.

'By the bed. Why?'

He picked up the handset, crossed to the window and dialled the number above the Chinese restaurant opposite.

'Set meal for two please; for Flat 2, 32 High Street ... Yeah, right opposite. How much? Okay, thanks.'

'Oh my action man, I do like a fella who's decisive. I take it I won't have to finish dressing after all?'

He said nothing but took her in his arms again. They kissed deep and long. His hands wandered, exploring her body. Ringing from the doorbell didn't penetrate their consciousness. The delivery boy tried again, this time leaving his finger on the button.

'Yeah, I'm coming. Sorry, busy with the ...' He opened the front door. He was greeted by a large brown paper carrier bag, going transparent in patches where the oil from the food was seeping through. 'Great, thanks. Wow, that was quick. Here.' He shut the door.

'Bedroom or dining table?'

She emerged from the bedroom fully dressed. 'Dining table, I think. You'll have to wait for your afters.'

Jimmy unpacked the food—silver foil cartons occupied most of the free space on the table.

'You've not heard anything more from Bogart and Maigret? I guess they got their story, and are now on their way back to Moscow or wherever.'

'Let's hope so. It was all a bit creepy. They missed the best bits. You know, the locks and roulette wheel. And the farm gate. That was impressive, Jimmy Kavanagh. Why do you think all this stuff is happening now?' Barb served herself mindful of spilling any on her clothes.

'Not sure really. I know it has something to do with the tower. It was falling directly on you. I couldn't let that happen. I had to protect the one I love.' He blushed.

'So how long have you had feelings for me?'

'Since the day I started at Zylog. Since I first saw you.'

'But that's,' she counted on her fingers, 'nearly two years ago. Why didn't you do something about it before?'

'I didn't know you felt the same. Let's face it, every bloke in the office fancies you, even Mike.'

'Didn't I know that! But that has certain advantages, especially at half yearly appraisals, or getting expenses signed off like the Grosvenor.'

Jimmy considered what she'd said. 'So that's why I ended up at The Crown.'

'Anyway, what about these powers of yours? How did you know you could shift that tower?'

'I didn't. When the electric cable snapped, I felt a thump in my chest. Some sort of discharge. That's what alerted me. I saw what was happening and I knew I must do something. I ran, waving my arms, kind of frantic like, thinking all the time, no, no, no, not this way, move damn you move! And it did. Like the gate today. I never actually touched it.'

'So in your ..., what age are you?'

'Thirty three.'

'In all those years, nothing like that has happened before?'

'Well, no,...yes,...maybe, I'm not sure. Over the time I was growing up, all sorts of odd things happened, but I never connected them, or tried to control them. Not like now.'

'Right, so what other odd things have happened?'

'There's quite a few really, I don't know where to start'

'Try the beginning.' Barb titled her head and raised an eyebrow.

'Okay, I was born at an early age close to my mother ...'

'Yeah, yeah, very funny. Kavanagh—that's Irish, isn't it?'

'My mum, Kitty, short for Catherine, came from a fishing village, Dingle. It's in County Kerry in the far south west of Ireland. Beautiful place, big fishing community. We used to go often as kids. We'd spend the whole summer there. She was the youngest of seven, so I had loads of aunts, uncles, cousins etcetera, who made a complete fuss of me. Being a boy, and youngest of three, I was treated special. My sisters always thought it wasn't fair. They reckon I got away with murder while Mum told them off for everything.'

'So you were born in Ireland?'

'No, at that time most of the young Irish thought England was the place to be. Loads migrated here before the war all looking for work. My dad too moved south from Yorkshire. He worked in a hospital in Colchester, down Essex way. Whereas Mum came to England in 1938 to Wolverhampton with a cousin, I think; Mary was her name. We always called her Aunty Mary; she was a nurse as well.'

'When did your mum and dad meet?'

'I'm not sure when but where is easier. Both ended up in a mental hospital ... working, not patients. It's not far from here—Kingwood Common, a few miles north of Henley. Nursing was a protected occupation, so they spent the war years there. In fact, we had a staff house in the grounds until '62 when we moved to Sonning. They married at some point, my sisters were born and I came along in 1952.'

'What about odd things happening? You said there were many.' Barb sipped at her wine.

'The first thing,' Jimmy drew quote marks with his fingers, 'was when I was only eighteen months apparently. I don't remember much. Dad loves telling the story of his Magno Man.'

'What?' She looked quizzical. 'Magno Man!'

'Okay, our current Queen came to the throne in 1952, but her actual coronation wasn't until June '53.'

'So?'

'Hang on, I'm getting there. There was great excitement and interest from everybody, the whole country. Since the war people were trying to rebuild their lives and homes, quite literally. There'd been so much bomb damage.'

'What's that got to do with the Queen?'

'A boom in televisions ... we got one.'

'So what's that got to do with the price of butter?'

'Well it wasn't like today's TVs. For a start, the picture was tiny but the cabinet it came in was massive. I don't know if you know but TV's work by an electron gun moving across the screen and exciting the phosphorous coating on the glass. It glows and that's what we call a picture.'

'Okay Marconi, thanks for the science lesson.'

'Well the point is, both the cathode ray tube and the large speaker for sound, housed in the bottom of the cabinet, generate very strong electromagnetic fields.'

'Does this story have a conclusion or shall I pour some more wine?'

'You asked! Yes, wine please.'

Barb poured, and sat back down. 'You have my undivided attention.'

'At the time I was only crawling. To stand I had to hold onto things. The TV fascinated me, according to Mum. At any opportunity I'd be in the front room playing with the knobs and dials. She'd hear the sound, then I'd hear *Jimmy, how many more times do I have to tell you, leave that thing alone* echoing from the kitchen. She'd appear in the doorway: *You'll break it and where will we be then! Now come away with you.* With that she'd take my hand and lead me back to the kitchen to keep an eye on me. Of course she'd soon be distracted and I'd escape again.'

'So what are you saying?'

'Well after the other night I've been thinking about what happened, and of course, with the locks and roulette wheel. It appears I'm magnetic.' He watched her face for a reaction to his conclusion.

'Magnetic! And you think you playing with the TV is what did it?'

'Well sort of. You see, Dad called me Magno Man because of what happened with the new fridge a few months later.'

'More wine? I think I'd better open another bottle. Thank goodness tomorrow's Saturday.' She refilled their glasses.

'It was August and Mum decided cooling stuff in the pantry ...'

'What, where you had a wire mesh for a window and that would keep things cool? That's what we had, I remember it well.'

'Anyway, ... didn't work and she wanted a fridge, with a freezer unit. I remember when it arrived, the delivery men brought it in the back door but they had to take nearly everything out of the kitchen to manoeuvre it into place. It was very impressive, as tall as Mum, white with chrome handles on both the fridge bit and the freezer compartment on top. It came with loads of bits— shelves, ice tray, egg holder, butter dish thing and, most exciting to me, an ice lolly maker kit. All we needed to do was just add orange juice.'

'Little things.'

'Give me a break! Our own ice lolly maker—what could be better?'

Barb took on the challenge. She opened her eyes wide and pouted while fluttering her eyelids. Jimmy stood, extending his hand, hoped to lead her off to the bedroom.

'Not so fast Jimmy boy, I still don't know where this story's going!'

'What I didn't know,' he sat down and resumed, 'was from filling the moulds to them actually becoming lollies takes a fair time, several hours. Mum must have been driven mental by my continuous questions. *Ready, ready*, every few minutes. My knowledge of the physics of cooling was lacking. Eventually she got fed up with me and sent me into the garden to play in the sandpit with Cinders, our rabbit. Because of the heat, I had my knitted swimming trunks on.'

'Ummm...sexy.'

Yeah very fetching they were, yellow and white stripes. I can still see them today.'

'Glad I can't.' She laughed at the thought.

'So from the sandpit I could see into the kitchen. Mum was moving around doing her stuff. At one point she disappeared from sight; it felt like she'd been gone for ages. She was failing in her duties. How would we know if the lollies were ready? Somewhat perturbed, I went to investigate. I reached the back door but she wasn't visible. I ventured in. Still nothing. As a small child, seeing over or around things was difficult. The kitchen table, with its four chairs and covering of plastic flowery cloth, made it impossible for me to see. I had to negotiate the whole room to see if she was there, and since she wasn't it was down to me to check the progress of the lollies.' Jimmy took up a fork full of noodles, Barb had to wait for him to finish.

'Right, as it happened, the chair closest to the new fridge was at an angle to the table, not pushed in neatly like the rest. I had little bother pushing it across the floor and hard up against the fridge door. My next challenge was to find something to help me climb onto the seat. It came in the form of a single step ladder Mum kept in the gap between the cooker and the wall. Apparently this ladder was the handiwork of a neighbour who loved working with wood, and produced a range of useful household items in the shed at the bottom of his garden. Well, handy it was as it provided me the necessary lift to climb onto the chair seat.

'Undaunted by my new-found height, although I did stop to look across the kitchen with an uninterrupted view afforded by my location, I set about my task. Even standing on a chair my combined height left me too short to enable me to get purchase on the freezer door handle. It meant getting up on tiptoe and stretching for all I was worth. Being new to standing, such a feat was not easy, especially as I needed to balance to heave at the handle. All I could do was to press myself hard against the fridge. My whole torso, arms and thighs were in contact with the shiny metal door. I heaved, nothing happened. I stood taller and heaved again. The chair wobbled but the door remained steadfastly shut. I applied every ounce of strength whilst reaching the tallest I'd ever been.

'Something had to give and it wasn't the door. Instead, my heaving had set the chair off balance and it was now on a new voyage of discovery without me. The bang of the wooden chair striking the kitchen cabinet alerted Mum. It sounded as if the house had exploded.

'I liked finding things out so I'd been in a variety of similar situations, proportionately greater than my age, and was only too aware that often crashes and bangs were accompanied by a fall or a knock or some other unpleasantry, frequently involving pain. I waited to take up my new position, as determined by gravity. Opening my eyes—I'd instinctively shut them as the crashing chair announced itself—to my utter surprise, I was still able to see across the table without interruption. I wasn't lying on the floor in a heap of mangled arms and legs, with blood oozing from some orifice. I was still pressed up hard against the fridge door with my feet dangling untethered. I was defying gravity! This was a first, and for one so young, a very disturbing predicament to find myself in.

'It wasn't unpleasant. There was no pain or noise, just an unerring sense of attraction to the fridge door. My exposure to strong magnetic fields of the TV and speaker cabinet made me a human fridge magnet. Not that I knew it at the time, nor did Mum. The noise had brought her racing back into the kitchen. The sight of me pressed up against the fridge, some three feet off the ground with no visible sign of support did it for her. Like it would for any loving parent, it put her into a state of panic. I knew she'd spotted me by her scream. *Jimmy!*

'Utter astonishment mixed with disbelief provoked the response. She was rooted to the spot. I was held fast against the door. Something had to give. It was me! Seeing her transfixed, and hearing her scream alerted me to the fact that something was wrong. I wanted my mummy above all else. I needed to feel the protective security of her arms holding me tight. I wanted to hear those words of comfort: *there, there, everything will be alright.* These urges were greater than the force of the magnetism. I peeled away my arms and twisted my body towards her. Less of me remained in contact with the fridge. The force of gravity took over, not in a sudden way, no crashing to the floor, but just a gentle descent. The sight of me sliding down the fridge spurred her into action. I never reached the floor. She scooped me up as a reflex response. She had no time to think. It just happened. I was safe, she was relieved; we were both confused as to what had occurred.

'After checking me out to ensure no bones were broken, she asked me what happened. Not too surprisingly I couldn't give an explanation. In truth I had trouble compiling a sentence at that age, never mind going into the ins and outs of magnetism versus gravity, even if I knew. She satisfied herself with some self-generated explanation about how hot it was and how I must have been sweaty and the sweat acted as an adhesive. She was happy, I knew no better and Dad accepted it as she recalled the story over tea. Thereafter Dad insisted on naming me Magno Man—not that he knew I was magnetic. He'd trot out the story in front of friends and family whenever he could fit it into a conversation. No family occasion was complete without hearing *did I ever tell you about the day Jimmy got stuck to the fridge?* And off he'd go.'

'Oh my God, you were a human fridge magnet!'

'So I guess that was the start of it. In fact, if I accept I'm magnetic, a lot of other things fall into place, but hey, enough of me. It's late, and if I remember rightly you're wearing some very fine underwear. I just need to refresh my memory.' He took her by the hand, flicked the light switch and headed for the bedroom.

'What about the dishes?'

'Tomorrow …' Jimmy pulled Barb into his arms.

* * * * *

Matt and Brad were beside themselves with frustration. 'It's been a couple of days since that guy—what did she say his name was?'

Brad flicked through his log sheet. 'Kavanagh.'

'Yes, him, did whatever he did, and all we know is the Russians are on to it, but what they're on to, and what they're doing with Sheila is anyone's guess. We need to lean on her, make her earn her money, otherwise we'll miss the boat.' Matt rolled a silver dollar coin across his knuckles. 'Darn Brits. Do you think she's pulling the wool over our eyes?'

'Is it catching, talking in clichés?' Brad smiled.

Matt grunted. 'Come on, let's go to The Mitre. I'll bet my silver dollar we'll find her there.'

Leaving their front door they noticed the Russians' house was in darkness. Rather than going round the long way they just walked past. For spies, they weren't very observant. The standard lamp, so obvious from the street, concealed a miniature wide-angled lens attached to a fibre optic. It delivered a crystal clear, night vision enhanced picture to a TV monitor in the kitchen of the Russian's house. A second lens, mounted on the curtain rail of the front upstairs bedroom, faced their house while a third was hidden in the ceiling rose of the light fitting in the back bedroom; the planned destination for Jimmy Kavanagh. All three feeds were saved to video recorders and triggered by movement sensors. The Russians were out but their technology was very much at home—and primed.

Entering The Mitre, the sound of piano, accompanying a diverse range of singing voices, spilled into the night. The two Americans exchanged glances.

'What's the plan?' Brad whispered rather pointlessly, given the din.

'Let's see if we can find somewhere to watch without being too conspicuous. We need to get her attention and tell her to come back to the Mews. If that fails then we might need to persuade her. Get my drift?' Matt sought acknowledgement from Brad.

'I guess so. Look, in that corner. There's a long table—we can squeeze on the end. I'll get the drinks, you get the seats.'

'Okay, Bourbon—make it a double.'

Brad headed for the bar, scanning the crowds for Sheila as he pushed his way through. Nobody took much notice; they were more interested in the song, something about being a Londoner. Closer to the bar, he had a better view of the piano and who was standing around it.

Hey, she's real pretty, he thought. *Doesn't she scrub up well?* Brad spotted Sheila. She had a fine voice and was happy to share it. What Brad hadn't expected was her accompanying singer. Dressed in a charcoal grey suit, all six foot three at least, some two hundred and fifty pounds, with thick swept back silver hair, was the older Russian. His left hand held a shot glass while his right flailed around like an opera singer reaching a crescendo. He was in full voice. Brad got to the bar and stared in disbelief.

'Oi mate, wot can I get ya?' The waiter followed his eyes. 'Yeah, he's good, great voice, or is it our Sheila you're looking at?'

'Two Bourbons, doubles please.'

'Sorry mate, will Johnny Walker do?'

Brad rolled his eyes. 'I guess so.'

'That's six quid.'

Brad handed him a tenner and left with his drinks.

'Gee mate, that's real generous, thanks.'

Either Brad didn't hear, or he didn't care; telling Matt about the Russian was more important. 'There he is, for everyone to see, singing away as if he owned the place, as large as life.'

'And Sheila?' Matt enquired.

'She's looking great, all dressed in red. She's one fine woman.'

'That's as maybe, but we need to speak to her. With him at her side there's no chance.' Matt took a swig of his drink. 'Jesus Christ, what's this crap? I said Bourbon!'

'You forget this is England, that's all they've got.' Brad drained his glass. 'Another?'

Matt did the same. 'I guess so.'

While waiting to be served, Brad tried to get Sheila's attention.

'You ain't got a chance with her, mate,' the barman said, 'every fella in here fancies our Sheila and who can blame them. Gorgeous she is, gorgeous.'

'Okay, thanks for the tip.' He took his drinks and returned to Matt.

'Have you a pen and paper?' Matt had an idea.

'Yeah, sure.'

He scribbled a note, folded it then wrote *for your eyes only.*

'What's it say?'

'Just that we need to see her and to be at our place tomorrow at three thirty sharp. *And don't forget, we know where you live.'*

Brad laughed. 'I like the last sentence. Subtle enough to tell her we're watching her.'

They slipped away, pushing the note through the café door letter box before heading home the short way.

Back at The Mitre, Sheila and Vladimir had finished their song, to a round of applause. 'Vlad, it's been fun and you've such a good voice, another Pavarotti, but I must go now. Early start as usual.'

'My dear, pleasure is all mine. We look forward to seeing you after shopping. Good night.' He bent down and kissed her on both cheeks, 'Until tomorrow.'

She wasn't expecting that: 'Yeah okay..., tomorrow.' She disappeared through the side entrance to the café, as the two Russians walked home. Vladimir had a spring in his step.

'She is so fine,' Vladimir said.

'Come on, you are old enough to be her father or grandfather.'

'I know, but some women like older men. We are mature, experienced, more knowledgeable on the needs of women.'

'What would the English say? You live on cloud cuckoo land.' Oleg chuckled. 'It will not happen.'

'But I can dream.'

The Russians opened their front door; the sound alerted Brad. He rushed to the window, but not fast enough to see who went in. He strained hard, listening to the noises from the speaker. He could make out two sets of footsteps but nothing resembling the click clack of stilettos.

The whisky had made Matt sleepy, and he woke with a start. 'Is she with them?'

'I don't think so.'

'That's good. I'm going to bed. You take this watch and wake me if you think there's anything going on.'

Brad settled down on the sofa. The drink had done the same for him too.

At 44 Lancaster Mews, Oleg and Vladimir retired to the kitchen for an hour of watching video recordings. Oleg jotted down the times the Americans left and returned.

'I wonder where zey went.'

'Zey were only gone,' he did some maths, 'seventy minutes, so zey did not go far. Maybe an evening walk.'

'Do you really zink so? Zese are top America's

agents, out walking, taking promenade? Zey are spies, not tourists.'

'Seventy minutes is sufficient to get to US embassy in Grosvenor Square and back. Perhaps zey went to check in, you know, get latest data.'

'Well we had much better evening.' A smile returned to Vladimir's face as he thought of Sheila. 'I expect she is all tucked up in her bed now.' His smile filled his craggy face.

'Stop, enough, we have work to do.'

CHAPTER 5

ROTATING HAMMOCK

'I must get a man in to sort this bloody latch.' Sheila stood on tiptoe and swore at the door, 'Every sodding morning it's the same.' Looking down, she noticed the folded sheet of paper. 'Wot's that, *for your eyes only? I don't believe it. Wot muppet would write that?'* She flipped open the note and read it. 'No way, I'm out shopping then.' She found a pen on the counter and wrote under the message *Sorry, no can do. I've a date with Miss Selfridge and I'm out in the evening. Sunday morning's out, it's my only chance of a lie-in. Then mid-day I'm always with my mum up in Tottenham, so four o'clock any good?'* She re-read the note, crossed out four o'clock and replaced it with *16:00 hours.* That ought to impress them, she thought. Signing it *Sheila* she drew a smiley face.

She checked the wall clock. *Yeah, it'll only take a few minutes,* she thought. Running down the cobbles wasn't easy in three inch heels, nor quiet. It didn't require any surveillance equipment to hear her coming or going. She arrived back panting.

'Where you been this time of morning darlin?' The milkman was waiting for her. 'Don't forget I need paying today.'

'How much do you want?'

'For the week, or all of it?' Milky had given up

hoping he'd ever get the whole bill cleared, but he had to ask.

'All of it, of course.' Sheila beamed at him. 'I can clear all my bills now.'

'Wot, you come into some money? Your old mum's not died, has she?'

'Hope not. She's cooking me roast tomorrow, can't do without that.'

'Sixty pound fifty all told.'

'Cor blimey! I hadn't realised. 'Ang on a minute.' She disappeared and came back with six tenners. 'And fifty pence,' she said, taking it from the till.

The milkman held each one up to the light. 'Make these yourself, did ya?'

'Oi wot do you fink I am!'

'Bleeding clever if you can make real-uns like these.' He laughed, placing the money into his leather satchel. He ticked her off in his book. 'That's great, thanks, see ya darlin.' He skipped down the mews rattling the empty bottles as he went.

She busied herself; the usual selection of customers came and went. It was getting light as Vladimir and Oleg arrived. The café was busy, but apart from taking their orders, and a polite good morning, nothing was said. Vladimir was feeling delicate, nor was it appropriate to talk.

She took them an extra coffee. 'Have these on me.' Standing back at the counter, she saw the Americans walk by. They stopped at the door and Matt put his hand on the handle. Seeing Vladimir and Oleg, he retreated. He held up four fingers and mouthed okay. Sheila smiled in acknowledgement.

'As usual my dear, zat was excellent.' Vladimir pushed a tenner into her hand. 'Keep change.'

'Feeling a bit better, are we?' She smiled one of her radiant smiles.

'I am now.' They got up to leave. 'See you later.' He winked at her as they disappeared through the café door.

You should be ashamed of yourself gal, acting like that, she thought. *But wot the heck, it does 'im no 'arm and me lots of good.* She slapped her jeans pocket where a wad of tenners was stashed.

* * * * *

'Come on, it's after eleven, the day's almost over.'

'But it's Saturday! Just another hour ...' Jimmy's plea was lost in the duvet.

Barb stretched over him, grabbing for his wallet. 'Only on one condition.' She waved a Durex in the air.

His face appeared from under the covers. 'What, again!'

'You boys these days have no stamina. Maybe while I'm at the clinic you can talk to the doctor about your sex drive.'

'What's wrong with my sex drive?' He sounded quite indignant.

'John and I ... sorry, I didn't mean to say that.' A blush moved up her cheeks.

'What about you and John? You've started so you might as well finish.' Jimmy's tone had an edge.

'It's just he, we, were more suited in that department.'

'What's that supposed to mean? You were at it like rabbits?'

'No …, well maybe, yes, I suppose so.'

'I believe in quality over quantity.'

'John managed both.' She looked wistful.

Jimmy sensed their break up had left a big hole in her life. 'I don't know what happened between you two, that's your business, but I'm not John.'

'No, you're right,' she paused whilst she thought, 'but you still might want to get yourself checked out.'

He slid his arm around her waist.

'No Jimmy, not now, the moment's passed.' She threw the covers back and headed to the bathroom. He watched her. *She really is beautiful and so sexy*, he thought. He drifted back to sleep. She left him to it.

Alone with her thoughts she busied herself with breakfast. Barb had a pang of guilt over John; lovemaking had been an important part of their relationship. Actually, she reflected, *maybe that's all we had; that's why it never lasted*.

'Jimmy, toast and coffee's ready.'

He came to. 'There in a minute,' He called, hauling himself out of bed. 'Seen my boxers anywhere?'

'On the floor by the bathroom door.'

He appeared at the dining table. 'You got any cornflakes? I really fancy a bowl.'

'Cereals are in the first cupboard on the right.'

He wandered into the kitchen. 'Can't see any.'

'See the list on the counter? Just add them on

there.'

'Are you going shopping?' He was back at the dining table.

'Of course. It's Saturday, all those boring jobs have to be done sometime. Why don't you come too? I was thinking of trying the new Sainsbury's down the A4 near Taplow.'

'Can't wait.'

'Sarcasm isn't very helpful. Now get yourself dressed.'

'Bet John didn't go shopping.' Jimmy muttered, but Barb heard.

If looks could kill: '... that was a bit unnecessary.' She grabbed the crockery off the table and stormed into the kitchen. 'Bastard!' She had tears in her eyes. He neither heard nor saw. Those feelings she'd so successfully suppressed after the breakup were actually just below the surface. Her new relationship had rekindled them.

Jimmy appeared dressed and ready to go. She was in the kitchen stacking the dishwasher. He held out his hand, looking for her to take it. She turned, looking him full in the face, they held their gaze.

'Sorry,' they both said together. He held her, she held him back, they melted into one. He kissed the top of her head, inhaling deeply the scent of the new woman in his life.

'Sainsbury's?'

'Sainsbury's.'

*   *   *   *   *

Turning into Sainsbury's car park it appeared the whole of Maidenhead had the same idea. Eventually they found a space. Jimmy got a trolley. Barb went straight to the entrance to wait for him. She saw him coming towards her. As he got closer she could see he wasn't touching it—just walking in front with his arms by his side, palms facing backwards. The trolley was following him like a dog on a lead—but with no lead. Anyone else looking would think he'd just pulled it or something, but she knew what he was doing.

'Any more tricks up your sleeve?'

'Saves getting your hands dirty,' he laughed.

Just inside the main door was a display of Ambrosia Creamed Rice Pudding—several hundred tins stacked in a great pyramid. Jimmy set his trolley in motion but supermarket trolleys tend to have a mind of their own and without a firm guiding hand they can display wayward behaviour. A child, oblivious to the world around him, ran between the trolley and Jimmy, causing Jimmy to lose control. The trolley continued its journey, unabated. It was too late to do anything so he didn't wait to see the outcome. He quickly turned on his heels and head for the exit, and the trolley park to retrieve another one.

Barb, who had been studying her list trying to decide which aisles to visit, was brought back to the here and now by the clatter and commotion. Mothers grabbed for toddlers, older kids watched and yelled in amazement, and pensioners scurried as best they could to avoid the tide of tins advancing across the floor towards the large revolving doors. As they rotated, more and more tins amassed being swept along in never ending circles. Some rolled onto the pavement outside only to be popped surreptitiously into passing shoppers' bags. The crowd of errant tins grew to the point where they completely overwhelmed the revolving door. It jammed, but not beaten, it pushed forward until the pressure sensor killed the power. It released, waited and tried again, and again, and again. Only the swift action of a Saturday boy shelf-stacker hitting the emergency stop button brought the door to a halt.

Jimmy, along with many other shoppers, was stuck on the outside looking at the unfolding scene. Those on the inside, who had paid for their shopping and were struggling with their overstuffed bags, couldn't leave. Several other would-be shoppers, separated by the jammed doors, milled around not knowing what to do. Without a trolley there was no point in venturing off down the aisles. Some people wanted to be helpful and were now collecting cans. Unsure of what to do with them they passed them to the Saturday boy. He soon disappeared under an armful in danger of becoming too heavy to hold.

'Hope you're satisfied with yourself.'

Jimmy tried to read Barb's lips, but failed. He shrugged instead. 'I didn't do it on purpose,' he mouthed back to no avail. It was a good quarter of an hour before normal service was resumed.

'Okay, looks like I need to be more careful in the future.'

'Shhh, someone will hear you. Right, fruit and veg.' Barb headed off with Jimmy behind her, pushing the trolley. 'I want to see two hands on that handle all the time.' She sounded like his mother.

'Yes Mummy,' he said under his breath.

The rest of the shopping trip was uneventful.

'Do you fancy a coffee or a Danish?' Jimmy asked. They headed for the cafeteria, finding a table near the trolleys. 'My treat.' He said, returning with a tray. 'They've a great selection.' He set about his Danish pastry; the sort filled with custard.

* * * * *

'You know what we were talking about last night, about when you were young. What happened after Magno Man?' Barb licked away the custard from the corner of her mouth

'Not a lot really, well not until I was six. I had a very strange experience with a hammock.'

'A what?' She wasn't sure she'd heard him.

'A hammock ... In post-world-war Britain things were different—but not for me or you I guess, since neither of us were born until seven years after the hostilities ended.

'Rationing ended July 1954. Didn't it?' Barb chipped in.

'In our house Dad would get all sorts of military surplus. Many shops selling this sort of stuff sprung up around the country. Much of the surplus came from US sources. They had landed millions of tons in the UK during their war involvement. After the conflict much of what wasn't used, lost, stolen or just spirited away found its way to these shops. One such item ended up at our house: a hammock. It was a basic camouflage type with metal rings at each end where the ropes providing support were tied off. These in turn could be connected by a single rope to a tree to enable it to swing freely. To a brave six year old like me this was Nirvana.

'Dad hung it in the garden. Of course my imagination ran away with itself. I devised all sorts of stories and had a multitude of adventurers. For a complete summer it became the total focus of my fantasies. That was fine until the days started to get shorter and cooler. Deprived of my favourite toy, after much disquiet and badgering Dad eventually mounted a couple of heavyweight zinc plated 'eyes' in the walls of the laundry room. One on either side so the hammock could be suspended between them if Mum wasn't in there. She had a new Hotpoint washer, a tumble dryer, and an old hand mangle mounted on a butler's sink, plus various items all useful for keeping our clothes clean, fresh and ironed. On washday she would set these devices off knowing their cycles would take several hours; none of this 40 degrees heat like today, it was all washed at, or near boiling point.

'To enable me to quickly attach or detach my hammock Dad bought a pair of snap hooks with swivel ends. This allowed the hammock total freedom of movement, even to rotate if needs be.

'I remember on one particularly cold wet Saturday afternoon, Mum needed to get the laundry sorted and I wanted to play in the hammock. She went first setting off a washing machine full and a tumble dryer load. The room was chilly so she put on the wall mounted electric fire, both bars. It was overcast so she had the light on. To cap it all off the radio was on too. In that small space there was enough electricity being consumed to keep the local power station running at full tilt.

'Left to my own devices, I soon had the hammock mounted. I climbed in and closed the top; that was a feature of this style of hammock as it meant soldiers on patrol could keep dry. Inside it was more like a small tent suspended off the ground. I was playing my favourite game — hiding from baddies who were trying to find my secret location. Keeping very still so as not to alert them to my position I lay prone, silent, expectant.

'At first the gentle movement was, I thought, just residual motion from where I'd been settling down. The laundry machines were humming, the electric fire was heating up the room and the radio was playing for all it was worth. All these appliances were fed electricity via the ring mains; the copper wires running around the room feeding the different sockets. Remember I was magnetised by the TV. In this high electrical energy environment, I believe the two interacted. The copper wires in the walls were like the turns in a motor carrying the current and I provided the magnetic field. Encased in the hammock that could turn freely, the inevitable happened — as described by Faraday over 100 years earlier. It started to rotate. Remember; school, science?'

Barb sort of nodded. 'No not really.'

'The pump on the washer kicked in, so increasing the current load significantly. The hammock rotations gathered pace—not just swinging back and forth, nor gently turning but full rotations at a speed up to 50 rpm in line with the mains frequency. I was the core of a human electric motor. Flummoxed, I had no choice but to go with it. Feeling totally disorientated, nauseous, and frightened, yet excited, I just hung on very tight. The duration of the pump running was determined by the amount of water to drain. Usually this took a couple of minutes and was always accompanied by a lot of clatter as the drum hit resonance. The sound was very distinctive and could be heard around the whole house. Once it ceased Mum would know it was time to return to the laundry room. On cue she arrived. The rotations stopped and I was left swinging. To her it appeared nothing was wrong since that's what hammocks do.

'She asked how the game was going and did a few shoot 'em up noises to get into the spirit of things. I didn't reply and she didn't really notice as she was focused on the washing. Inside the hammock I lay dazed, speechless, not knowing what to think. My knowledge of science was very rudimentary even if I was to think that way. For me it was just a game, a very unusual game and one I couldn't explain. It never happened again as I didn't know the conditions needed to repeat it, although I tried. It was an experience I'll never forget and was added to the list of unusual things that happened to me as I grew up.'

'That's incredible.' Barb wasn't sure what to think. 'Aren't you curious as to what is happening to you? To be magnetic you need iron. Isn't that so?'

*   *   *   *   *

Closing time couldn't come quickly enough. One old chap, a regular, whose wife died several years ago, found his mug and plate cleared away a good half hour before three thirty.

'Sorry Bert, special occasion, closing early.'

Shelia's smile was small compensation. He was disappointed. She saw.

'Tell you wot, 'ave that one on me.' She felt less guilty, he felt more happy.

Fortunately the shops in Oxford Street stay open late. She had a lot to get and many decisions to make. Between Selfridges, Debenhams and John Lewis, she managed to get everything. Given the number of bags acquired, and the time, Sheila hailed a taxi. '44 Lancaster Mews' she said to the driver. *That felt good, I could get used to this,* she thought.

The taxi driver kept looking at her in his rear view mirror wondering if she could afford it? *That's expensive there.* Noticing all her bags, he changed his mind.

The throb of a London taxi on tick-over is distinctive and loud. Both Matt and Brad watched from the bedroom window as it disgorged its passenger with baggage. Brad took dozens of pictures, getting close-ups of each carrier bag, the open door of the house and hall, Sheila handing over money to the taxi driver, and the taxi driver himself just in case.

Vladimir and Oleg, watched the TV monitors in the kitchen, and kept well out of sight until the front door shut.

'Okay, where do you want these?' Sheila called down the empty corridor.

'Just coming, my dear. I will show you bedroom.' Vladimir appeared and scooped up a handful of bags. 'Zis way.'

The hall, stairs and landing were all in darkness. She noticed there were no bulbs in any of the fittings.

'Why no lights?' she asked as her foot missed a step. 'Bollocks. Sorry, it just slipped out.'

'Zat is not a word I am familiar wiz. What are bollocks?' Vladimir asked, slowly and deliberately, practising the pronunciation.

'You remember 'itler?'

'Da of course, what has zat to do wiz it?'

'Well he only had one.'

'One? Oh yes, I see now. In Russian we call zem *mudak*.' He laughed. 'Here, zis door.' He pushed it open. 'Come in.'

Street lighting illuminated a single bed, chair, dressing table and wardrobe.

'You got a bulb in 'ere?' She went for the light switch.

'Not yet, my dear,' he said, pulling her arm away. 'We must shut door and curtain first.' The street light disappeared behind the blackout curtain. The room fell into total darkness.

'Well that wasn't too clever. I can't see nuffink now.'

'Just wait.' He pulled a small torch from his jacket pocket. 'Zere, see.' He shone a thin beam of light onto the switch. 'Close door first, zat is better.'

'Are you skint or summat? You can't see a knat's arse in this light.'

'Knat's arse? Why would you go looking at knat's arse?'

'I meant it ain't very bright.'

'Why you not say? Zis would be like football stadium floodlights, in Moscow. In fact, most apartments only have one bulb altogether. Rest are sold off to buy vodka.' He looked sad. 'Drink is real problem. If it does not kill you it makes you blind. Zen you do not need light bulbs.'

'Err, that's sick, that is.'

'Anyway, we leave you now. Would you like tea or vodka?' Vladimir waited by the bedroom door.

'Tea with milk, oh and 'ave you any of those chocolate Digestives like the Americans do? I've 'ardly eaten all day.'

'Oleg bought Marmite. Would you like some?'

'Yeah great, a couple of slices, toasted.'

'Put light out so I can go into corridor. When I bring up tea, put out light before letting me in, okay?'

Alone with her purchases, she needed to sort out what she'd bought. She hung the items that needed hanging on the outside of the wardrobe; make-up and jewellery went on the dressing table while underwear, accessories and shoes on the bed. She surveyed them. Her face lit up with excitement. *Oh I must pee first.* Standing by the door, she switched out the light.

The monitor went blank. 'Now what she doing?'

'Quick, switch on night vision.' The picture returned but Sheila was nowhere to be seen.

'Where is she?' Vladimir's whisper was more a shout.

'Bollocks,' echoed down the stairs.

'What did she say?' Oleg didn't understand.

'She is talking about Hitler.' Now Oleg was more confused than ever.

Vladimir opened the kitchen door. 'Hold on my dear, I am coming wiz torch.'

'I just need a pee, that's all.' As the beam of the torch illuminated her she could see she'd kicked the night stand. 'No damage done.'

'At end of the landing. Zere.' He pointed out the door handle with his torch light.

'Stay there, don't come any further.' She disappeared from sight. 'Wot is it with you spies and Izal, is it part of your toughening up?' She shouted through the closed door. Having flushed and rinsed she reappeared, before disappearing back into the bedroom. A thin glow came from under the door. Vladimir got back into the kitchen just as the image changed from night vision to normal colour. Her jeans were the first to come off. Both men stared, transfixed, not even blinking. Next was her jumper.

'Zis is wrong, we should switch off.'

'True Vladimir, but we have not had a chance to test equipment. Wait until I see if I can focus and zoom.' Oleg pushed the controls on the mixing desk. First her very full breast filled the entire screen, 'Ah good, zoom works.' He fiddled some more. 'Look,' he said triumphantly, 'she has little blonde hair on her nipple.'

'So focus works zen, now turn off.'

'I need to test sound.' He increased the volume. They could see her holding up her new knickers.

'Ah they're so sweet, Jimmy will love these.' She bent down as Vladimir hit the off switch.

'What you do zat for?'

'Because Mother would turn in her grave if she knew I was watching zat—sorry Mama.' Vladimir looked to Heaven.

'But your mother is not dead.'

'I know, but if she was, she would.'

'Come on, zis is once in lifetime opportunity.' Oleg's hand hovered over the on-switch.

'You can watch but I am going to make her cup of tea and Marmite toast.'

'What, my Marmite?'

'She had nothing to eat all day.'

'But … But …'

'It is small price to pay; look what you get back in return.'

Oleg switched the monitor back on; Sheila once again filled the screen.

CHAPTER 6

DEW DROP INN

'Sundays, I love Sundays. You know, doing nothing, footie on the telly—Spurs are playing—reading the paper.' Jimmy picked up the remote—Barb sighed.

'What?' He didn't know what her problem was.

'Have you seen outside? The sun's appeared after I don't know how many days of rain. You've been sat at your desk all week …'

'We went to Sainsbury's yesterday.'

'That doesn't count. Come on, there's masses of great walks around here. You've got the Thicket, Pinkneys Green, Knowle Hill, Henley by the river and loads more.' She thought for a bit. 'I know—what about the Dew Drop Inn, Honey Lane?'

'Where?'

'It's a real olde worlde pub, Henley Brewery owned; they do a fantastic Sunday roast. Home cooked, as good as your mum does. We can drive to Hurley, and leave the car there. From the car park a path leads across the field and through the woods. It's about a mile and a half. What do you say?'

'Have I got a choice?'

'And I thought you were my action man, my hero. You're just like all the rest, damn football mad. If I said the pub's got one of those projector tellies and a dartboard, would that help?'

'Have they?' He got up from the sofa. 'Right let's go.' He rubbed his hands in glee.

'You really think I'd suggest a place like that? Of course they haven't.'

'What, they've no telly or dartboard?' Jimmy's enthusiasm melted.

'Certainly no telly. They may have a dartboard.' Barb was disappointed in him.

Jimmy's hand was resting on the remote control. Barb saw—he noticed—she kept looking. He got the hint and moved his hand away.

'Right, get your coat and scarf,' he said, 'it might be sunny but I bet it's chilly.'

Barb drove. Hurley was only a few minutes away, especially on a Sunday, but the bad atmosphere made it feel much longer. Parking, she switched the ignition off. Jimmy was out the passenger door like a dog from a starting gate.

Don't slam ...' She said it too late. The slamming of car doors really annoyed her. Jimmy walked off in the direction of the Public Footpath sign without looking back or waiting for her. She went to the boot for her wellingtons. It was wet underfoot. By the time she was ready he'd disappeared out of sight over the brow of the hill. She walked slowly, using the time to think about her, Jimmy and, surprisingly, John. He kept coming back into her mind.

On the brow of the hill the path split. The straighter, more obvious path took you through some woods towards the pub while the right fork went north in the direction of Henley. Barb went straight on into the woods. In November, with no leaves on the trees and with the sun shining, it was bright. She never considered her safety, and had no reason to. Lost in her thoughts, she carried on. The route was well known to her. It had been a favourite walk with John. Although she'd not done it for a long time, it had a satisfying familiarity. She passed the large oak looking like an Ent, menacing, scary. *Tolkien has a lot to answer for* she thought. She knew it was just a story, and anyway the pub came into view right after it. The large blue sign with gold writing, *Dew Drop Inn, Brakspear*, was in desperate need of paint but other than that the brick and flint building hadn't changed. The only entrance was via a black, wide, low wooden door. Even she needed to duck. Her finger found the latch; there was a familiar sound—a metallic clunk, as it released. She pushed—the warmth of the fires, one in each bar, the smell of freshly cooked food and the sound of cutlery on crockery, accompanied by the low hum of conversation, assailed her senses.

She pictured her and John at the table next to the fire. It was everyone's favourite table; it had to be booked well in advance unless you were extremely lucky. Today it was occupied. Looking around there was no sign of Jimmy. She retraced her steps to the entrance and this time went left into the Public Bar, not that there was much difference. DH Lawrence was serving—not really, but his doppelganger. It was odd seeing him there. He'd been the landlord since her very first visit. She found it difficult not to ask him about Lady Chatterley's Lover or Sons and Lovers, or one of his many other titles. She'd read a lot, especially since John was no longer in her life, but that had all changed now—or so she hoped. *Where is Jimmy?*

'Can I help, my dear?' DH's lookalike spoke to her.

'Any chance of a table for two? We've not booked.'

'For you my dear, I'm sure we can fit you in. I'll get Betty to check.'

Does he remember me or is he just this welcoming to all his customers? Barb thought. 'Thanks I'll wait.'

He disappeared into the back, before reappearing to say: 'She reckons in about ten minutes, okay?'

'Yes, absolutely fine.'

'Where's John?'

He did remember her! Barb face reddened, and she looked down not wanting to make eye contact.

'Oh I see, sorry my dear' he hesitated. 'So who's your new man?' Now he blushed. 'Oops, a bit presumptuous there.'

'No, no problem, it's no secret. His name's Jimmy but it's still early days. Actually I was just looking for him. I can't see him here or in the other bar. He set off at great pace. You see, we were parked at Hurley and walked up.'

'Good for the appetite! You'll be hungry then. I'll tell Betty to give you extra.'

'At the moment, it's only me ...' She scanned the bar again.

'Maybe he's in the Gents. Give him a few minutes.'

A tapping sound on the bar indicated someone wanted serving. DH moved off.

Barb sat on the stool, not sure what to do next. Five minutes passed, then ten, followed by fifteen.

'Betty says the table's ready. Sorry it's not next to the fire.'

She smiled. 'That's okay. Which one?'

'By the window. Betty's there, she'll show you.'

Barb went through; she was greeted like a long lost friend. 'We've missed you. It's been a while. Sorry to hear about you and John. Anyway, that's all in the past now you've got Jimmy.'

News travels fast around here, she thought. 'Thanks—only I can't find him. We sort of had a tiff and he walked off. He doesn't know these paths but since it's straight up from Hurley ...'

'Yeah, I heard you'd walked. I'll pop an extra slice of meat on your plate. So he's got himself lost. Well it's a good afternoon for exercise. Don't worry, he's a grown man, it'll do him good. That'll teach him for rowing with you. You don't deserve that.' Betty left, clearing an adjacent table en route.

Barb waited for a while, then checked the time— one thirty.

'Do you want yours my dear or are you going to wait?' Betty asked.

She hesitated. 'Umm.'

'It's no trouble, though we've got a party of eight at two.'

'I'll take mine. Thanks, sorry to mess you about.'

Betty returned with a plate of food. 'Here, get

yourself around that. Bleeding men, we love them really.'

'What about your husband? He seems really nice.'

'Who, DH?' Betty saw the look on Barb's face. 'Ain't you noticed, or don't you read much? Everyone says so; you know, the author chappie, DH Lawrence. I don't see it myself but all the regulars renamed him DH and it just sort of stuck.'

'Well I did, I've always thought so myself. Just assumed it was me.'

'You'd better eat up before it gets cold.' Betty left, she could hear DH calling her.

*   *   *   *   *

'Where's this frigging pub?' Jimmy muttered as he walked. Another fork lay up ahead. The left path headed further into the fields and away from any woods. He tried to recall what Barb had said. He was sure she said it was in the woods. He strode off on the path forking right; it felt like he was going the correct way. He was still heading north towards Henley, though every step took him further away from her. He noticed the time: *crikey, quarter to two. She said it was only half an hour.* The sun disappeared. Off to his left were menacing black clouds. Another path crossed his. He stopped.

'Eeny, Meeny, Miney, Moe. No, that's not going to help. What did dad say?' Jimmy tried to recall. 'I know, *go right and you can't go wrong*. Right it is.' He set off with a new sense of purpose. After only a few strides he stopped.

It didn't feel right. He turned, and walked back to

where the paths crossed. Going right now would take him in the direction he was heading prior to turning. He took it. Heading north again felt much better. With one eye on the advancing storm and the other on the clock—it was now two thirty—he kept up a brisk pace. He stopped to admire the new vista as the hill dropped away. Henley, with the Thames in the foreground, its old road bridge, the clock and Town Hall were all clearly laid out before him.

'Oh that's all I need,' a large raindrop hit his face. He pushed on with greater urgency; the drops were coming more frequently; hunger made itself felt. The hill was steep and the path slippery. He couldn't stop. It levelled out on reaching the Wargrave Road. He knew it wasn't far now. Once over the bridge he headed for the phone box. It stood on the right, opposite the Little Angel pub. He started dialling. 01628 ... he'd forgotten the rest. Actually he hadn't committed Barb's number to memory. He hung up and redialled, this time Directory Enquiries.

'What name please?'

'Cooke'

'With or without an 'e'?'

'With.'

'Initial?'

'B for Barbara.'

'Has she got a middle name?'

He was silent.

'Hello caller, are you still there?'

'Yes, sorry, just trying to remember her middle name.'

'Which town?'

'Maidenhead.'

'Just one moment please.'

He started rummaging in his pockets. 'Shit. No pen.'

'Right that's …'

'Sorry, stop, I've no pen …' Desperation sounded in his voice.

'Do you want this number or not?' The operator was nonplussed about his lack of a pen.

'Yes of course. I just need a pen.'

'Have you got one now?' She sounded exasperated.

'No, but go on.' He breathed on the glass.

'01628.'

He started to write then stopped, he could remember the code.

'864125.'

He repeated the numbers as he wrote. It was impossible to hear with the sound of the rain beating on the glass. Once he had six digits, he put the receiver down without a bye or leave.

He dug into his pocket, dumping a pile of loose change on the shelf. Pushing the coins around he separated the bronze from silver, sorting the silver into tens, twenties and fifties.

He dialled. It rang once, twice, a third time, 'Please be in.' It was answered on the fourth ring. 'Yes, hi Barb,' he said, waiting for confirmation but there was only silence. The rain was now a drizzle; he could hear her breathing. 'Barb …'

'I was worried.' She sniffed.

'You been crying?'

'Where are you?'

'Henley.'

'Henley! How the hell did you get there?' She couldn't believe what she was hearing. 'That's miles. I waited for you at the pub. It got embarrassing in the end, thinking up excuses for you. I've been back here for ages.'

'Could ...,' he was tentative, 'could you come and collect me? Just it's Sunday service. You know, the trains are every hour. And I'd have to change at Twyford.'

'Where are you?'

'Opposite The Little Angel. It's been chucking it down. I'll wait in the phone box till I see your car. Thanks.' He put the phone down.

Barb arrived some time later. 'On the way here I've been trying to figure out why you went to Henley. The pub was straight up. I saw you at the top of the hill. By the time I'd got my wellies on you'd gone. I got to the pub, but you weren't there. I expected you to walk in any minute. DH and Betty were quite worried in the end. They even offered to get their Land Rover out.'

'DH and Betty?' Jimmy didn't understand.

'The landlord and his wife.'

'Sounds like you know them pretty well.'

'Used to. We'd come often, once a month at least.'

'We. Who's we?'

'Oh it doesn't matter, it was a long time ago.'

'John, by any chance?'

She chose to ignore him. 'That still doesn't explain what you were doing in Henley.'

'Well at the top of the hill, the path forks. I just

had this feeling, well more than a feeling really, it was an urge to take the right fork.'

'That's odd. Why the right?'

'Don't know. I've noticed before that whenever I'm walking, it's always a struggle unless I go in a particular direction.'

'What direction?'

'In this case it was Henley. What was worse, I noticed the storm clouds coming in from the west.'

'West, you say? Were they on your right or your left?'

'West.'

'No. As you walked, were they on your right or left?'

'Left, why?'

'Then you were heading north.'

'I suppose so.'

'And that felt comfortable?'

'Yes. Actually I came to another path crossing the one I was on, so I took, my dad's advice and turned right.'

'What, your dad was with you?'

'No, course not, but he always said, when faced with a decision on which way to go, always go right and you won't go wrong, so I went right.'

'And?'

'Well after only a couple of strides, it felt all wrong.'

'So from heading north, after turning right, you'd be going east.'

'If you say so.'

'That felt all wrong?'

'Absolutely, so much so I turned around, came back to the junction and continued in the direction I was going.'

'North?'

'Yes, eventually ending up in Henley.'

'Right, Magno Man.' She'd figured out what was happening. 'What conclusion can we draw?'

He thought for a while. 'I like Henley?'

'Dummkopf. I thought you were the bright one.' She started to laugh.

'Go on, tell me.'

'Have you got no idea?'

'No, none.'

'Are you ready for this?'

He wasn't sure. 'I suppose so.'

'You're a compass.'

'What do you mean?' He was doubtful.

'How does a compass work?'

'Well the little needle thing spins on a pin and somehow points north.'

'The needle is a magnet and pivots freely so it always rotates towards the earth's magnetic north. That's you, that's why you find it easier to walk north. Any other direction and the earth's magnetic field pulls on you.'

*　*　*　*　*

'She said sixteen hundred hours.' Matt checked his watch again. 'It's seventeen thirty. She's giving us the run around.' He paced the hall. 'Damn women, they're so unreliable.'

'Are you talking about the ex-Mrs Serrano again? She fits the bill, both unreliable and in giving you the run-around.'

'I'll have you keep your damned nose out of my personal affairs, Special Agent Mason. You do your job and I'll do mine.' He came and sat on the sofa. 'Them Commies have given us nothing; I checked the wire. This whole thing's under the radar and Langley doesn't like it. They're asking questions I can't answer.'

'Shush, listen.'

Click clack, click clack, was followed by rat-a-tat-tat.

'God damn it, doesn't she realise this is a covert operation! She might as well stand on the street corner with one of those advertising boards, you know, like in Oxford Street, with a big arrow on it saying *Golf Supplies Here*, or whatever. Answer it, otherwise I might ...'

'Sorry I'm late, I was having Sunday roast with my Mum like I told you and the Victoria line was closed for maintenance so they bussed us instead ...' Sheila drew a breath. 'Cor, I'm still panting. I ran all the way from Paddington. Fought it would be quicker than changing again for Lancaster Gate.'

'Thanks for the update on the London transport, most useful. Now I come to think of it, that's the most useful you've been to us so far.' Matt pushed his face uncomfortably close to hers.

'Wot'd you mean?' she said indignantly.

'I mean we've given you fifteen hundred quid, in pounds, sterling as you asked ...'

'Oh, are pounds and sterling the same fing? I didn't know that.'

'Give me strength. Brad, take over before I ... I do something I'll regret.'

'What he's saying is we're no further forward understanding what's going on than we were before you got your money.' Brad played the nice guy.

'That's your fault, innit. I gave it to you on a plate. I turn up in a taxi, I knew cos of your equipment you'd see. You couldn't help but 'ear, given the racket they make. I even waved—didn't you notice? Then with your camera upstairs you could take loads of photos. That's all good ... wot do you call it?'

'Info, yeah I suppose so but apart from knowing you went shopping at Selfridges, Debenhams and John Lewis, and that those Ruskies don't have a light bulb in their hallway ...'

'You could see that? I noticed too and asked Vlad why. He said no house in Moscow has any bulbs, except one maybe, cause they sell them to buy vodka. Actually he was quite sad at that.'

'Are you, what do you say, milking the piss?'

'No taking the piss—you milk cows, silly.'

'Where were we?' In his head he was thinking how easy it was to steal state secrets or kidnap a politician compared to getting any sense from Sheila.

'You clocked how long I was in there, didn't you?'

Brad checked his log. 'Nineteen ten to twenty one-o-six. Nearly two hours. So what were you doing?'

'Trying on my new outfit, everyfink from top to bottom,' she slapped her bum, 'and beyond.'

'Those Commies paid for all that stuff?'

'Well, Vlad did.'

'You two are becoming quite friendly. We saw you last night in the pub singing together. Very sweet.'

'Wot, you were there? Why didn't you come over and say hi? Vlad had too much vodka to care. We could 'ave 'ad one of those truces, like in the Second World War when the Germans and Brits played football. We did it in 'istory at school.'

Brad gave her a withering look. 'I don't think so, and it was the First World War, Christmas 1914 to be exact.'

'Cor you knows your 'istory, don't you? So can I go now? I need a shower after all that travelling across London. Oh, and don't offer to wash my back; no's the answer but fanks anyway.'

She rose to go. Brad caught her arm tight. 'Not so fast. We still have no idea what's going on. What's the new outfit for?'

'Vlad's just a generous bloke that's all.' She kept a straight face.

'Are you his ...' he chose his words carefully, 'woman?'

'Nah, course not.'

'So why the clothes?'

'He told me to tell no one, Mum's the word. Actually I told Mum today at lunch. She's a great cook, she learned all she knows in Australia. She often cooks lamb, I guess that's why.'

'I don't believe it. Now we're talking Australian sheep! Just stay focussed.' Brad thumped his fist on the coffee table. Everything jumped. An old copy of the New York Times slipped onto the floor.

'There's no need for that,' she slid along the sofa out of his way.

'Has she said anything yet?' Matt was back into the room.

'Nothing of any use, but she's just about to.' Both men stared at her.

Sheila was running out of excuses and started to feel uncomfortable. The room was silent. She shifted herself on the sofa, her skin squeaked on the leather. She smiled, they didn't; her mind was blank.

The sound of footsteps came from the speaker. She was off the hook.

'Get your coat, you're coming with us. Quick.' Brad stood at the window to confirm the Russians were leaving. 'They've just opened the door. Get in the hall now.'

Sheila was sandwiched between Brad and Matt. Brad opened the door sufficiently to see where the Russians had got to. He slipped out into the street.

'Come on, quick, keep close to the wall.' Sheila and Brad kept moving. Matt stayed to close the door securely. Passing number 44, she looked directly at their camera and mouthed, *Thank you.*

By the time she and Brad made it to the café, Matt had caught them up.

'Go home now. I don't want to see you at 44 tonight, or any other night unless I give you the say-so. Now scram, we'll be in touch.'

Sheila did as she was told.

* * * * *

From her bedroom window she could see all the comings and goings in the Mews. She needed to contact Vlad. She decided a note would be easiest. Naked apart from a towel wrapped around her wet hair, she switched out the bedroom light and waited. The blind afforded enough privacy without obscuring her vision. Two men in trilbies and trench coats came into view. She took her note and, wrapping it around a plastic hair curler to give it weight, and let it fall, aiming it just in front of them. Startled, Vlad plucked it off the ground and placed it, unread, into his pocket. *I'll read that later,* he thought. Never looking up, the Russians' pace hardly faltered. When the Americans came past the whole building was in darkness. They suspected nothing.

'Good, she's in bed. That's one less thing to worry about. Here, we'll go the long way round to avoid them.' Matt had had enough. 'You take early watch. Don't wake me up till one, or not at all if you think there'll be no more action tonight.'

In the kitchen of 44 Oleg was tucking into a plate of Marmite toast and watching a re-run of Sheila's striptease.

'Look, we have freeze-frame, step through one at time, and even zoom. Our boys make some amazing equipment.' He'd overlooked the *Canon* label stuck on the casing.

'I seem to have missed zat bit of news. When did Japan become part of Republic?' Vladimir said sarcastically.

Oleg chose to ignore him. 'What she say in her note?'

The Yanks are getting hacked off with me not telling them stuff.

'What is hacked off, Vladimir?'

'Unhappy, I think.'

'Zat makes sense. What else?'

He read on: '*I need a cover story about the new clothes, they've got pictures of me getting out of a taxi. And they said I can't visit you again without their permission.* She has put smiley face at end.' He studied the note and handwriting. 'She does not seem too stressed, just not sure what she can do.'

'Tomorrow we will have breakfast at her café and leave reply zen.'

'Good idea, Oleg. What will it say?'

'Well, instructions about Thursday operation and photograph of Kavanagh, otherwise we do not need to contact her again.'

'Photograph? Yes, I suppose. We do not want her getting wrong man. Have you got photograph?'

'I tried to get one from video tape but it is not clear. In fact whole tape is no use for our purposes, except I did find launch of Windows interesting. I would like my own PC.'

'PC, what is PC?'

'Vladimir, keep up wiz times—personal computer. Part of demonstration showed a card game, Solitaire I zink. Maybe we get Moscow to send us one.'

'Sometimes, Oleg, I wonder if you are right man

for job. What next? How will we get photograph?'

'We need to go back to Maidenhead wiz my Pentax. We can't use the bad picture we have from his passport.'

'What about cover story for clothes she bought?' Both men went quiet.

'I know what ... no, zat is no good.' Oleg dropped his head.

'Ah, I know.' Vladimir looked pleased with himself.

'Come on, what you think?'

'She could say she is my date for a ball at Russian Embassy.'

'But you hate dancing.'

'I love singing. Anyway, zis is only pretend.'

'So what is ball for?'

'It is celebration of great Russian event. I do not know, she does not need to know, Americans will be happy wiz zat.'

CHAPTER 7

GOING FISHING

It was still dark out. The usual hum of traffic from the Bayswater Road was absent. Only the odd bus or delivery van was moving.

'We will leave our shoes off until we are out front door. Remember to tiptoe, we do not want to alert zem.' Vladimir switched off the kitchen light. Both men, with trilby, trench coat and shoes in hand, negotiated the hall towards the front door. Vladimir rotated the knob of the Yale lock until the latch cleared the strike plate. Light appeared around the edge of the door as he pulled it open. The hinges behaved themselves, no protesting squeaks. Vladimir still had hold of the knob. Oleg was able to pass him out. He set off up the Mews, not looking back until he was sure the Americans couldn't see him.

Vladimir put his key in the lock so he could pull the door to and stop it snapping shut. Silence was imperative. He removed the key, pushing on the door to satisfy himself it was locked. He tiptoed across the Mews before making his way up it towards Sheila's. Oleg waited there for him. It was even too early for her. The café was in darkness. Vladimir took the envelope from his coat pocket and slipped it into the letter box as quietly as he could. They finished dressing before disappearing into the shadows of the building adjacent to the café. It was built on an incline; the ground floor was supported on pillars, which provided an excellent place to hide.

'We will wait here.' Vladimir checked his watch. The luminous face glowed in the dark. 'Five twenty. If we stay here for ten minutes and zere is no sign of zem, we know we have caught zem nappy.'

'Nappy?' Oleg checked he'd heard right.

'Yes it is one of zose English sayings; ask Sheila when we see her next.'

The Mews lit up. 'It must be five thirty, we must go.'

Sheila had turned the lights on in the café.

They emerged from the shadows. 'All clear.' They set off at a brisk pace for Paddington Station. Neither spoke again until they were on the concourse.

'Let us go in First Class. We have better chance of getting compartment to ourselves.'

The train was virtually empty. The backside of London suburbs rolled past the window. They watched in silence. Reaching Slough, things didn't get any better. Only as the train passed over the Thames on one of Brunel's finest achievements did the scenery improve. From the train they could see the 18th century road bridge over the Thames, with its arches and Victorian lamp posts. At Maidenhead Station no one was there to check their tickets. Oleg headed for the taxi rank.

'Nyet, it is only short walk. We can find High Street again.'

'You zink you can remember where are Zylog offices?' Oleg sounded doubtful.

'One of my jobs back in Moscow was teaching

pigeons how to find zeir way home.' Vladimir smiled at his own joke.

Oleg still wasn't convinced.

It was light now and more people were about. Some school kids were larking around but they passed by without stopping.

'Zat was long time ago; we do not have as much fun like zem.'

Lloyds Bank came into view. 'See, I told you so.' Vladimir was pleased with himself. 'Okay, let us wait here. Apartment of his woman is over zere. Can you see any lights on?'

It was in darkness. 'Entrance is around back, come on.' Vladimir led the way. 'Have you got camera ready?'

Oleg opened his coat like a pervert flasher. Hanging around his neck was a Pentax, with high speed, 80 to 500 mm telephoto lens.

'I have loaded 800 ASA film so will not need flash. Too obvious. Wiz a long lens we can keep discreet distance.'

'Da, great.' The finer points of photography passed Vladimir by. 'As long as you get good pictures.'

The entrance to the flats, eight in all, four on each level, was via concrete stairs and an open landing running the length of the block. Each door had a number large enough to read from a distance.

Vladimir scanned the numbers. 'Zere.'

Oleg followed his finger to the lower level, second door in from the stairs. He lifted the camera to his eye, zooming in tight.

'Stop, not here, you are too obvious.' Vladimir

pulled him by the sleeve towards cover afforded by a rubbish skip.

Oleg had a good line of sight and was using the camera like a monocular to survey the scene.

'What can you see?' Vladimir was getting impatient.

'Nothing yet, everything is in darkness.' Oleg kept the camera to his eye with his finger resting on the shutter release. The automatic metering and focus took care of any variations in light and distance as he moved his attention between the two windows and the door. Vladimir kept a look out just in case anyone around took interest in what they were doing.

'Zere, look, now.' Oleg saw the kitchen light come on. The sink was in front of the window and the taps were visible. 'Zere, an arm holding kettle. Now her, Barbara. By look of her, she has only just got out of bed.'

'Zese English do not know how good zey have it.' His watch showed seven forty five. 'We would have been at work by six!'

'Vladimir, you are getting old. You were never at work by six. You are starting to believe your own propaganda.'

'Can you see him? Is zere anyone else wiz her?'

'I have not seen him, oh … bathroom light is on. It has funny glass in window so you cannot see in.'

'Have you taken pictures yet?'

'What, of a door and two windows? No, why would I do zat?' Oleg continued looking through the viewfinder.

'Because we may need to break in—you rule out

nothing. What did zey teach you at Spy School?' The sound of the mirror in the reflex mechanism moving up and down as he pressed the shutter release confirmed to Vladimir that Oleg was doing his job.

'More rather than less is my motto.' Oleg said. He paused. 'Why is standing around so much part of spying?' He shifted his weight from foot to foot. It didn't help.

'Shhh, just keep zat camera to your eye.'

'But it is getting heavy.'

'Stop complaining, you are ...' He never finished his sentence. Barbara opened the door. He was struck by her hair, naturally blonde, flowing over her shoulders. And the Burberry coat and scarf, so distinctive, so elegant. Only her top half was visible, the landing wall obscuring the rest. She pulled the door to, turning the key in the Mortice lock.

'Did you see zat? She is careful wiz security.' Vladimir couldn't take his eyes off her. 'Zat picture on her desk did not show her beauty.'

Walking the landing to the stairs, she disappeared from view as she went down the first half flight. Turning the corner, she reappeared. A pair of black leather knee high boots and an attaché case completed the outfit.

Oleg clicked away.

'I hope you have got more rolls of film wiz you,' Vladimir said. In truth, he was pleased Oleg was taking so many. He fancied a couple for his own private collection; *after all, why should the lads back in Moscow have all the fun?*

Barbara turned away from them and down the

passage leading onto the High Street. Vladimir checked his watch: eight twenty five. 'Make note in your book, Oleg.'

'What, now?'

'I zink we follow her to the office, but discreetly.' They set off for the passage, turning down the High Street towards the Zylog building. 'Damn, I cannot see her. Come on, more quickly, we need to catch her up.' Vladimir hurried. They reached the traffic lights at the bottom of the High Street where it intersected with Forlease Road before becoming Moorbridge Road. While waiting to cross, Vladimir happened to glance back.

'She is behind us.' Panicking, he pulled Oleg into a shop doorway, hoping she'd pass without seeing them. Half a dozen people walked with her, all carrying take-out coffee and sandwich bags. Barb was occupied chatting. Jimmy wasn't amongst them.

'Zat was too close for our comfort.' Vladimir let himself breathe again.

'Why worry? She does not know us. You are too nervous.' Oleg was right—their behaviour would make anyone watching suspicious.

Opposite Zylog House was a hoarding surrounding a building site, waiting for work to commence. The ground had been levelled but nothing else had been done.

'We need to find a way into zere.' Vladimir pointed at the building site. 'You stay here, I will walk up to look.' He strolled down Moorbridge Road, trying to look invisible. Although plenty of people were turning up for work he was conspicuous by his size, plus the trilby and trench coat made him stand out. He saw his reflection in a plate glass window and thought the same. Carrying his hat and loosening the coat's belt and buttons, he felt he blended in better. Having gone a hundred yards, he turned back to check on Oleg. Seeing him engaged in conversation was the last thing he'd expected. Uncertain of what to do, he stopped and watched. He was too far to be sure.

'What is he doing, talking wiz him?' The shock caused him to blurt out the words. It drew a curious look from a passer-by. Vladimir just smiled.

He was in a quandary. He took a few paces back towards Oleg, stopped, thought, then turned away. Walking slowly forward his mind was whirring: about what to do? He stopped again, did a half turn, then thought better of it. He was waiting for an idea but none arrived. He took several paces forward. Stopping and turning, Oleg wasn't in sight, nor was the person he'd been talking to. Vladimir panicked and ran back to where he last saw him; all the time scanning the faces of on-comers or looking beyond and up the High Street — nothing. He slowed. Now what? He crossed at the traffic lights; a red man was showing. He heard a screech, followed by shouting.

'Oi, look where you're bloody well going. You'll get yourself killed.' He saw the driver staring at him. Vladimir mouthed a *sorry*. His apology was returned with two fingers.

At the bottom end of the High Street were many small shops — a baker, dress shop, flower shop, the usual sort you'd expect. He checked each as he passed. No

Oleg. He walked quicker, now slower; turning, he retraced his steps. He spotted Oleg's trilby and coat placed on a low wall in front of a new, yet unoccupied building. Modern in style, it had a large expanse of white rendered wall. Standing with his back to it was Jimmy Kavanagh. Vladimir was close enough to be certain. Oleg was a few feet in front, camera to his eye, taking pictures. They were engrossed. Vladimir ducked into a doorway; he wanted to see without being seen.

Oleg had Jimmy adopt several poses—full face, half turning left, then right, smiling, a more serious look, hands by his side. It resembled a shoot for a magazine. Completed, there followed a shaking of hands and a brief exchange of words. Jimmy walked away to re-join the High Street and headed in the direction of his office. Oleg collected his coat and hat while Vladimir waited in the doorway until Jimmy was out of sight. Oleg sat on the wall studying his camera.

'What happened? Come on Comrade, tell me.'

'What could I do? You had walked away towards zat building site when I felt tap on my shoulder. It was him. He recognised hat and coat. He asked me what I was doing here. My camera was visible and he noticed. So I said we needed picture to go wiz article. He agreed, happily. I was looking around for good backdrop, something plain, and he suggested here. I had taken some pictures, he said he must go to work, I said zank you, he left. Zat is it really.'

'Did he say anything else? How did he look? Annoyed you were following him, suspicious perhaps, curious even?'

'No, nothing. He was very pleasant, comfortable. I zink he enjoyed himself. Actually he asked for any good ones to be sent to his office. I agreed.'

'Did he mention me?'

'Not really. He did say *where is your partner in crime ...*'

'See, he knows it was us who stole zat video.' Vladimir had panic written all over his face.

'No of course not. It is one of zose English expressions, he meant nothing.'

Vladimir contemplated what Oleg said. 'We have what we wanted, let us get back to Mews.' Vladimir set off up the High Street once more. Oleg followed a few paces behind as he fought with his hat, coat camera and lens.

'Hold on will you, what is hurry?' Oleg shouted. Vladimir stopped walking but Oleg was too preoccupied to notice; he bumped into him.

'Hey watch where you poke zat lens ... Have you seen zis?' He did a sweeping gesture with his arms. 'Zere, look above doorway; great black bear. It reminds me of home' He read the sign: 'Bear Inn. It is pity it not open. Vodka would be good after zis morning.'

*   *   *   *   *

Matt and Brad burst through the café door. It was empty apart from Bert, who was lost in his memories, aimlessly stirring his mug of tea. He didn't notice them. Matt flipped the sign to *closed* and secured the latch. Brad disappeared through the plastic curtain. Matt followed.

'Where is she?' The kitchen was empty.

'There,' Matt said, pointing at the door to the yard. He pushed on it—it swung open. A quick glance revealed no sign of Sheila.

'She must be in her flat.' Brad was up the stairs two at a time. He had his revolver in his hand. He had no intention of using it but wanted to show her he meant business. The landing had four doors: three were shut. He was drawn to the open one. With his back pressed against the wall, he progressed his way towards it, conscious of keeping quiet. Brad heard Matt reach the top of the stairs. Without looking back, he waved his hand in a *stay put* way. Brad stood at the open door, on the hinge side. Through the gap between the door and the frame he could see Sheila sitting at the dressing table. Her reflection in the mirror revealed she was concentrating on applying mascara. Avoiding getting it in her eye required her full attention. Here was his opportunity.

With the speed and dexterity of a praying mantis, he leapt from his hiding place to a position where his hand covered her mouth and the barrel of his gun pressed against her temple. The muffled squeaks told Matt he'd struck. The mirror revealed to her the seriousness of the situation.

'Where are they?' Matt had joined them. The urgency in his voice said he wasn't joking. 'Those Commie bastards have given us the slip. Now tell us or Brad here will do his worst.'

Fear registered in her eyes. She struggled but he had a firm grip around the top of her shoulders, bearing down to further restrain her. Her attempts to speak were thwarted by the hand clamped over her mouth.

'He'll release you but first you must promise not to scream or he'll have no excuse but to shoot you. Do you promise?'

She nodded.

'Really?'

She nodded again but much more violently.

'Take your hand away real slow. If she so much as squeaks, you know what to do.' Matt watched her every move.

Her look of fear receded as Brad released his pressure.

'Now that's a good girl. So where are they?' Matt knelt next to her. Brad still had hold of her around her shoulders.

'Ow the 'ell do I know? You bastards come crashing in 'ere like this, scaring me 'alf to death ...'

'Hey, enough now. Tell us what we want to know and we'll leave. Promise ... Brad, let her alone.'

'Look, I can't tell you wot I dunno. I'm not bleeding 'oudini.'

'He was an escapologist.'

'I know that, I meant the other one. You know, wot's her name, yeah that Mystic Meg.'

Matt signalled to Brad and he took up the stranglehold again. 'Stop giving us the run around and start talking.'

Before she had time to speak they all heard her name being called from downstairs.

'Sheila, can you hear me?' It was Bert. 'I'd like to go home now.'

They froze.

'Sheila.' Bert repeated, louder this time.

'He's coming up the stairs. Quick, go down to him. And not a word—we're listening.'

'Sorry Bert, got sommat in my eye, 'ad to sort it out.'

'Oh I'm sorry dear. It's just I need to go now and the door seems a bit stuck.'

'Come on, down we go, I'll sort it out.' She released the latch. A couple who'd been waiting outside came in.

'I thought it was a bit strange. It said *closed* on the door. That's not like our Sheila, I says.'

''Ad a spot of bother with the tea urn. No tea, so it ain't worth opening. Anyway it's all okay now.'

'I thought you said you had something in your eye.'

'Yeah, that too Bert.' She patted him on the back. 'See ya tomorrow.'

'But I haven't paid.'

'Go on now, have that one on me.' She closed the door after him.

Turning to her new customers: 'So wot's it gonna be?'

'I heard what you said to him. We've been standing out there for a good ten minutes dearie.'

'Okay, so wot would you like?'

'Two teas and two toasted teacakes.'

She went into the kitchen to pop the teacakes into the toaster. Matt and Brad were there.

'We're not finished with you yet ...' Matt was

interrupted by the doorbell.

'Where is my Sheila?' Vladimir and Oleg were back.

The kitchen fell silent. Each wondered what to do next.

'Sheila, where are you? We are very hungry. One of your all day English breakfasts would be most welcome.' Vladimir was heading towards the plastic curtain. Matt could see him coming. Without warning he spun Sheila around and pushed her through it. She stumbled into view.

'Sorry Vlad.' She straightened herself up. 'Just in the yard, didn't 'ear you come in.'

'Everything alright my dear? You look little red in face.' He bent down to kiss her cheeks. 'We have just returned from Maidenhead. Did you see my note?'

Sheila flashed her eyes, trying to tell him she had company in the kitchen. He didn't realise.

'We have some good pictures of Jimmy and his woman.'

'He 'as a woman? Galfriend or wife?'

'Not wife. She is very beautiful. Blonde, wears expensive clothes. Zey work together at Zylog.'

In the kitchen, Matt and Brad were feeling very pleased with themselves. Brad was taking notes.

'What did you think of excuse for your new outfit. Do you zink zose Yanks will believe? We often have parties at Embassy so zey should accept what you say.'

'Wot if they ask about wot's being celebrated?'

'Oh I not know, just say it is Lenin USSR day.'

'Wot, you celebrate that? It was one of my

favourites when I was kid growing up. Ow does it go? *Back in the USSR, You don't know ow lucky you are.* John Lennon was fab. Do you like 'im?'

'I am not sure what you talk about, my dear. However, you are happy. Now Thursday, I expect seeing you straight after you close here. You said you were getting your hair done, when is zat?'

'Wednesday. I'll be a new woman by the time I've finished.' She preened herself. 'So you want two full English, with tea or coffee?'

'Coffees, my dear.' Vladimir joined Oleg at the table. Sheila went into the kitchen. Matt and Brad had slipped out the back. On the worktop they'd left a note: *Thanks for the info.*

'Bastards. I hate those bloody Americans,' Sheila muttered as she prepared the orders.

'Sheila my dear, is that toasted teacake coming?' Her other customers were fed up waiting.

'She popped her head through the curtain. 'Yeah sorry, as I said I've 'ad trouble with the urn, it needed to re'eat.' She now realised she had a bigger problem. To tell Vlad about the Americans, or stay schtum?

* * * * *

The digits on the office wall clock flicked over to 9.00 as Jimmy appeared at the top of the stairs, panting.

Rob saw him. 'Just made it, Jimmy boy. It's not like you to be late.'

Jimmy checked the clock. 'I'm not late, dead on nine.'

'Yeah, but you're usually here by half eight.'

'Had something to do on the way in.'

'Well it wasn't Barb, she's been here for ages.'

Barb shot Jimmy a look saying *defend my honour*.

Jimmy smiled at Rob's comments. 'Now that's not needed, show the lady some respect.'

Jimmy wandered over to her desk and leant in close. 'So what was that all about this morning? Locking me in and all.'

'I'm not your keeper; you're in my flat. As you just said, show the lady some respect.'

'Yeah, sorry but you locked me in.'

'Well, Magno Man, I knew you'd have no problem with that. I just thought I'd make a point.'

'Is it about yesterday, the Dew Drop, Henley and everything?'

'No, it's more about football and your lack of consideration for me.'

'We went for a walk.'

She stared at him.

'Okay, maybe not together but …'

'I don't want to be taken for granted. It's important to sort out stuff from the start. I need to know who you are.'

'What?' A line appeared on Jimmy's forehead. 'We've worked together for nearly two years.'

'No, we've shared an office. That's not the same thing as getting to know each other. You've no idea who I am …'

'Well, you're beautiful Barbara Cooke, leading sales person for Zylog Systems, every man's heartthrob.

What more do you want?'

'Who's my favourite author, what's my favourite colour, name a cassette in my car, when's my birthday, where do I come from? Shall I go on?'

Jimmy skulked back to his desk. His phone went. 'Jimmy Kavanagh, can I help you?'

It was Barb,

'Just one more thing. Mike said I can take an extended lunch. I have an appointment at the birth control clinic. I thought you might want to come with me.'

He paused before responding. 'Isn't that, you know, private woman stuff?'

'I don't want you to come with me to the clinic,' she heard his sigh of relief, 'but I have to walk through Kidwell's Park from here.'

'You're not afraid, are you?'

'Course not. It's just that the park has one of those kiddies' roundabouts, the sort you stand on and scoot with your foot. Personally they make me sick but kids seem to love them, going round and round as fast as they can.'

'What's that got to do with me?'

'I thought you might test out the compass theory.'

'How?'

'You be ready at one-o-clock and I'll show you. Are you up for that?'

He nearly said, *Do I have much choice?* but thought better of it given yesterday's tiff. 'Of course, my love.' He put the phone down; Barb wasn't convinced of his sincerity

Rob walked past his desk. He was pushing the thumb of his right hand into the palm of his left. 'She has you right there, mate. I know the signs; I've been married for ten years.'

In frustration Jimmy swept his hands across his desks. All the metal objects jumped into neat lines, except his phone. The handset fell off and landed on the floor talking to itself: *On the third stroke it will be nine forty five and thirty seconds.* Somehow he'd dialled the speaking clock.

*   *   *   *   *

'Come on, you ready?' Barb was standing by his desk.

Jimmy stood up and looked out of the window to see if it was raining.

'We need to get going.' Barb was halfway down the stairs before he had his jacket on. 'Are you coming?'

'I'm not sure I've much choice.'

She didn't hear him, but Rob did. He sat there screwing his thumb into his palm. Barb, with all her beauty, was waiting. *I must be daft,* he thought to himself, *she's gorgeous.* 'Here I come.' He bounded down the stairs two at a time.

The kids' playground was empty; it was a school day and too cold for young mums to gather.

'Here.' Barb pushed the roundabout ride; it rotated freely.

'So what are you saying?' Jimmy wasn't sure what she had in mind.

'Tell me two things about magnets.'

He thought. 'Yeah I know. One, they are red,' he

hesitated; she raised her eyes skywards, 'and two, they're sold in Woolies.'

'And I thought you were the clever one. All that computer stuff and your degree, and that's all you know about magnets? What about north and south poles?'

A glimmer of recognition showed on his face. 'It's been nearly twenty years since I did school boy physics.' He played dumb on purpose.

'So what about poles?'

'Well, if I remember correctly, every magnet has one of each.'

'Do you think that includes you?'

'If I am one, then I must have.' He was less certain now about being magnetised.

'What's the other thing about poles?' She examined him intensely as he thought about her question. 'Jimmy, come on, give me strength. Opposites attract. My eight year old niece could have told you that.'

'You got a niece? I didn't know that.'

'As we discovered this morning, there are many things about me you don't know.'

He blushed. 'Yeah sorry … So what do you want me to do?'

'Just stand on the roundabout as close to the centre as you can. Now wait.' He stood, arms by his side but nothing happened.

'How long do I need to wait?'

Barb was busy looking up at the sun. 'It's just after one and the end of November, so south is there-ish.' She waved her hands, turning to face south. 'If that's so, the north's behind me. On my right is the west and left is the east. She pointed to both in turn. 'That makes you facing north east-ish.'

'Should me being on the roundabout make it spin towards north, if what you say is right?' He started to climb off.

'No, no, stop. Think about a compass. The needle is the magnet, like you, with a north and south pole. It pivots like the roundabout but you're standing up, vertical: the needle is horizontal. While standing it won't work. Lie yourself across the hand rails with the centre pivot in your stomach.'

'It'll hurt!' His complaint drew no sympathy.

'Go on wuss, it'll only be for a few minutes.'

Jimmy struggled to hook one foot around a hand rail. He positioned his stomach over the central upright and lay stretched out, grabbing hold of the hand rail diagonally opposite. Before he got comfortable, the roundabout started moving unaided. It stopped once his feet were pointing in a northerly direction.

'There, see that, you're a magnet and a compass!' Barb didn't hide her excitement.

'Okay, yes it rotated, but my head's not facing north, rather the complete opposite.'

'Well of course. What was the second thing I asked you to remember about magnets?'

'The opposite attract. So my feet are my south pole and my head is my north pole. That's why I swung around this way.'

'If you were from Australia, your head would be your south pole and your feet your north, so in the northern hemisphere, as a compass, your head would face north.'

'Assuming I was lying down, but if I went to Oz as I am now, my head would point to the south … I think I see.'

Barb looked at her watch. 'It's late, I'm off to get my coil fitted. See you back in the office.'

Jimmy scooted himself around 180 degrees before lifting his feet off the ground. He swung back through a semi-circle. He played for a few more minutes until he realised he hadn't eaten.

'Rob,' he said, now back at his desk with a sandwich, 'You know stuff?'

'What now?'

'If for instance you were magnetic and lived in the northern hemisphere, like here in Maidenhead …' He paused waiting for some response.

Rob grunted through a mouthful of baguette.

'And say you met a girl who was also magnetic but came from somewhere in the southern hemisphere like, say, Australia, do you think you'd be attracted, you know like magnets, where opposites attract?'

* * * * *

'Rob, you seen Barb this afternoon?' Jimmy was concerned.

'Yes, sorry mate. She came in about three. Said everything's okay, all fitted and working but wanted to go home for a rest. What's fitted and working? She had something done to her car?'

'Sort of. I'll tell you when you're older.' Jimmy

grinned at him.

'Cheeky git. Oh yes, she asked if you could get something for tea. See, I told you mate.' Rob sat there screwing his thumb into his palm.

'Thanks for telling me.'

'Well I've told you now, so what are you going to get her, couple of Big Macs?'

'That'd suit me but I think she'll expect something more special, something from Marks and Spencer's.'

'You really know how to treat a lady.'

'Yeah, thanks for the vote of confidence. Right.' Jimmy checked the office clock. 'I was late in this morning, don't want to be late twice in one day. See you.' He disappeared down the stairs and out of the office. He found himself in Marks and Spencer's food hall.

'Beef with cashew nuts, maybe? Vindaloo? No, that's not her. Toad in the Hole—excellent, but not her. Salmon, dauphinoise potatoes and broccoli. That's the one.' He paid then left.

He rang her doorbell as a warning he was coming in—using his palm to release the door lock: 'Hi Barb, got your message from Rob.' He put the dinner in the kitchen and a bottle of Vino Sol in the fridge. She hadn't appeared. 'Are you in, darling?' He strode into the lounge. No sign of her; he noticed her bedroom door was shut. Tiptoeing, he approached it quietly and turned the handle. She was fast asleep. Watching her for a few moments before creeping out, he made a cup of tea and put the telly on.

Later he went back to her room. 'Barb.' He rocked her gently. 'Barb,' he tried again.

Barb yawned as she spoke. 'What time is it?'

'Seven thirty. Dinner's ready, it's on the table.'

'Have I been asleep all that time?' She threw back the duvet.

'It's getting cold, you feeling okay? Do you want it on a tray?' Jimmy showed her the care she hoped for.

'No, I just need a second to wake up. Pass my dressing gown please.' She yawned again.

Jimmy left her. Returning to the dinner table he lit the candles on it and the other dozen around the room. No other lights were on. The stereo was playing a track off a Bread album, *Make it with you*. Old, but appropriate, he thought.

'Oh Jimmy.' Barb's face was a picture in the candlelight.

He took her in his arms, feeling the warmth of her body as he held her tight. She lay her head on his chest. The music took over. They moved slowly, dancing, holding, enjoying the feeling of each other until the track ended.

'Come on, let's eat before it gets cold.' He led her to the table and pulled her chair out.

She looked deep into his eyes. She'd gone to some other place.

'Penny for your thoughts my darling.'

'Am I going to make it with *you*?' She'd been to this place before and was scared of getting her heart broken again.

'Hey come on, eat up.' Jimmy tried to make light of the situation. 'So what happened at the clinic?'

'I hate those places. It's all a bit in your face. Legs

204

in those stirrup things and a gaggle of people working down there as if it's an everyday occurrence.'

'I suppose it is for them. See one and you've seen them all.' He let out an embarrassed laugh. The piece of bright pink salmon on his plate caught his attention. 'It's not really a dinner table subject.'

'What about you in the park? That was exciting. See, you're not bad at directions, it's just you prefer to go north—like a compass. Now you know that, it'll be easier to understand what's going on.'

'More wine?' Jimmy lifted the bottle.

She pushed her glass towards him. 'Remember in the office I said we know little about each other?'

'Yeees.' He wondered what was coming next.

'And how I said it was important to get this stuff sorted early on.'

'Yeees.'

'Well maybe this is a good time to find out some more.'

'Yes.' He sounded relieved.

'Oh stop saying *yes*. I'm not about to get the thumbscrews out. I was thinking it's early, we could take the bottle to bed and you could regale me with interesting things about your past.

'Yes.' He realised he'd said it again. 'No, I mean yes, great, excellent idea ... I'll do the dishes.'

'No, just stick them in the sink. I'll blow out the candles. See you in bed.'

Now he was confused. Did she mean, see you in bed to talk, or see you in bed ... to not talk? He looked for his jacket. He called to her, 'Seen my jacket? I need my wallet.'

'You won't be needing them. Remember where I've been today.'

*   *   *   *   *

When Jimmy arrived in the bedroom Barb was sitting up, duvet pulled to her chin, with a glass of wine in her hand. 'Come here, Jimmy Kavanagh. I want to get to know you.' She patted the bed.

Conscious she was watching his every move he was especially attentive, laying his clothes in a neat pile on a chair, not on the floor. He put his socks and shoes together. Naked, he slipped under the covers, waiting for a sign from her as to what to do next. In anticipation, he slid his hand across her stomach.

'Not yet big boy, have some wine. I want to hear more about you, especially after today in the park. What other weird things have happened?'

He sat up and took his glass. 'Remember I told you about being a fridge magnet and an electric motor in my hammock; a sort of related event happened one day at my primary school.' He took a drink.

'Where did you go to school?'

'It was in the village of Stoke Row, north of Henley-on-Thames. The whole school had only 40 pupils. This was insufficient to stream by ability or even divide by years. The only distinction was 4 to 7 year olds and 8 to 11's. Ms Bates, the head mistress, taught the older children while the rest were cared for by Mrs Greenaway. The school provided lunch. It came ready cooked, shipped in large aluminium containers. Mrs Hayden was the dinner lady. Her two sons Desmond and Graham were also at the school. They got preferential treatment like first in the queue, extra-large helpings or two chocolate-coated rice-crispy balls for pudding. It wasn't fair.'

'I see food played a big part in your life even then.' She smiled to herself.

'Well we all have to eat. As I was saying, academic rigour didn't feature highly. Today they'd call it a hands-on learning experience. The vegetable garden adjacent to Ms Bates' schoolhouse was well tended and productive. Project work was the order of the day and in the strictest Blue Peter fashion, the children spent much of their time drawing, cutting, bending and gluing an array of materials found in the classroom.

'One project involved creating a table-top zoo. Each animal was big and sturdy enough to stand by itself. The elephant was my responsibility. It was similar in size and appearance, minus the standy-up ears, to a domestic rabbit. My pet rabbit, Cinders, provided the inspiration. Crafted from scavenged cloth and stuffed with old nylon stockings, my elephant took shape. I'd cut left and right halves. All I needed to do was pin them together prior to hand sewing.

'Other children were engrossed in making their animals. We all worked on a long trestle bench that doubled as a lunch table. In the centre were pairs of scissors, pinking shears, glue pots with brushes, a small stuffed hedgehog with sewing needles for spines, and a large circular plastic pot with hundreds of steel pins in a veritable rainbow of colours. The dress code for boys was grey shorts, white shirt, long grey socks and in winter a grey jumper. Shorts were worn all year round and this day was no different.

'I needed to pin my elephant ready to start sewing. The plastic pot was more than a stretch away. Rather than asking someone to pass it to me, I climbed off my seat and onto the bench. Crawling on all fours, I headed off towards the stash of pins. The trestle table had seen many years of service and was showing signs of wear. Having a seven year old boy bearing down his full weight was the last straw for one of the fixings that held the legs to the top. It failed. The failure, accompanied by a loud bang and rapid drop in height of the corner I was on, was complete.

'My flat crawl took on a new, almost vertical angle as the corner from where I was approaching succumbed. Everything resting on the table went first upwards, soon followed by a reversal of direction as gravity took over. Most disturbing was the plastic container of steel pins. In the absence of a lid they had dashed for freedom, showering me all over. Losing my grip, I slid towards the ground. Given there were so many pins I was lucky not to suffer more. One did manage to land point down in my arm. I reacted by jumping up and running from the table.

'Without hesitation, I plucked it out, to my great relief. In doing so I noticed the rest of my arm, my other arm, legs, in fact everywhere skin was exposed was covered in pins. Not sticking in but more lying on me akin to soldiers in ranks: all lined up in rows.

'With my arms stretched out I ran around the

classroom shaking and kicking in a vain attempt to dislodge them. Ms Bates saw.

'Jimmy, what are you doing? Stand still boy. Actually this wasn't very helpful when all I could see were pins. The other children wanted a closer look and began chasing after me. Ms Bates continued with her admonishments while I became even more confused as to what was happening or what to do next.

'Graham Hayden, eleven at the time, was due to leave the school for the secondary modern in a couple of months. He had plenty of experience with the sort of things boys play with. Struck with the idea of using a magnet to collect up the pins, he went into the science cupboard.

'This cupboard housed a number of magnets of various sizes and strengths. Assessing the situation, he decided this was a case for a more dramatic solution: the large electromagnet. This magnet was seldom rolled out, let alone switched on. Past experiences suggested it was a bad idea. Invariably something untoward happened. In Graham's mind, this was a drastic problem that needed a drastic solution: an emergency with no time to waste. He didn't. He had the magnet plugged into the mains and fired up before Ms Bates even noticed.

'Scissors are steel, like the cutlery used for lunch, as well as the serving utensils, and in fact, what isn't appreciated is how much iron or steel is around: wastepaper bins, staplers, letter openers to name but a few. These objects are normally found lying where they were left waiting for their turn to be used. It was the smaller objects which were first to react to the electromagnet force. From stationary, harmless things, they set off at great speed in a very clear direction but with no obvious purpose. Magnetism doesn't differentiate but attracts all suitable entities with the same enthusiasm. Soon the air was thick with flying detritus. Children screamed while jumping for cover behind or under anything to avoid the airborne onslaught. The noise drowned out Ms Bates' hysterical screams to turn off the electricity, while I was doing something reminiscent of an Irish jig. My pin-laden body was food for the magnet. It appeared it wanted to devour everything metal in the vicinity. I was being whirled across the room by this invisible force. Fighting, I grabbed for anything which offered potential sanctuary. My journey was delayed when I caught hold of a desk until my grip weakened and once more I was off. With magnetism, the closer an object is to the source the greater is the attraction and for me, the more useless it became to fight.

'Good fortune appeared in the guise of a heavy wooden desk and a couple of chairs knocked over in the mayhem. My leg trapped, wedged firm. I was held fast albeit hopping. Quite literally, I was being pulled relentlessly towards the magnet but my progress was impeded by my ensnared leg. What did complete the journey was the layer of pins that had previously been adorning me. The electromagnetic force was significantly greater than the force I was emitting so they deserted me en masse. Graham cut the power and everything fell to the floor with a clatter. By now I'd been hopping for several minutes and was into a steady rhythm. Despite the lack of magnetic pull I kept it up until rescued by Ms Bates. Her relief at my lack of injury save a small pinprick, was obvious. My relief that it was over was the greater but everyone's understanding of what had just happened was equal. No one knew of my magnetism, and everyone just assumed it was an oddity.'

'If you weren't magnetised before, which you obviously were, by the time Graham, what's his name …?'

'Hayden.'

'Yeah by the time he'd finished with that great big magnet, you definitely were … are, even.' She picked up the wine bottle and looked at it. 'Sorry no more.'

* * * * *

'That's a shame. What are we going to do now then?' Jimmy scooted down under the covers.

'I guess there's nothing for it but to put the latest bit of birth control kit to the test,' Barb said as she scooted down next to him.

'Did they show it to you before …, you know.'

'Yes, of course. They spent some time explaining how it works, where it fits. It's quite literally a copper wire coil placed at the top of my vaginal canal.'

'Wow, steady, too much information.'

'You did ask! Anyway you need to know. If I got pregnant, then you'd want to know.'

'Well less of the science lesson. A theory is only a theory until it's tested.'

'It's hardly romantic, you fumbling around down

there.'

'I know, I'm just not sure about this.'

Barb rolled her eyes, 'Take it slow, just inch your way in, no thrusting.'

'You say such romantic things at times.' Jimmy smiled to himself. 'How does that feel?'

'So far so good …, go on a bit more.'

'Now …, still okay?'

'Yes fine, what can you feel?'

'At the moment, only you. And that's so much better than those frigging rubber boots.'

'Yeah but they have their place. Now push more …, just a little. I think I can feel the coil.'

'Yeah me too, well it's something hard, not uncomfortable. So does my …' He wasn't sure which word she'd find acceptable.

'Penis.' She helped him out.

'Yeah, penis, fit inside or something?'

'Sort of, the coil's in my vaginal canal and that's where you put your penis.' She emphasised the word *sort of*.

'Still feel okay?'

'You can push more in if you like, but slowly still.'

'I'd like to but I've no more to push in!'

'Oh, that's it?' Disappointment registered on her face.

'Well you know what they say.'

'I don't, but I feel I'm about to find out. What do they say?'

'It's not the meat but the motion.'

'Well let's put that to the test, but slowly. We

don't want you bouncing around the room like Zebedee.'

He wasn't sure how to interpret her remarks.

'Come on, I'm only teasing.' Barb gave him a reassuring smile.

'Okay, on the count of three.'

'It's not the Apollo launch,' she laughed out loud.

'We're in danger here of having to abort the mission. How can a man perform under these circumstances?'

She clasped a hand around his neck, pulling his head towards her. They kissed long and hard. She used the other hand to caress the full length of his back.

'Better?'

'Yeah much.' He maintained a steady rhythm.

'Oh … Oh … Oh … Oo … Oh … Oh … Stop.'

'What! Have I hurt you?' He was most concerned.

'Can't you feel it?'

'What, the coil? Not really.'

'No, not the coil, more the … I'm not sure how to describe them. I've not felt anything like it before.'

'Good or bad?' He tried to help her form a description.

'Neither. Different, not bad, sort of stimulating.'

'Stimulating's good, isn't it? Pleasant or unpleasant?'

'Well again, not unpleasant, but there's a sort of surge, up through my body, one for each of your strokes.'

'A surge with each stroke!' He didn't really understand.

'I'm not sure how else to describe it. Okay, each time you thrust, I get this sensation shooting through me, a tingle, as if I've touched an electric wire. Not that jolt you get from the mains, but more the sort if you put your tongue on a battery's terminals.'

He thrust a couple more times.

'Yes, exactly in unison with your stroke.' She smiled and winked at Jimmy. 'I think this needs a lot more testing.'

* * * * *

'No, I cannot let you in.' Oleg was quite insistent.

'But you not understand?' Vladimir hopped from foot to foot. 'I'm desperate for piss.'

'Colour film processing takes time. If I open door pictures will be ruined. Hold on.'

'I said you should take zem to Boots, zey did great job on my holiday photographs.' Vladimir couldn't contain himself and banged on the door. 'Come on, man.'

'Two more minutes.' Oleg slid the bolt back. 'You are worse zan child.'

Vladimir rushed past him. 'Ah, zat is good … when you get to my age and have prostrate size of egg!'

'Now do not touch anything.' Oleg said assertively. 'I will dry prints. Make me tea and Marmite toast. By time you finish I will be done. We can have a look zen.'

'Please.'

'What?'

'It is good manners to say please.' Vladimir looked over his shoulder at Oleg.

'You are telling me about manners, when you piss in my dark room.' Oleg waved his arms dismissively.

'Get my toast …, please.'

Vladimir picked up a picture. 'She is so beautiful, look at her.'

'No,' Oleg slapped the back of his hand, 'zey are not dry yet.'

'Zis camera is better zan Polaroid. Look how you captured zose cheek bones, and her mouth, it makes you want to kiss it.' Vladimir was back in his fanciful world.

'Here.' Oleg pushed some more prints in front of him. 'Look at Jimmy Kavanagh. I am very happy with them. For Sheila, I have cut up a picture leaving head and shoulders, zat way it will fit her handbag.'

'Clever thinking. We can deliver zose to her later wiz note about Thursday.'

Oleg passed a sheet of paper to him. 'I have set out timetable, here is one for you:

15.00 *S arrives at No. 44 to change.*

16.00 *V leaves for Grosvenor House Hotel, travelling by taxi from Bayswater Road.*

16.15 *V at GHH, locates presentation room of JK's event and where hospitality will be served.*

16.30 *O to take pictures of S for record purposes*

16.45 *O and S take taxi from BW Road to GHH.*

17.15 *O and S meet V in foyer to brief S re JK's movements*

17.30 *Windows deployment seminar, Day one ends*
       S to join delegates as they move to Hospitality Bar
       O and V place themselves to keep an eye on S

18.30 *(Target time), S and JK leave GHH for Lancaster Mews*
       O and V to follow — alight taxi at top of Mews
       S & J walk down Mews to No. 44
       O and V take over — S to go home

Vladimir studied the timings. 'Zis is very good, only two questions.'

'Okay what?'

'Why we get taxi from Bayswater Road, and if JK does not play game by 18.30, zen what?

'We cannot have taxi come here as it is too obvious. Agree?'

'Da, and two ...'

'Delegate dinner is at 19.00. If offer of sex does not trap him, we know zat food will. All men are same, only want two things.'

'What are you suggesting?'

'If Sheila does not seduce him by seven, she will make sure he is drunk so we can, let me say, escort him out of hotel as he goes to dinner.'

'You mean kidnap him?'

'If necessary, I suppose. But I am sure Sheila will do her job well.'

'Well she could seduce me any day.'

'Vladimir, smile from Moscow lavatory attendant would seduce you!'

'For plan to work, she need money for taxi fares and drinks. Also front door key for here.'

'And once inside, what zen?' Oleg needed to hear the details from Vladimir.

'She takes him to bedroom, what else? I know zat is where I would take her.'

'God help me man, keep mind on job. Yes we would all like to ... you know wiz Sheila, but zat is why she is here.'

'Da, da, make sure your hair is kept on, I can

dream.' Vladimir smiled as he thought of him and her together. 'Have you envelope?'

'Drawer in kitchen table.' Oleg pulled it open. 'Here.'

'So money, say £100.' Oleg looked surprised. 'GHH is expensive. Key zat is spare, his picture and her table of times.' Vladimir put the items in the envelope; he licked and sealed it before standing it against the teapot sat in the middle of the kitchen table. He took it back. 'Have we pen?'

'Drawer in kitchen table.' Oleg took a bite of his Marmite toast.

Vladimir added, *Sheila, good luck. Vlad,* with a smiley face and two kisses. Underneath he wrote, *(01 272 8213)*. He admired his handy work. 'I will put zis through her door. No time like present.'

Oleg laughed, 'You sounding more English every day.'

Vladimir didn't bother with his hat and coat; he'd only be a few minutes. Tiptoeing down the hallway, he opened the front door as quietly as he could. The American listening device picked up the click of the lock releasing.

*   *   *   *   *

'Did you hear that! They're on the move.' Brad was by the window. 'Only one at the moment, the big one, Vladimir. He's not got a coat; I guess he's not going far.'

'Thanks for the running commentary.' Matt was slumped in a chair trying to figure out what the Russians were planning.

'Should we follow?' Brad looked for guidance.

'No coat and only one, you say. Is he carrying anything?'

'Not that I can see.'

'He's going to the shop for milk, you wait and see.' Matt continued his pondering.

Brad remained vigilant. 'Look, he's back already.'

'Is he carrying anything now?'

Brad strained to see. 'No, nothing.'

'I bet my silver dollar he's been to Sheila's.' Matt sounded confident.

'Well he hasn't had time to talk to her.'

'Because he didn't need to, he's dropped her a note, a letter or whatever. Damn and blast, we warned her not to visit those Ruskies, so they're using written communication.' Matt thought for a while. 'Did your dad ever take you fishing, Brad?'

'Fishing?'

'Yeah, you know, with a rod and line.'

'He did, but I've not done it for a long time.'

'Well you're about to right now.' Matt smiled. 'We need a pole, twine and some chewing gum. Can you manage that?'

Brad disappeared. Matt was aware of him moving around the house. Doors creaked, drawers opened and closed, cupboards were searched. He reappeared.

'Look, I've found this stick on the back patio, it came out of a flower pot. We've got no twine but I've improvised. You know that old rug upstairs in the back bedroom, the one with all those patterns and colours?'

'Yes, the Turkish one.'

'Well I noticed a few threads were loose, so I pulled them out and twisted them together. The gum I had in my pocket, that was easy.' He was feeling pleased with himself.

'Not a cheap fishing set then! That carpet is worth over a thousand dollars.'

'I didn't know!'

'Anyway, tie the twine real tight to the end of your stick and take two pieces of gum and start chewing. Keep chewing until you reach Sheila's. Once there, tie the gum to the other end of the twine, then go fishing.'

'What am I fishing for?' Brad still hadn't formed a connection.

'The envelope, note or whatever that Commie bastard put through her letterbox. Go now, as quick as you can before she finds it.'

'What if I'm seen, you know, by people in the street?'

'Look, you're a covert agent, be covert. Anyway, on a Monday night, no one's around, they'll all be watching East … whatever.' He couldn't think of the title. 'That new TV programme they all watch.'

'Coronation Street.'

'Maybe. Just go to it. I'll keep watch on our friends while you're gone.'

Brad disappeared again. Within minutes he was back. 'What do you think?' He paraded in front of Matt.

'God damn it man, what are you wearing?'

'I found them in a cupboard when I was hunting for the fishing stuff.'

'What's that say on the front?'

He pushed out his chest. '*Chelsea FC*, it's a soccer shirt and so's the baseball cap.'

'Look, those jeans are half way up your leg. Brogues and sunglasses? Are there no sneakers? And take those sunglasses off, it's pitch black out there. This is London, not LA.'

'It's a disguise. What happens if Sheila sees me?'

'She'll laugh her little cotton socks off.'

Brad slipped into the Mews, staying away from the street lamps. He got to the café; it was in darkness. A light was on in her flat. He waited in the shadows of the pillars of the adjacent building. The Mitre was quiet. Matt was right—everyone was watching TV. A taxi went down Lancaster Gate but the driver never glanced at the Mews. Brad found her letterbox. Through the glass in the door he could see the envelope, just as Matt predicted. He took his make-shift rod from his trousers and gave several good chomps on the gum before attaching it to the line.

Squatting by the door he fed his rod, with line, into the letterbox. Since his rod was fifteen inches long and the line about twice its length, the chunk of gum was still on the wrong side of the door and not dangling from the end of the rod. He pulled it back to try again. This time he'd push the line through the letterbox before the rod. Pulling it back, the letterbox snapped shut. Its distinctive sound was heard in the flat. Sheila ignored it. Brad ran for the shadows, leaving the end of his rod protruding from the letterbox. He waited—no lights came on. He returned to his task. What he hadn't realised was with the line so long, he wasn't able to get sufficient movement in the rod to lift the gum into position. He pulled it all back again. The line snagged. Giving it a good tug, the letterbox clattered again.

Sheila was now curious. Leaving the lights off, she crept down to the kitchen. The plastic curtain kept her hidden but she had a clear view of the door, letterbox and, more importantly, of the figure crouched outside. She spotted the shirt. Bastard Chelsea supporter, she thought. She was well known to be a Tottenham fan, as that was where her mum lived. I bet he's up to no good. By the kitchen door was the broom used to sweep up. *Right my laddo, it's your turn for a surprise.* She squatted, holding the brush end. Inching her way along the counter, she moved within striking distance. Pausing, she waited for whoever it was to push open the flap. He did. Bang! Without wavering she rammed the broom handle, with all the force she could muster, through the letterbox into the face of the perpetrator. He fell back clutching his head as Sheila ducked back into the kitchen, broom very much at the ready. He stood and, still holding his head, dashed down the Mews. Stopping, he spun around and ran back the other way onto Lancaster Gate.

'Good riddance, you bastard,' she shouted. She doubted the guy would hear but it made her feel better. The nerve in her right leg had gone into spasm and started shaking uncontrollably. She took a deep breath, and another. Slowly calm returned. Letting go of the broom she went to go upstairs. From the corner of her eye she noticed the envelope. Stooping to pick it up, she saw the fishing rod and through the door glass, a pair of broken sunglasses. *They look like something those Yanks wear,* she thought, *what are they up to?*. Recovering the rod she pocketed the envelope. Opening the door she took one more look up and down the Mews before heading back up to her flat.

In the sanctuary of her bedroom she examined the rod; it was botched together in a hurry. She held the envelope. Using the handle of her metal comb, she slit it open: money, keys and timetable. On the bottom of the timetable, Oleg had written; *Money for taxi and drinks, key for No. 44. It is crucial to stick to the times given. Any questions contact Vladimir.*

Seeing the timetable brought the whole thing home to her. Up to now it was about the money and getting back on track after dumping her useless boyfriend. She'd played with clothes and really enjoyed herself but now she had a knot in the pit of her stomach.

Wot if he doesn't fancy me? she thought. He 'as a galfriend so why would he fancy me? I've only got an hour—how quickly do those *femmes fatlees* take? I've never picked up a bloke before, they always make the first move. He maybe, he maybe, he maybe …, 'elp! she screamed inside, 'wot 'ave I done?' She'd said *yes* once too often and now Vlad was depending on her.

Putting everything back in the envelope she noticed the telephone number. She wondered if she should ring him and tell him that she couldn't do it, that she was just not good enough. *But wot about the sodding Yanks?* She still had to deal with them. *Unless you pick up the phone,* she told herself, *you've no chance of making the call.* Her hand rested on the handset. Wot do I tell him? *I know, my mother's been taken ill and I have to go right now to look after her. No, once you start lying, it just gets worse and worse. The truth then, you've lost your bottle. Sorry to 'ave messed you around, goodbye. Do you fink they're gonna let me get away with that?*

Ring, ring, 'Jesus wot's that?' The phone under her hand burst into life. 'Mum, 'ello, I was just finking of you.' She waited for a response but got silence instead. 'Are you okay Mum?'

'Is this 8728270?'

She knew the voice: Vlad. Shit! She panicked and put the phone down. It rang again. She picked it up and listened.

'Sheila, what is wrong? It is me, Vlad ...'

'I can't do it.' She said, slowly and deliberately.

'What do you mean, you cannot do it? What cannot you do?'

'You know, the 'ole fing. Going to the Grosvenor, chatting up Jimmy wotever 'is name is. Bringing 'im back 'ere.' She had tears in her eyes. 'I've let you down ... sorry.'

'My dear, you have not let anyone down. What made you zink like zis?'

'The note, seeing the times and wot you want me to do.'

'But it is only as we discussed.'

'I know, but now it's more real. I've never done nuffing like this. I'm scared, especially after today. They held a gun to my 'ead ..., in my flat! And just now, they tried to steal your letter. I caught one and smashed him with a broom 'andle.'

Now it was Vladimir who was silent. His brain

was in overdrive. 'Gun! When?'

'Late morning. You know, when you came for your full English.'

'Zey were zere? Where? Why did you not say?'

'I tried, but you took no notice. All that stuff you told me about Jimmy, his galfriend, Zylog, pictures, they 'eard it all and made notes.'

'Notes.' Vladimir was seething. 'And now, what happened?'

'I 'eard the letterbox rattle so I came down to investigate. Took 'im by surprise. He run off 'olding his 'ead.

'Did he get letter?'

'No course not, but it put the willies up me.'

'Sorry, willies, are we talking about Hitler again?'

'No, silly,' she laughed. 'Frightened, I was.'

'Okay I must zink. I talk with Oleg. We will contact you. Now act normal like nothing has happened. Bye.'

She was listening to dial tone.

*   *   *   *   *

'Jesus Christ, what happened to you?' Matt jumped up at the sight of Brad. The swelling around his face meant he could only see out of his left eye. Bruising was starting to show.

'I fink my 'ose is 'roken.' He was difficult to understand. The blue Chelsea shirt was now red with his blood.

Matt picked up the phone. 'Who's on emergency

duty tonight? We've a man down here … No not dead, but we need medical assistance … 12 Lancaster Mews, quick and make it discreet.' He replaced the handset. 'Hey buddy, sit down. Let me get you something to stop the bleeding.' Matt turned to leave the room just as Brad collapsed, striking his head off the corner of the coffee table. He was out cold.

The distinctive sound of rotor blades throbbing overhead announced the arrival of US special services Delta Force en masse. The Mews was bathed in search lights, as men dressed in one piece black combat gear, full face ski masks, gloves and heavy duty mid-calf leather boots shimmied down ropes suspended from helicopters. Each had a semi-automatic rifle, stun grenades, blades of various sizes designed to kill a man with minimum fuss and any number of other death-inducing implements. Within seconds, the Mews was in lock-down. Nothing could move in or out. Across the roofs of adjacent buildings shadowy figures stood watching and waiting. Matt went to the front door.

'Step outside.' A voice growled at him.

'Hey buddy, go easy, it was me that made the shout for assistance.'

The Commando, using his gun barrel, pushed Matt down the hall, 'We only have your word for that.' They'd been joined by several other soldiers.

'Here sir, he looks real bad. His face is all puffed up like he's been hit real hard. He's covered in blood, it's splattered around the furniture,' one of them said.

'What you got to say for yourself?' The Commando growled. Matt hesitated. 'ID.' Matt was shell-shocked. The Commando put his nose to Matt's. 'Now!'

Matt fumbled for his dog tags.

'Hands away from your body, keep your arms raised, assume the position.' The Commando pointed to the kitchen table and Matt complied. Another Commando came behind him, kicking his feet further apart. Matt managed to stop himself falling forward. Two more commandos stood guard. The leader went to see Brad for himself. He lifted his hand to his mouth and spoke at his wrist. 'Ambulance status.'

Another Commando standing at the window saw it arrive. 'It's here, sir.'

'Right, you and you, take his head and feet.'

Brad groaned as they carried him out to a large estate car. All its windows were blacked out. It displayed no number plates; it was totally anonymous. The tailgate rose up as the gurney extended. It was dark inside but the outline of another person was visible. As quietly as it came, it was gone. Another equally anonymous car had been waiting on Lancaster Gate and it now moved forward. By the time it reached number 12, Matt had been cuffed and brought to the front of the house. The back door opened and a Commando pushed him in. Within seconds he was secured inside. The car purred up the Mews; only the sound of rubber on cobbles told you it was moving. Before it turned onto Lancaster Gate, the searchlights were extinguished, all the Commandos melted away and peace returned. The sound of rotor blades was now just a memory.

Across the road Oleg and Vladimir observed the whole theatre in astonishment. It was all captured on video and would provide great info for the guys back in Moscow.

'I need to speak to Sheila.' Vladimir sounded concerned.

'Phone her.'

'I've tried, it's engaged.' He put his coat on.

'Not so fast, look out there.' Oleg pointed to number 12.

Following the removal of Matt, a squad of cleaners had moved in. Two black transit vans were parked out front. Like the other vehicles, neither had distinguishing marks. The house was being stripped of anything linking it to the CIA, including Brad's blood, clothing, listening equipment and cameras. Even the locks on the front door were changed while the whole building was swept for listening devices. The operation lasted less than an hour; it was completed in virtual silence. Everyone was trained for a specific task and carried out without need for further instruction. As quietly as they came, they were gone.

If it hadn't been so serious, the two Russians would have given them a round of applause. The Bolshoi, renowned for producing outstanding choreographed ballet, had nothing on these guys.

'Now what?' Oleg sought direction from Vladimir.

'Well at least problem Sheila was having has gone away.'

'What do you mean?'

'Sorry, wiz all zis excitement I had no time to discuss telephone call we had. She got, as English say, cold feet and wanted to stop operation. It was mostly fault of Americans, but now zey have gone.'

'For now,' interjected Oleg.

'Zen all is well. I must see her.'

*   *   *   *   *

Sheila felt the same. Although her flat was at the opposite end of the Mews it was on the first floor and up an incline so she had a pretty good view of the whole proceedings. She'd been hanging out of her bedroom window concentrating hard on the unfolding events at the far end of the Mews. She failed to notice the Commando crouched by a large chimneystack on the roof of The Mitre opposite. He removed his dark glasses, revealing a pair of eyes to Sheila. The whites were in such contrast to everything else it was as if they were floating in space. He must have heard her gasp. Flashing a couple of times as he blinked, they disappeared behind the glasses once more. Pulling her head in, closing the window as she did, she felt less visible, safer with the light out. Her phone went.

'Is that you Vlad?' she whispered, conscious of the Commando outside.

'Sheila, what are you playing at? Who is this Vlad, have you got a new boyfriend? Why didn't you mention him when you were here?'

'Mum, shhh, they're everywhere. The 'ole Mews is overrun by some military guys, Americans I guess. We've 'elicopters, blokes sliding down ropes all carrying guns, and goodness knows wot. They're stopping anyone coming or going from the Mews. It's like a war zone.'

'Are they firing guns?'

'I've not 'eard any, but they've those silencer thingies and telescopes.'

'I'm not sure they're telescopes, but I know what you mean. Back in Sydney when they thought the Japs were coming after Pearl Harbour, we were told to get under the bed, you know.'

'Do you fink I should now?'

'Well my little possum, I don't want no harm to come to you. Look, I'd better go now, call me later darl when they're gone.'

'No Mum, don't go. I'll crawl under the bed like you said. Please don't 'ang up, I need a friendly voice right now.'

'Oh my sweetheart, hey I'm worried about you. Do you want me to come over?'

'No, there's no point. They won't let you down the Mews.'

'And you can't get out?'

'No, I'm trapped. Wot was it you used to say? *We're banged up 'ere tighter than a dingo's arse.* I miss Oz, Mum. I wish I was there now.'

'That's twenty years ago at least. You were only a young slip of a thing when we left. My little Sheila, yeah I miss it too sometimes. If it hadn't been for that damn father of yours going off with that farm hand, that shearing queen from Brisbane, we'd still be there.'

'Shhh, the lights have gone and the 'elicopters too. I fink they're pulling out. Look, I'll let you go now, speak soon. Love you.'

'Bye, my little darl. Give Vlad a call. There's nothing like a pair of strong man's arms in a crisis.'

'I will. Bye Mum.'

Sheila dialled Vladimir's number, which rang once before it was answered. *'Sorry all calls to this number are withheld.'* She held up the handset in disbelief. She dialled again more slowly. It started ringing. *'Sorry all calls ...'* She replaced the handset. She was now concerned. Maybe the Americans had come for them. Through her unopened window she could see very little. The guy opposite had gone. She unhooked the latch, inching the window open wider. The guards were still patrolling the Lancaster Gate end and it looked like two black transit vans were parked outside Vlad's. With no search lights it was difficult to see.

CHAPTER 8

DIDCOT POWER STATION

Before she could open up her café, Sheila had to wash down the pavement and door to remove the blood stains. She collected the broken sunglasses, standard CIA issue, and binned them. They reminded her of the glasses all those soldier guys were wearing last night. She had the BBC's Radio 2 playing; the news came and went with no mention of the incident in the Mews. She switched to Capital Radio; still no mention. Jack, the paper boy, delivered the usual half dozen red tops she got for her customers, but there was nothing in any of them either. *Odd, maybe it'll be in the later editions,* she thought to herself.

The milkman arrived. 'Hi darlin, everything okay? Here's your milk.' He took his empties and left without another word.

Am I going mad? Sheila thought, starting to doubt her own memory. She flicked through the papers once more. The ring of the café doorbell was so familiar, she was oblivious to it.

'My dear.' Vladimir touched her on the arm to get her attention.

'Oh God, you frightened me!'

'Sorry my dear, I want to see you are alright.'

'Look, there's nuffink in the papers about last

night. Tell me I ain't dreaming. It did 'appen, didn't it?'

'Of course it did, my dear. Zere is nothing in papers because Americans imposed news blackout.'

''Ow can they do that? Bloody cheek.'

'Moscow TV were very grateful for footage but we are not to delight in zeir difficulties.'

'Wot are you doing here? I fought it was you the Americans were after. I was 'anging out my bedroom window trying to get a better view when suddenly, from across the other side of the Mews, this pair of eyes appeared. Those ...' she hesitated. 'Wot were they?'

'Commandoes. Delta Force, zey call zem.'

'Yeah, them. They were on the rooftops everywhere. All in black they was; you could 'ardly make them out. They even wore sunglasses. I fink that's wot 'appened. The Commando on The Mitre's roof must 'ave taken his off. Suddenly there they were, this pair of eyes, sort of 'overing in space. Gave me a real turn. I found a broken pair outside my door this morning when I was cleaning up his blood.'

'Sorry? Cleaning up blood?'

'That's wot I've been trying to tell you.' Sheila stopped to catch her breath.

'I think we must start at beginning. Breathe slowly, hold it ..., now let it go. Once more to make sure.'

'That's better.' Sheila could no longer feel her heart banging in her chest.

'Did they get envelope?' Vladimir needed to know if the Americans had intercepted it.

'As I said on the phone, no. Wot 'appened was, I was watching telly, Eastenders, when I 'eard the letterbox rattle. I didn't take no notice. You often get junk mail. Then only a couple of minutes later it 'appened again. I fought, sod this for a game of monkeys.'

'You had monkeys? I never saw monkeys. Did Americans bring zem? I would not be surprised, zey would use anything to take advantage.' Vladimir was confused.

'No, no, there weren't no monkeys.'

'But you just said.'

'I know, just pretend I never mentioned monkeys.' She rolled her eyes skywards. 'Right, where was I? Oh yeah, the letterbox rattled, so I crept down in the dark. From the kitchen I could see this bloke squatting down. The first thing I noticed was his Chelsea shirt. I fought he's gonna shove dog shit through. See, I'm a Spurs fan since Mum lives in Tottenham.'

'Ah I see.' He didn't, but wanted her to finish her story.

'So I fought, you bastard, I'll get you. I took the kitchen broom and, crouching by the counter, I crept as close as I could to the door. He pushed open the flap and *Bam!*' Sheila slammed her hand down on the table; Vladimir recoiled in surprise. 'I smashed 'im in the face real 'ard. Well he fell back 'olding 'is 'ead. After a bit he managed to get up; bleeding everywhere. Then he ran down the Mews towards you, got a few steps, turned and ran out into Lancaster Gate.'

'What did you do zen?'

'I stood 'iding in the kitchen, shaking, I was. I didn't know if he'd come back or wot. The guy wasn't really a Chelsea supporter.'

'Why you say zat?'

'Cos they'd be pushing stuff in, not trying to get it out. I fink it was that young American from number 12. After I 'it 'im, remember I said he started running down the Mews, then he realised wot he was doing, you know, giving the game away, so he ran the opposite way.'

Sheila dropped her shoulders, and relaxed her mouth. She appeared better having told her story.

'Can I have breakfast? At least cup of tea.' Vladimir looked wistful.

She looked passed him. 'Where's Oleg, will he want one?'

'Yes, he has been up all night reviewing video footage. I needed to see you so, left him alone. He will be here soon.'

The café doorbell jingled. 'Ah speak of the devil. So what did you find?' Vladimir beckoned to Oleg.

Breathless, he couldn't speak. 'Need … to … get … my … breath.'

'For a spy he's very unfit,' Sheila laughed.

'Nyet, he is not really spy, he just likes to play wiz gadgets. So what have you found?'

'Da, man zey put in ambulance, he was young agent. What was most odd was he was wearing football shirt, blue, well it would have been blue but it was covered in blood so it was difficult to see.'

Sheila gestured to Vlad. 'See I told you. Bloody Yanks.'

'Bloody Yanks, I like zat,' Vladimir chuckled to himself. 'What else?'

'Well other one was arrested by those

Commandoes, taken away in handcuffs. I zink maybe zey had fight.' Oleg was pleased with himself.

'Sorry Oleg, you're wrong there. It was Sheila here who put him in hospital.' Vlad cuddled her in gratitude.

'Steady on, let me go and get your breakfasts cooking.'

'Is she back working on operation?' Oleg eyes followed her into the kitchen.

'I have not asked her but I zink so. Shhh here she comes .... Ah my dear, tea, you are life saver.'

'I been finking, if the young one's in 'ospital, serves him bloody right. I didn't like him, he kept looking at my pants.' Sheila saw both men were confused. 'No, not to worry. Anyway, if he's in 'ospital and the other one's been arrested ...'

'And number 12 has been closed down,' added Oleg.

'Then they're out of the frame and I ain't got no worries about Fursday now.'

'So you are back with us?' Vladimir asked, tentatively.

'And raring to go.'

'Zat is good news. Sheila dear, you make an old man very happy.'

* * * * *

Jimmy and Barb arrived at work together, somewhat later than their usual eight thirty, but both with very broad grins.

'Hey it's the love birds. All's well in the nest, by

the look of you two.' Rob gave Jimmy a knowing wink.

'Wait till you take your missus on that cruise, you'll know what being in love feels like.'

'Love or lust?' Rob hoped for a reaction from Barb.

'Do they have to be separate?' Barb cooed at him. His face reddened as he busied himself.

Barb's phone rang; Jimmy took the opportunity to ask Rob for his help. 'Look mate.' He paused and thought, 'I've got a little problem, well, not really a problem.' He checked to see if Barb was still on the phone.

'What is it, Jimmy boy? Do you need some advice from your Uncle Rob? A man of the world, a hit with women, the man who taught Casanova all he knew.'

'No, no nothing like that. It's more about physics.'

'Physics? What you on about?'

'Magnets and copper coils.'

'Coils?' Rob's inflection said he was surprised.

'Shhh, keep your voice down. Yes, you know, see I've forgotten basic school-boy stuff. I can remember doing some experiments with magnets and copper coils.'

'Are you alright or is this a wind up? I've got work to do.'

'It won't take long. All I want to know is what happens if you move a magnet in a coil?'

'Is that it? Is that your question? That's easy.'

'Well?'

'Because of induction, a current is generated in the coil. If you connected each end to a meter you'd see the meter swing in time with the magnet being moved closer or further away. That's how electricity is generated, obviously on a much bigger scale, but it's the same principle.'

'Right, thanks.' Jimmy returned to his desk, contemplating what he'd said. Rob was just confused.

Barb saw the two of them chatting and called to Jimmy: 'You're not talking about us to him, are you?'

'No of course not Barb, that's private stuff. We were just chatting.'

'So what were you just chatting about?'

'Oh you know, stuff.'

'Not about my coil, I hope.' Barb looked across at Rob and he smiled back at her.

'Course not.'

'He knows, doesn't he?'

'No, really. I asked him about how electricity is generated.'

'You think I was born yesterday? Have I got *mug* tattooed on my forehead?

'Okay. I asked him if you have a moving magnet in the vicinity of a coil ...'

'See, I knew you were talking about me!'

'No, it wasn't like that. I talked in general about magnets and coils. It turns out that's how you generate electricity.'

'Are you saying I've got Didcot Power Station between my legs?'

'Course not, don't be silly, but it does explain why you kept feeling those little tingles, okay?'

'I suppose so.' She returned to her desk to consider this.

'Hey I think this is yours mate.' Rob was standing next to Jimmy holding some paperwork.

'What's this then?' He took it from him. 'Oh yeah, conference details. Thanks.'

'Barb, you there?' Jimmy couldn't see over the half height partition without standing up. He got no reply. He stood up. She had her back to the office and was staring out the window, deep in thought. He went to her. 'You alright?'

'Yes, fine. Just trying to understand what's happening to you.'

'How do you mean? Nothing's happening to me, I feel great.'

* * * * *

'You know, last night with the tingles. Yesterday lunchtime and the compass thing, Sunday's walk and you going off like that, not to mention the Sainsbury's trolley, the farm gate, the car locks, my flat locks and of course the tower. And never mind the roulette wheel. That's a lot of unusual stuff.'

'I guess so, when you put it like that.' Jimmy shrugged his shoulders.

'I want to know why? You explained about being a baby fridge magnet, the hammock and you as a pin cushion.'

'And there's more—like my skin, for example.'

'What do you mean, your skin?'

'Look at me. I've not always been this colour. I've often been mistaken for Spanish or Italian, you know, that Mediterranean sallow skin look, like a permanent

238

tan.'

'What were you before?'

'Just everyday common English white.

'So what happened?' Before she'd finished speaking she was regretting asking the question.

'In '62 we moved close to the river in Sonning-on-Thames. One thing my parents dreaded was me ending up in the river unable to swim. The local baths ran classes for all ages and I was soon signed up. I took to water like the proverbial and loved it. I became quite proficient, so much so that my teacher suggested to Mum I might like to join the squad for more serious training. Of course she was proud, as was Dad; me, their son, chosen for swimming training. Whenever my father relayed this fact he would puff out his chest to say *that's my boy*.

'Initially training was on a Sunday morning. Soon it became three sessions a week; quite a commitment. The more time I spent in the water the more competent I became. Confidence in the water carried over into other aspects of life. The training, the discipline and the camaraderie with the other squad members had a positive effect on my growing up.'

'Do you still swim now?'

'Yeah, of course, weekly. Anyway, Dad had a fine head of hair, dark brown in colour, almost black from a distance. I inherited the same except mine's finer in texture giving it an even darker and thicker look.' He flicked his hands through it. 'It was a fact that never crossed my mind until the summer of my twelfth year. In 1964 the English discovered the package holiday to Spain, and Torremolinos in particular. We'd never flown, or even been abroad before. In fact, Bexhill-on-Sea was the furthest we'd ventured.

'Swimming was a major part of my non-school time; extracurricular activities kept me in the water virtually daily. My continued exposure to water was unabated and gradually I noticed an all over change to my skin colouring. A medical person might think *jaundice*. Strangers thought my parents were Mediterranean. This led to questions, since they were most obviously not. *Is he adopted?* was quite frequently levelled at me by those who didn't know us. The response from me, or Mum and Dad, was a quizzical *What are they talking about?* I knew I was English through and through. If I didn't know any better I'd say I was going rusty; my skin was turning an orangey hue like a well-tanned Adonis. In Spain, the black hair and olive skin combination meant locals thought I was Spanish.

'The early years of the package holiday held a great divide between the pasty faced Northern Europeans, who neither spoke nor understood Spanish, and the local Spanish who had little or no knowledge of the English or their idiosyncratic ways. The English wouldn't put in the effort for two weeks per year to change the situation. If the Spanish wanted to communicate, they had two choices: learn English or be spoken to slowly and loudly.

'When the Spanish spotted me, fresh off the plane, and later with my pale skinned, sunburnt family, they made a beeline for me. My complexion and hair colouring stood out a mile. I had to be Spanish in their eyes. Taxi drivers, street vendors, shop owners and restaurateurs took one look at the family and drew a deep breath in readiness to launch into their version of English. Once I was noticed, their apprehension shifted to relief followed by a high-speed stream of colloquial Spanish directed at me. What was a twelve year old English boy supposed to do in such a situation? I had no idea what was being said, let alone cared.

'Shrugged shoulders and eyes cast to the floor weren't the responses they expected or hoped for. The Spanish were unprepared for the English. A *When in Rome* attitude prevailed amongst them. Getting an insolent reaction from a child was definitely not what they wanted. The language and cultural void was wide.

'On one occasion the owner of a gift shop was so frustrated she took hold of my arms and shook me, all the time muttering some incomprehensible phrase. She did *an English*: she thought if she said it repeatedly, with increasing volume, then somehow the penny would drop and I would miraculously burst into Spanish and give her the answer she so badly wanted. It stuck with me all those years. I later found out *¿Cómo estás disfrutando de su visita a nuestro país?* was this woman's attempt at making us feel welcome. It certainly didn't; it was more like the start of a diplomatic incident.

'Despite these somewhat awkward and uncomfortable introductions to tourism, come the following year the difficulties were mere history. We were now experienced and committed travellers. Dad dined out on these stories until it was time to repeat it all again twelve months later. I didn't let the grass grow under my feet and mastered the phrase 'Soy Inglés' in a vain attempt to deflect the Spanish from speaking to me. However, my continued bronzing, my growing muscle mass from swimming training and my additional two inches in height gained over the intervening year, coupled with my Spanish phrase, convinced them even more I was local. If they had their way my parents wouldn't have seen much of me as I was constantly asked to hang out or play football, being a welcome and much needed addition to their team.'

'Okay yet another unexplained thing that's happened to you.' Barb viewed Jimmy in a different light.

'Actually, I came over to show you this.' He passed her the papers Rob had given him.

'What are you saying?'

'I'm not here Thursday or Friday; it completely slipped my mind. I'm back at the Grosvenor. This time Microsoft are doing a Techie Conference on …,' he leaned over her shoulder and read the title, 'Windows Deployment and Support Strategies.'

'Riveting!'

'Look, you sell it, I'll look after your customers.'

'Yeah I know, only joking.'

'So I won't be here Thursday night, that's all. Looks like I'm booked into …,' he peered over her shoulder again, 'The Crown.'

'Well, just you behave. You blokes are all the same. A night on company expenses in London and you're like a rampant dog on heat.'

'Hey that's not fair. I'm being accused of stuff I've not even done.'

'I'm just saying be careful.'

* * * * *

'How you doing, soldier?' Brad was just coming to as Matt arrived at his bedside. He managed a grunt but little else. 'You're in the hospital under our embassy. The doc says your nose is broken but should mend okay; your right eye looks undamaged but until the swelling goes down they can't tell. You lost a lot of blood but they've pumped some back in. Oh, and your head's going to hurt where you cracked it on the table. Other than that you'll be out of here by Christmas.'

'Christmas?' Brad's words were lost in his bandages.

'Only joking. Easter! No, really, after the weekend. The guys upstairs want to talk to you about what happened. Can you lose your memory until you talk to me first? I'll keep coming by to see how you're getting on.'

Brad was left alone with his thoughts. It hurt to even think right now. All he wanted to do was sleep. He did.

Matt had been called upstairs for a debrief.

'Special Agent Serreno.'

'Yes sir.'

'Stand easy, Matt. I know you and Agent Mason were working on something involving the Russians and paranormal events. Is that right?'

'Yes sir.'

'The file's pretty thin. Can you fill me in?'

'I know, sir. I'd rather not at present sir. We were

on the verge of a breakthrough when your men—how should I put it—gate crashed the party.'

'Do you think the response was excessive? We had an emergency call on a secure line saying a man was down. What else did you expect?'

'It was a covert operation from a safe house. Now both are blown out of the water.' Matt thought the pen-pushers were out of touch with field work.

'Do you think the Russians saw anything?'

'Saw anything?! It will be broadcast on Moscow TV. As usual the Yanks will be the laughing stock of the Commie world.'

'Well I'm going to recommend we close this operation down, redeploying you two once Agent Mason has recovered.'

'So what am I supposed to do now, play Tiddlywinks?' Matt stormed out of the office, slamming the door as he went. 'I hate bureaucrats.'

*   *   *   *   *

By the time he'd returned to Brad's bed, he'd formulated a plan. 'Brad, you awake?' He gently rocked his shoulder. 'We need to get you out of here. It's Tuesday and we know the Russians are planning something on Thursday, okay?'

Brad grunted.

'So tomorrow evening, after the doctor's been, there's a shift change—we can slip out then. Can you walk?' Matt stared into his good eye and Brad nodded. 'I need to get you some clothes and shoes—all our stuff's in the lab waiting for analysis. What's your shoe size? No don't bother, I'll put in a requisition. They'll have your measurements and deliver it here. Right, I've things to do.'

The UK Citizen's Database, held by GCHQ Cheltenham, was available to the American Secret Service. Matt went to the computer suite to do some research. Searching by employer, he pulled up a list of staff for Zylog Systems, Maidenhead; their only UK office. He ignored the non-professional staff, cutting the list down to ten. He scanned down the names: Jimmy Kavanagh, Technical Support Analyst. Matt recognised his name from the news report and overheard conversations at Sheila's. He printed off his picture and details.

'Right Jimmy Kavanagh, which one of these three ladies is your girlfriend?' Matt didn't realise he was muttering to himself. 'Mary Jalanski, Book-keeper; Sonia Davies, Personnel; or Barbara Cooke, Software Sales.' He brought up photographs of each one. 'Oh no, sorry Mary, I'm sure you're a lovely lady but you're twice his age. Sonia, yeah, better, closer to his age but you're married. Now Barbara, yes, jackpot! You lucky fellow. That's our girl.' Matt printed off her address details plus picture. 'I'm looking forward to meeting you, sweetheart.' He logged out of the system and switched off the terminal. 'Maidenhead, here I come.'

Without Brad, and unsure what the Russians were up to, Matt headed straight to Paddington and bought a ticket—he didn't want more trouble from the guy who goes by the book. Walking towards the taxi rank at

Maidenhead Station, he saw a lady struggling with a number of large shopping bags.

'Hi Ma'am, can I give you a hand?' He smiled at her.

'Thank you young man, but I'm getting a taxi. It's just here.'

'Can I ask you, I don't know Maidenhead, I want to get to the High Street, is it easier to walk or do I need a taxi?'

She looked him up and down. 'Big strapping fella like you can walk it quicker. The one-way system will take forever.'

'Which way do I need to go, Ma'am?'

'Here.' She pointed. 'Across there, see the pub on the corner? That's Queen's Road. Follow it to the end and then you're in the High Street.'

'Most grateful Ma'am; now have a nice day.'

Matt read the address from Barbara's details. With some detective work he found the flat. He tried the door but it was locked. He rang the bell and waited; no reply. He rang it again for good measure—still nothing. He noted the kitchen and bathroom windows and the deadlock on the door. Using the micro camera attached to his wrist, he snapped shots of all these things. Back on the High Street, his next challenge was to find Zylog Systems, Moorbridge Road.

'Yeah, that's easy mate. Moorbridge Road's straight down over the traffic lights and you're there.'

'Thank you, most helpful.' Matt's trip to Maidenhead was proving far more useful this time.

He walked the full length of Moorbridge Road,

not stopping at Zylog. He scanned the faces of all the pedestrians he passed but recognised none as either Barbara Cooke or Jimmy Kavanagh. When Moorbridge Road ran into the main A4 Bath Road he stopped, checked his watch and considered what to do next.

Thirteen fifty. Unless you're on one of the long executive lunches, you Brits go around twelve thirty. I'm guessing I've missed the chance of seeing them till they finish after seventeen hundred onwards, he pondered his thought. Resigned to hanging around, he wandered back towards the High Street. Passing Zylog's building, he scanned each floor and large plate glass windows in turn without trying to look too obvious. First floor centre came up trumps. There she was, Barbara Cooke, looking better in real life than any photograph. He didn't want to be spotted; satisfied, he headed back to the station. *See you Thursday,* he thought.

* * * * *

'Jimmy,' Barb said, sidling up to him, 'I was mean to you earlier. I'm going to cook you a real treat tonight. It's my surprise. Once we finish, you walk back to the flat, let yourself in and I'll go shopping. How does that sound?' She waited for a hug or a smile, or a *great,* or anything. Nothing was forthcoming. 'You alright?' she asked, studying him. 'Did you hear what I said?'

'Yeah sure, sounds great, looking forward to it.' He wasn't convincing.

Barb titled her head and creased her brow.

He saw the look on her face.

'Hey, come here.' Standing up from his desk to

cuddle her, a spot of blood landed on his papers. He threw his head back before grabbing the bridge of his nose. She didn't have time to ask if he was okay; he'd disappeared to the Gents toilet.

'What's all that about?' She directed her question at Rob.

'You've not seen him get a nosebleed before? It happens quite often. If he's quick he can stop it before it gets too bad. I remember one time, six months or so ago, when we had to get him to A&E to get it cauterised, it just wouldn't stop.'

'I don't remember that. Where was I?'

'Out on a customer visit, training course or something.'

Jimmy returned to his desk. 'They're such a pain. I caught it just in time.'

'Has this been going on for a while?' Barb looked concerned.

'Forever; as a kid I always got them. The slightest knock or even a hard blow of my nose would start one.'

'What about the trip to hospital? That's a bit scary, what did they say?'

'Not a lot really. Asked a few questions, took my blood pressure, said it was a bit high but dismissed it as …, what do they call it, white coat syndrome. Apparently it's common for people to have high blood pressure in hospital as they get anxious about being there.'

'Why don't you slip away? Rob will cover for you. Mike's out so no one will know. I'll be back as soon as.'

Rob agreed. 'Yeah fine, I owe you one anyway for all those roulette chips. Get out of here. See you tomorrow.'

'Great idea, I'm feeling pretty knackered. A nap will be welcome.'

Jimmy went back to Barb's flat. Unlocking both locks was easy for him. The lounge was his destination and the sofa in particular. He got his nap.

Later Barb arrived home and busied herself in the kitchen. If Jimmy had been awake he would have appreciated the smells and all her hard work. After how he'd fussed over her, she wanted to do the same. Table laid, candles lit and some blues-jazz on the stereo, she thought it was time to wake him.

'Jimmy.' She rocked his shoulder. 'Come on, dinner.' she whispered. 'Wake up, or you won't sleep tonight.'

The response he gave lacked coherence.

'Come on, it'll get cold.' She was more forceful.

'Yeah, sorry I was dead to the world. What time is it?'

'About half seven. Dinner's ready. I hope you like paté, I've done fois gras.'

'Sounds good so far. We ate loads of different paté at home. Liver of any description was a big favourite.' He was more alert now. 'What's to follow?'

'Hope you like shellfish. It's mussels and chips with garlic mayonnaise.' Barb looked for his approval.

'Hey, you been speaking to my mum?'

'What do you mean?'

'Fish, and particularly shellfish, were always served at home as I was growing up. Mum came from a fishing village, I'm sure I told you. We'd have mussels, cockles, clams and even oysters on occasions. Excellent.' He was now at the table. 'Wow, this looks … Well I don't know; thanks.'

'Wine?'

'Yes okay.' He hesitated.

'What is it?'

'No, just when we had mussels, we used to have Guinness, a sort of tradition I guess. You haven't got any, I suppose?'

'You suppose right. You finished it the other night. I'll try and remember for next time.'

'Hey no big deal, wine'll do just fine. Gosh, this fois …'

'Gras …, goose livers, a real French delicacy. Mind you, it's very rich.'

'But very moreish.'

'Yeah well, don't fill up. We've got pudding as well.'

'Which is?'

'Which is a surprise. I'll just say it contains most girls' favourite ingredient.' She gave a cute little smile as if she could taste the ingredient now.

'What, champagne?'

'No silly, that's what you wash it down with … So what else did your mum give you?'

'She used to torture me and my sisters.'

'Sisters?'

'Yes, Sue and Trish, both older than me. When I was about eight, they'd have been teenagers. She'd give us a daily dose of cod liver oil, a great pudding spoonful, and an iron tablet. She said I didn't need it but to make it fair I had to take one. The whole lot was capped off with a large spoon of black molasses. I've no idea why but she said her mum fed it to her and it never did her any harm.'

'An interesting logic.'

'An interesting cocktail!. What else was odd was she never allowed us sweets, except on special occasions like birthdays, Christmas or Easter. Then it was always chocolate, the dark stuff, not milk. For treats, she'd give us prunes or dried apricots. To this day I still eat them when I fancy anything sweet.'

Barb cleared away the main course. From the kitchen she called to Jimmy: 'Close your eyes.' She came in holding a dark chocolate mousse. 'I know it's not your birthday, Christmas or Easter, but I'm sure your mum won't mind. Surprise!'

His eyes lit up. 'Barb, how did you do it? One way or another these are all my favourite things ... Come here, you.' He leaned in; their kiss lingered.

She pulled back to look into his eyes. 'I think Didcot Power Station needs turning on.'

Jimmy was embarrassed. 'Sorry my love, not tonight.'

* * * * *

The pictures taken with the micro camera provided Matt with the details he needed, particularly the makes of locks on Barbara Cooke's flat door. In no time he'd sourced the skeleton keys.

Arriving at Brad's bed, Matt saw he was sitting, though looking beat up.

'Okay, it's me Brad.' Matt thought it appropriate

to make himself known. 'Over the last twenty four hours while you've been sleeping it off, I've been busy. I've pulled the records of Jimmy Kavanagh and his girlfriend. You wait till you see her, she's a real looker.' Matt held up the picture from her record, 'See what I mean, buddy?'

Brad smiled, though you couldn't tell.

'I went back to Maidenhead yesterday and saw where they work. Tracked the route she takes back to her flat, mapped it, its location and entry and exit points. Yeah, I've just collected a set of door keys.'

Brad nodded to show he'd understood.

'Can you speak?' Matt listened for a response.

'Some, but it hurts when I move my face.' Brad's voice was barely audible.

'Okay but I need you to speak up a little.' Matt wasn't sympathetic.

'I'll try.' It was a marginal improvement.

'Have the guys upstairs talked to you yet?' Mike hoped it was a *no*.

'They asked a load of questions but I did as you said.'

'Great, so buddy, what really happened? You know, how come you're so beat up?'

Brad had been thinking about how to answer this question. Did he tell the truth, which would make him look incompetent, or fabricate a non-truth? He chose the latter.

'You know that soccer shirt, the Chelsea one I was wearing?'

'And the cap.'

'It turns out there are guys out there who don't like Chelsea, or their supporters.'

'But you're not a Chelsea supporter.'

'They didn't stop to ask. I was bent down with my fishing rod, just about to retrieve the letter …'

'So there was one. Commie bastards, I knew it all along. And?'

'On Lancaster Gate, at least three, maybe more guys were messing around. I'd seen them but took no notice. One spotted me, or the shirt really, and ran over. I was crouched peering into the letterbox, concentrating on hooking the letter. He saw my head as a soccer ball and kicked it like he was taking a penalty.'

'Jesus Christ. Damn football hooligans. These Brits are wild.'

'I don't know how long I was down before I came back to the house.'

'It must have been a while. You'd lost a lot of blood; that's why you passed out. It didn't help hitting your head on the coffee table.' Matt thought about what happened. 'The guys upstairs will be happy with that. I feel better about telling them—you know overwhelming odds, taken by surprise, I'd be too embarrassed to tell them Sheila did this to you.' Matt laughed; he didn't know how close to the truth he was. 'I don't reckon she could knock a flea off a raccoon's back.'

Brad was glad his head was covered in bandages so his blush remained invisible.

Matt moved in closer. 'Your clothes are in the closet. Once the doc's done his round …,' he picked up the chart off the end of the bed, 'at nineteen thirtyish, I'll be back. New staff come on duty then. They have a hand-over session so no one will be around. Get yourself dressed. I've a pool car parked off Grosvenor Square. We'll leave via the ambulance emergency entrance. Just hope there's no more soccer hooligans out tonight,' Matt chuckled. 'See you later, buddy.'

*   *   *   *   *

The doctor arrived to do his rounds.

'Nurse, Mr Mason here, is he showing any signs of regaining his memory?' The doctor peered in Brad's left eye using a torch to test the reaction of his pupil. 'Good, now what about the right eye? Let's remove the bandage. Mr Mason, how are you feeling?'

'So, so. It hurts when I talk.'

'The swelling's going down but you've got a real shiner there. Looks like you did a few rounds with Mohamed Ali and lost.' The doctor smiled at his own joke.

'Ouch.' It hurt Brad to smile.

'Sorry, Mr Mason. I think we'll leave the bandage off the eye for the time being. Can you see with the right?'

'Yeah, though it's blurred and I've double vision.'

'Can you remember any details of how this happened?'

'It's starting to come back.'

'Good, good.' The doctor added notes to the record sheet. 'Well that's it, see you in the morning. Plenty of rest now.'

By the time the doctor was down the corridor, Brad was dressed and waiting. His room door opened.

'Quick, the corridor's clear. Just keep close, let me do any talking,' Matt said.

The emergency ambulance exit housed two black, unmarked estate cars with two crew in each. One bay was empty and the other crew sat waiting for instruction. They were unable to leave their cars since every second counted in responding to a call-out. Matt knew no one would challenge them.

Brad felt a whole lot better in the fresh cool night air. He needed to be out on the job, not cooped up. The exit from the Embassy hospital was outside the heavily guarded perimeter fence. To anyone not in the know, it looked like the entrance to a subterranean garage so typical of large London houses. The pool car was parked close by. Within minutes they were around Hyde Park Corner, heading towards Harrods, Chiswick and the M4 Motorway. Matt was behind the wheel; Brad remained silent.

'Hey buddy, you okay?' Matt was feeling confident.

'So what's new?'

'Well I've booked us a room each at Fredrick's in Maidenhead. It's some fancy hotel, highly recommended. Anyway, we've a table for dinner at nine'ish—I said we may be late—then a good night's rest, ready for tomorrow.'

'But you've not said what we're doing in Maidenhead.'

'No, well I didn't want to bother you while you

were on the mend. We're going to get those Commie bastards to show us some respect. Let them do their operation with Little Miss Sheila, and we'll clean up.'

'How?'

'Jimmy Kavanagh will be begging to come to work for us because we'll have his real pretty girlfriend, Ms Cooke, as our hostage!'

CHAPTER 9

44 LANCASTER MEWS

'I hate frigging alarm clocks.' Jimmy pulled the duvet back over his head. 'I'm sure they're the work of the devil,' came from deep under the covers.

'That's as may be, but work of the devil or not, that's what we've both got to do today. Have you seen my quarterly sales targets? I think Mike's got it in for me,' Barb feared.

'He knows you're the best and carrying the rest.'

'It's hardly fair.'

'Sales isn't fair, that's why I do support.' Jimmy managed to get one leg out from under the covers. 'I hate cold dark mornings.'

'Hey Mr Grumps, we could generate our own heat and light, what do you say?' Barb cuddled closer to him.

'Now you come to mention it ...,' he sat upright, 'have I told you about me and my bedroom lights?'

'I'm all ears.' Barb rolled her eyes; she sounded disappointed.

'No, you know, you and Didcot, and what happened to me, now makes sense.'

'What, you had the same thing with another girl?' She sat up too, and stared into his eyes.

'No, course not, it was a Christmas Tree.'

'You are joking.' She gaped. 'Aren't you?'

'Okay not a Christmas Tree, but the lights from a Christmas tree.'

'Now I understand ..., not!'

He checked the clock. 'We've got a couple of minutes. What happened was in '67 nobody could fail to notice the *Swinging Sixties* were in full swing and in particular the *Summer of Love*. Every pubescent spotty youth was growing his hair, sprouting wispy chin stubble and dressing in all sorts of garish clothes like tie-dye shirts and loons. Everyone was an aspiring rock star; with no talent and no instruments but plenty of enthusiasm as they emulated their heroes. I was no different.'

'I remember that time, but I was too busy with my pony Freya, grooming, plaiting her mane and going to gymkhanas to get involved with that hippy stuff.' Her disapproval of his teenage years was clear.

Jimmy gave Barb a funny look. 'My bedroom was a sanctuary, where I could be anyone I wanted and do almost anything. It was pivotal to growing up. I painted the walls and ceiling black, stuck cardboard over the windows and a curtain over the door. With the lights out, even in broad daylight, the room was in total darkness. Actually more pitch black; so black you could almost feel it.

'I hated the bulb hanging from the ceiling. Instead I got hold of several sets of Christmas lights and strung them around the walls from skirting board to picture rail. They were all controlled by a single switch next to my bed — or so I thought.

'Now I realise what I'd created by stringing yards of wiring fastened at regular intervals around the room was, to all intents and purposes, an electrical generator with me as the armature.'

Barbara's face reflected her lack of understanding.

Jimmy noticed. 'At six feet tall and magnetised, each time I moved, my magnetic field would interact with the copper wires, inducing a current to flow in them. The result was clearly visible in the flickering of the several hundred miniature coloured bulbs.

'I first discovered the phenomenon soon after the decorations were complete. Putting the light switch by the bed on the opposite wall to the door introduced an unforeseen problem. Entering the room I would have to navigate it in total darkness. After all, I couldn't leave my door open for a moment longer than necessary otherwise my sisters or worse, parents, may look in or do the unthinkable and come in. Getting a torch crossed my mind but that was a bit sissy, and a candle was out of the question.'

'So what did you do then?'

'I developed a strategy of jumping so I could reach the bed and light switch with minimum likelihood of falling over any objects scattered around the floor. The process was to open the door, throw in my satchel in the direction of the bed and launch myself while simultaneously using a deft flick of my left leg to kick the door shut. If everything went to plan I'd make a soft landing on the eiderdown.

'But familiarity breeds contempt. After several days of successfully landing on the bed I became over-confident. This one attempt, instead of me landing square on the bed I hit it close to one edge. My flailing arms and legs acted as a generator, causing a few of the Christmas lights to sparkle momentarily. Nothing spectacular but just sufficient for me to glimpse the odd flashing bulb out of the corner of my eye. This was enough to raise my curiosity; enough to experiment. I found by standing in the middle of my room and spinning around with my arms held out all the lights would glow, flickering in turn as I rotated.'

'I'm not sure I should ask for any more stories about you growing up. This stuff's been happening to you all your life.' Barb slid her leg out of bed.

'There's more.' Jimmy was ready to tell her another story.

'Yeah but not now, or we'll be late. By the way, breakfast's on you.'

* * * * *

Wednesday in Sheila's café was uneventful. No American spies, and Oleg and Vladimir didn't turn up until midday. They only had coffee, and a round of Marmite toast for Oleg. Among her customers, the topic of conversation was still the raid by anonymous soldiers. The favoured rumour, started by Sheila, was it was a training exercise by the SAS, a mock hostage situation following the Libyan Embassy siege.

Sheila was more focused on shutting up shop. Her Vidal Sassoon hair appointment in Sloane Street was far more exciting. Bert would be unhappy at her closing early but it was a small price to pay for three hours of pampering.

She was right. Along with her hair wash, cut, styling and colouring, she had a facial and her nails manicured. The mouse brown, mid-length hair, she always wore piled on top of her head, was transformed into shoulder length, strawberry blonde hair that flicked up at the ends and swung as she shook her head. The salon also made her up to enhance their styling and colouring.

The woman she saw reflected in the mirror was beautiful but she didn't recognise her. Thursday's rendezvous with Jimmy Kavanagh had taken on a whole new meaning. It wasn't a job for fifteen hundred pounds, but a challenge, a way for Sheila to explore what might be, what she could achieve, who she could become. She loved her café but it was long hours, hard work and apart from the recent influx of spies, pretty mundane. Her bastard boyfriend stealing her savings, her means to escape her life, her key to her future, was the last straw. This Thursday, tomorrow, less than twenty four hours, could be the start of a whole new beginning.

She hailed a taxi. '44 Lancaster Mews please.' Watching the streets slip by—Knightsbridge, Hyde Park Corner and up Park Lane, past the Grosvenor House Hotel into Bayswater—felt so different. She'd seen these streets many times before, either from the tops of buses or as she walked along them, but it was different this time. She was no longer the outsider watching how the other half lived; she was part of it. She belonged—she'd arrived.

'Here you are Miss. Seven pounds sixty, and may

I say how stunning you look. Someone's a lucky man.' She paid him, plus tip. Within a few seconds the taxi and driver had disappeared out of sight.

She stood on the threshold with her finger poised above the doorbell to number 44. Apprehensive, she needed to share her transformation with someone. Her mum had come to mind, but Seven Sisters took a long time to get to by tube and a taxi would cost a fortune. The door opened; she'd forgotten they had cameras.

'Sorry, zis is private house, we are not expecting visitors tonight.' Oleg went to shut the door.

'Oi, stop it, it's me!' Sheila put her foot in the reducing gap. 'Oleg, opened up.'

His head emerged. With no hall bulb and the streetlight on the opposite side of the Mews, her face was in darkness. 'I am sorry, do I know you?' He still failed to recognise her.

Before she had time to answer, the door swung fully open. 'Oleg, fix yourself optician appointment, I would know zat voice anywhere. Come in my dear, and he says I am old fool.' Vladimir held out his arm in a greeting.

In the kitchen, both men stood back to admire the new look.

'Here, move little more under light.' Vladimir took her elbow, manoeuvring her to a better position. 'You are stunningly beautiful.' He said, salivating.

'That's funny, you're the second bloke to say that tonight. It must be true.' She did a full circle twirl. 'I feel like a million dollars. I can't wait to try my clobber on with this new Barnet.'

'English please, Sheila.'

'Oh sorry gents. I'm just so excited, I forgot you don't speak the lingo.'

'So it means?' Vladimir looked to Oleg. 'You need to take notes.'

'Right, *clobber* is my new clothes and all, and *Barnet*,' she pointed to her hair, 'is obvious, innit? Barnet fair—hair.'

'By time we finish zis assignment we will have extended English/Russian dictionary by big amount.' Oleg was in agreement. 'Well my dear, Jimmy Kavanagh will not be able to resist you.' *I know I certainly could not,* he thought to himself. 'Today we went to Grosvenor just to *suss lie of land*. Is zat what you say? We check out situation.'

She smiled at this.

'We have identified rooms for conference and where hospitality will be. I do not like surprises. A reconnoitre is always useful. Since Americans have gone from across road ...'

'Good bloody riddance I say,' Sheila hissed as she spoke. 'That younger one deserves everyfink he got. Bastard!'

'Zat is as it may be but now we can get taxi to collect us and drop us here without being watched. We will stick to planned times. It is easier at zis stage. If we change zem zere will only be confusion. Right my dear.' He helped her to her feet. 'Until tomorrow.' Vladimir went to kiss her cheeks.

'Oi, careful. This lot cost a ton.' She saw their confusion. 'Undred quid ... I dunno ow I'm gonna sleep in this. Maybe I'll 'ave to sit in the chair all night.' She giggled.

* * * * *

'Come on guys.' Mike was doing what sales managers do. 'End of month review, always an exciting time.'

Meeting Room 3 was full of the usual suspects all waiting in anticipation of who achieved target, or missed, details of forthcoming marketing campaigns, product launches, promotions, resignations, and general tittle-tattle that makes a team function successfully.

'And finally,' Mike continued, 'after the weekend, Barbara here will be clued up on the MSA suite of products. She's at a product training day this Friday, so long weekend for her then.' Mike made his usual inane grin but Barb looked back at him with daggers. 'Only joking,' he felt uncomfortable. 'And really finally, speaking of product training, Jimmy's back at the Grosvenor hotel.' General mutterings were heard all around. Mike picked up on the disquiet. 'No it won't be like last week, well I hope not, cause I'm not invited. He's in for two days of Windows Deployment Strategies. I think after that he'll need a Friday night drink at The Bear. Don't forget, my first round. Okay that's it. Thanks for all your efforts, now go do it.' The meeting room emptied.

'So that's another week of training you'll miss.' Rob playfully punched Jimmy on his upper arm. 'At this rate I'll be catching you up.

'Yellow Belt to Third Dan in two weeks? Pull the other one it's got bells on.' Jimmy slouched back in his

264

seat.

'What's this you're on about? What training and who's this Dan—your instructor?' Barb had no idea what they were discussing.

'Don't you know? Your lover boy here's a bit handy with his karate chop, and his feet and elbows, knees—come to think of it, just about any of his body parts he can use as a weapon.' Rob was impressed with Jimmy's skills, if not a little envious.

'I'm licensed to defend. If you use your martial arts to attack, you're likely to lose your licence.' Jimmy wanted to play down his martial arts skills.

'Licensed to kill, more like. He'd give James Bond a run for his money.' Rob couldn't help himself.

'How come I've not heard of this?' Barb saw Jimmy in a new light.

'Don't listen to Rob, it's nothing really. I started as a kid years ago, did pretty well. I'm still with the same club, down the Oxford Road in Reading, near Reading West Station.' He was being very modest.

'And Dan's your instructor?' Barb saw Rob and Jimmy exchange smirks. 'Have I just said a stupid girlie thing?'

'Well you're not to know. Dan's the grade, and I'm a Third Dan Black Belt.

'So how did this all start?' Barb asked the question but soon wished she hadn't. 'On second thoughts, maybe we should do some work.'

'No time like the present. Actually I'll give you the abbreviated version. Rough and tumble are all part of growing up. Whether it's falling off your bike, playing football or parachuting from a tree with a headscarf.'

Barb and Rob looked at Jimmy in disbelief.

'Yes I did that. Now listen—any youngster growing up will suffer cuts, pain and often cracked or broken bones. For me this was no different except for breaking bones. Many of my friends broke at least an arm, leg or rib but good fortune, the luck of the Irish or whatever, meant I never did. The opportunities were always there as the bruising bore witness. Trips to A&E were frequent but sprains or deep cuts were what took me there, not the requirement for plaster casts.'

'I broke my collar bone playing touch rugby.' Rob beamed.

'Yeah, very good. As I was saying, in our first house the windowsills were made from quarry tile. My bedroom had two single beds—mine and a spare. Separated by several feet of floor space. The spare was pushed up against the window wall directly under the sill. One evening between doing my teeth and getting my pj's on I thought about practising my long-jump skills. I was only eight. Standing on my bed I bounced a few times before launching myself at the other one. The clatter as I hit the floor provoked a response from downstairs. Not an *Are you alright?* sort of response or the sound of feet running up the stairs to see if I was hurt but more a *keep that blinking noise down* moan, *we're trying to watch TV, don't disturb us* sort of response. Mum and dad paid no heed.

'Anyway I was alright. I pulled myself back up onto the bed ready for another attempt. This time I'd a better understanding of the amount of force required.

Pacing the length of the bed, eyeing up the jump to gauge what was needed, I squatted ready to thrust myself skyward but chickened out. I paced the bed again, knowing it was going to be a big one. Concentrating, I could feel the bed beneath my feet. Balanced, calm and confident, the urge to jump was overwhelming. Suddenly I was in mid-air, committed, flying, no turning back. I passed over the edge of the spare bed destined to land safely, in one piece. I'd done it, I thought—I hadn't.

'What I didn't realise was, with a jump of such force, inertia takes over. I wanted to stop still and bathe in the glory. Unfortunately I was no longer in control but was subject to the forces of nature, like the sort of stuff I'd done in science at school. With my head over four feet from my feet, and my feet in contact with the bed, my head still had momentum. Since a divan is only three feet wide, in less time than I could do anything about it my forehead was bouncing off the quarry tile window sill.

The soft tissues went first but on the forehead there's very little. It transpires though, there are many blood vessels. The tile and the bone of my skull were in contact. My forward journey ceased. The pain was instantaneous, as was the gushing of the blood. The screams alerted my parents. This time they were up the stairs and into my bedroom before they knew they were there. It's a protective parent thing. Mother shrieked and father was mesmerised. On occasions like this, time itself seems to slow down. In reality my parents burst into action with towels to soak up blood, water and flannels to wash my face, cotton wool and bandages to help arrest the blood flow. Anything and everything to make me better.

'In 1960, telephones weren't that common but Terry's mum—Terry was my best mate who lived three doors away—had one installed a few months earlier. She was also a nurse, and insisted on calling an ambulance. The first aid stopped the bleeding but no one knew if I'd fractured my skull. At the hospital the wound cleaning removed several fragments of tile. The medical staff were concerned but only an x-ray, and an overnight stay, would determine the extent of the damage. No vomiting was a good sign and once the x-ray plates were developed it was clear I had no fractures. The scar above my right eye is permanent but it was remarkable how my skull remained undamaged. The nurses and doctors who plied the care all commented at one time or another. No cracking, no hairline fractures, nothing. It's as if my bones were made of some extraordinarily strong material like iron.

'This was another piece in the jigsaw—if only I was able to see the complete picture. What is apparent is I'm different from others.'

Rob and Barb looked at each other. 'So why martial arts?' Barb asked.

'Well, with strong bones like mine it seemed the obvious thing to do. And it helps me stay fit for swimming.' Jimmy mimicked a few karate style chops of good measure.

CHAPTER 10

BEN SHERMAN CALLED

'Why am I waking you up? Come on, get a move on. The train goes in twenty minutes.' Barb shook Jimmy several times. 'At times you're so infuriating.' She put her feet into the small of his back and pushed for all she was worth. He crumpled onto the floor before slithering into the bathroom. Barb pulled the covers over her head. *What's wrong with him?* Crossed her mind, before she fell back to sleep.

Jimmy made it to the train station, but only just. From the ticket hall to the platform were twenty steps, but at a run they felt like more. He wasn't the only one running for the train, and commuter camaraderie kicked in, with passengers holding the doors open to let everyone jump aboard. Even at six minutes passed seven AM, the train was virtually full. The fast trains from Maidenhead to Paddington only stop at Slough, and are mainly used by the serious travellers, those who prefer to make their commute bearable by avoiding mums, toddlers, school kids, sightseers, shoppers and concessionary fare passengers.

Jimmy found a seat, the last one in a compartment of eight; he caught his breath. Though he didn't travel this way daily, he'd done the journey enough times to know the drill. Reading, not talking, was the order of the day, whether it was a newspaper, that report you took home from work last night or the six hundred page novel you'd never find time to read were it not for this period of transition from home to working life. Today he had nothing to read. Resigned, he watched East Berkshire slip into Greater London. He sat patiently. At Slough everyone budged up in their seats, managing to fit another two passengers into the compartment. The corridors were filled to capacity, and Jimmy's view was now limited to one side only as standing passengers, jostling, swaying and lurching with the train's movement, made it impossible to see past. He'd had no breakfast but these conferences usually provided at least orange juice, coffee and a croissant. He didn't care, he was just glad to be on the train.

Iver came and went, next West Drayton, followed by Hayes and Harlington. *Good progress, no stopping or slowing.* He checked his watch—*we might even be early,* he thought. For no apparent reason the rhythm of the train changed; it slowed only marginally, but slowed nonetheless. *Come on driver, you were doing so well.* No one else noticed. *There*—Jimmy felt it again—as slight tug on the breaks. They were definitely going slower. The chap opposite looked up from his stack of papers. He'd felt it too. Glances were exchanged; no words, but a *here we go again* message was conveyed.

Crawling pace preceded the stop. A gentle stop with no sudden breaking, a nothing too serious halt, somewhere outside Southall. General fidgeting followed. Newspapers turned, books closed using tickets for place marks, important papers were put to one side. Seven thirty meant the sun was rising. Daylight was sufficient to see up and down the track. Some fellow stood, opened the top sliding window of the carriage, and peered out. A chilly draft caused everyone to shudder.

'I can't see nothing.' He reported to no one in particular. He shut the window and returned to his seat. Those standing in the corridor were more restless. The need to constantly shift weight to maintain balance while the train was moving makes standing bearable but now it was stationary legs soon turn leaden.

Time in these circumstances takes on a new dimension. Each stationary minute feels like five or more; by some means time seems to slow. Busy people always wishing for more hours in a day, would have their wish fulfilled.

The moaning started. Some chap chipped in, 'What I don't understand is the distance between Maidenhead and Paddington hasn't changed since Brunel built the railway in 1860. You'd think damn British Rail would have got it right 125 years later.' Everyone grumbled in a show of agreement.

Eight o'clock came and went, with no sign of a guard.

'You'd at least think they'd tell us what's going on.' Everyone nodded at Jimmy's comment.

By nine o'clock coats and jackets were off. Most of those in the corridor were sat on the floor, or propped up against any available support. All reading matter had been consumed; even the six hundred page book readers had had enough. Anyone who'd not had breakfast was now regretting it. The local, slow stopping trains were moving in both directions without problems. The main line high speed link had come to a halt.

The air in the carriage was stale and it was uncomfortably warm. The British stiff upper lip was softening. Still no news on the lack of progress. Resignation to missed appointments, onward connections or meetings were accompanied by searches through diaries or fat time-managers, looking for ways to recover from the situation.

Unannounced and unexpectedly, just before ten-o-clock, the whole train jolted violently backwards, sending everyone and everything in a variety of directions. With its now dishevelled, disquiet, and disgruntled passengers it moved gently forward, gathering pace all the while. Southall came and went, soon followed by Hanwell and Ealing Broadway just before Paddington. The train drew into the Paddington station. One and all pulled themselves together, regaining their composure before disgorging onto the platform as if nothing had happened. Only three hours late. Now the race was on to get a taxi. Four hundred commuters with the same strategy to make up lost time.

For Jimmy the Grosvenor House Hotel was a welcome sight. First stop, the toilet. It had been impossible to move on the train. Next the Conference Registration Desk. It was a big event and, judging by the number of unclaimed badges, there were still loads of late attendees. Jimmy scanned the ranks finding his before the conference organiser, Maggie did.

'I know you.' He recognised her from collecting the video tapes. 'Hi again. That friggin train stopped at

Southall for three hours.' He felt he owed her an explanation for his lateness. 'Must dash.'

'They're breaking for coffee now,' Maggie called after him. 'Just through there.' She pointed to the door on the right. 'You'll be early for that.' He was gone.

*   *   *   *   *

'Has Sheila got the day off?' The milkman breezed in with a crate and collected the empties. He was in a hurry. Giving the woman behind the till a cursory glance; he hadn't recognised her. Sheila's hairdo had survived the night and the comments, whistles and cat calls kept coming. Consternation amongst her regulars was rife.

'Cor blimey! You'd fink I grown another 'ead or summat.' In truth, she was enjoying the attention. She found her mind wandering, thinking about what she needed to do, how she was going to approach Jimmy and deal with his questions.

'Wot if he rejects me?' she said aloud, without meaning to.

'You got man trouble again, Sheila love?' One of her customers said, 'I gave them up years ago. More bother than they're bleeding worth. Mind you, they come in 'andy on a cold winter's night. Great for warming your feet on. Mine get like blocks of ice.'

Sheila smiled. 'If only it were that simple.' She busied herself, trying to make the day go faster. Half of her said, let's get on with it, while the other half went into panic mode at the very thought. She checked the clock one more time: it was only nine.

I wonder where Vlad is, she thought to herself. *Seeing him would be reassuring; confirmation it was happening today, that it was real and not just some crazy dream.* Ten o'clock came and went: no Vlad. I suppose he's down the Grosvenor, she appeased herself. Eleven o'clock: *Vlad where are you?* She could feel her anxiety rising. *I bet something's wrong — those bloody American's have taken him, or raided the Grosvenor.* She peered out the window, checking the rooftops just in case she was being watched.

She heard a noise from the back yard. She froze; her heart raced waiting to hear it again. There it was. She crept towards the back door, listening all the while. Her anxiety was turning to paranoia. Cautiously she rotated the handle until the catch released. Free to move, she inched it open.

'Sheila, is that you?'

'Course it's me; you really scared me. Wot you doing skulking around out 'ere?'

'It's Fursday, 'ow else your bins going to get emptied?' Dave lifted the dustbin onto his shoulders. 'See ya for breakfast tomorrow …, oh, I like the Barnet.'

'Yeah, silly me, I forgot.'

The café doorbell vied for her attention. Coming out from the kitchen she saw the look on Vladimir's face.

'Wot's 'appening Vlad, everyfink alright?'

'Coffee, strong, black please my dear.'

'That sounds serious. So tell me, it's not Oleg?'

'Nyet my dear, he will be here any minute.'

'So if it isn't Oleg, wot then?' She was concerned.

'Kavanagh, he has not come yet to conference. I

have been zere since half past eight. Table of name badges, including his, were laid out. By nine thirty many had been picked up, but his not. I waited hour and half, trying not to look conspicuous. I walked past table so many times one of organisers, Maggie her badge says, asked me if everything was okay. I zink he knows we are after him.'

'So wot we gonna do?'

'Wiz no Kavanagh, zere is no need you going.'

Sheila didn't know if she was relieved or disappointed. ''Ave you checked with 'is work? He might have called in sick or summat. When I worked I did it all the time, you know, if it was a nice day and we didn't want to go in, I'd just lie for an excuse.'

Vladimir was shocked. 'Back in Russia, if anyone did zat ...' He stopped himself. 'Zat is not point, point is what we do now?'

The rattle of the doorbell announced the arrival of Oleg.

'Why long faces?' Oleg was feeling very pleased with himself. 'His room is ready, all my video and listening devices are working. Americans are gone and here,' pointing to Sheila, 'we have irresistible beauty.' He checked with Vladimir for agreement.

'We do not know where Kavanagh is, he has not appeared at Grosvenor. It has been waste of time.'

Oleg thought for a while. The best he could come up with was, 'Coffee, strong, black, wiz no sugar.' He joined the long faces.

'Please,' added Vladimir.

Sheila disappeared behind the plastic curtain. She

reappeared with a coffee and a broad smile.

'Go on zen, tell us.' Vladimir could see she had something to say.

'Who was she?'

Vladimir was perplexed.

'The woman at the Grosvenor, you know you just told me about 'er. Name badge woman, the one who saw you.'

The penny dropped. 'Maggie.' His smile returned.

'Yeah, her. She'll 'ave a list of all those attending. Get back to the Grosvenor, use your charms to find out where Jimmy's got to.'

Vladimir drained his cup. 'Come on old comrade.' He got to his feet and headed for the door. 'Oleg, never mind zat, come on.'

When they arrived at the hotel the bellboy drew near to them. 'Good morning, gentlemen.' They couldn't hide their surprise. 'Sorry sir, didn't mean to startle you. I was just wondering if you managed to find him?'

'Well, no … who? We are not looking for anyone.' Vladimir regained his composure.

'Ain't you the gentlemen I spoke to last week? You were looking for that chap who saved those people.'

'Da … but.'

'It's my job, sir. I see hundreds, thousands of people passing through here every day but I remember faces. It's a gift, I suppose. Journalists, aren't you? Are you back to see him again?'

'Why you ask?'

'Well he's here. In the Microsoft Conference. Saw him go in after coffee break. If you hang on till one-o-clock, they'll break for lunch. You can catch him then.'

Before he'd finished speaking, Vladimir had his wallet open and pressed a fiver into the bellboy's hand. 'It is rare gift you have but much appreciated.'

'Thank you sir.' He was gone.

'Just to make sure, you go to where delegates are registered and check to see if his name badge has gone.'

'Why me?' Oleg sounded puzzled. 'You know what you are looking for.'

'Because zat Maggie will be suspicious if she sees me again.'

Oleg went, and returned quickly. 'I spoke wiz her, very helpful. She says train broke down, zat is all.'

'Right, so plan is back on track. We must to tell Sheila. Come on.'

* * * * *

'It's me.' Matt knocked again. 'Are you okay, buddy?' The corridor in the hotel was empty. Matt pressed his ear to the door. 'Hey Brad, open up.'

The lock released. Brad was naked except for a towel. 'Shower.'

'I was worried. You sleep okay?'

'No medication, things are painful, but hey, I'll survive.' Brad tried to smile but it hurt too much.

'It's …,' Matt checked his watch, 'nine thirty. Get yourself some breakfast. I've had mine already, then I went to Cooke's flat before following her to her office. There was no sign of Kavanagh. Now I know you're alright I'm going back to Zylog to find him. We need to know his movements so he doesn't spoil our plans. Just rest here.' Matt let himself out.

The Manpower temp on Zylog's reception was very helpful, just not very knowledgeable. The phone rang. 'Excuse me, sir, I just need to deal with this call.' Matt waited. Scanning the faces of anyone passing through, he saw no one he recognised.

'Sorry about that. How may I help you, sir?' She put on her best smile.

'Is Mr Kavanagh in?'

'Have you an appointment, sir?'

'Sorry no, I'm from Microsoft, flying back to Seattle later today, after the Windows launch. Mr Kavanagh's quite a star. I just want to thank him for what he did. It'll only take a few minutes. If he's busy, not to worry,' Matt lied convincingly.

She brought up the company calendar on screen. 'Sorry sir, looks like a wasted journey, it says here he's out of the office for two days on some course.'

'Shoot. Okay thanks.' Matt was on the verge of leaving. 'Does he have a cell so I can contact him?'

'A cell, sir?' She was confused.

'You know, cell.' He repeated himself, only louder.

'Well as far as I know, the only cells we have here are prison cells, and I'm sure he's not there.'

'Okay forget it. Does your computer say where he is?'

'Grosvenor House Hotel, wherever that is. Actually, he's with your company, Microsoft. There's a coincidence.'

'Thank you young lady, that was very helpful.'

Matt turned to leave.

'Oh sir, who shall I say called?'

'Me, ah yes,' he blushed.

'Your name, sir, what is it?'

'Ben … umm … Sherman. Yes, say Ben Sherman called.'

'Very good, sir.'

Matt left returning to Fredrick's hotel. He knocked on Brad's door. 'Brad … it's me …, open up.'

Brad dragged himself off the sofa: 'Have you seen this Good Morning programme? I thought our TV was crap, but this stuff is God-damn awful.'

Matt walked over to the TV, hitting the *off* button. 'It's the Grosvenor where those damn Commies are going to get Kavanagh. He's back there for a couple of days. I bet my silver dollar they're gonna snatch him.' Matt was very animated.

'So what do we do?'

'Shhh, let me think.'

Brad switched the TV back on.

'Hey buddy, give me a break.' Matt paced the room. 'Look, we're here now so this is our plan. Those Commies snatch Kavanagh, get the info, then using Cooke as a hostage, we get what we want from them. Okay?'

Brad nodded in agreement.

'So back to our original plan.' They were both relieved.

'Right, so lunch now, then we'll go together to her flat. I'll leave you there and then go to her office. As she finishes her work I'll follow her back here. If she gets any ideas of running, I'll take her down, otherwise you restrain her here.' Matt smiled. He was on a mission.

* * * * *

The skeleton keys were stiff but it didn't prove a problem.

'Hey, nice place she has here. An apartment like this in Langley would cost a pretty dollar. I'm guessing Zylog pay her well. According to her records, she's in software sales, lots of commission to be had.' Matt emptied his small holdall onto the dining table.

'So what we got?' He pushed the contents around. 'Two full face ski masks, two Berettas,' he dropped opened each chamber to check they were loaded, 'two pairs of regulation sunglasses, leather gloves ... Here,' he threw a pair to Brad, 'keep them on at all times. No fingerprints, remember. A gag and a pair of handcuffs.' He held the last two items up. 'Look, that chair there, bring it nearer the radiator. We can cuff her to that.' Matt checked his watch. 'Right, it's sixteen thirty, I'm going now. I'm locking you in, we don't want her getting suspicious. Close all the doors, no lights, and keep away from the windows.'

'Thanks teacher, I've done the course too.'

'I didn't mean nothing, buddy. I was doing a sort of mental check list in my head. Okay next time I see you, it'll be with her.' The Yale lock snapped to as the front door closed. The deadlock was less compliant but eventually capitulated.

Brad toured the flat, he paced the hall, looked

behind every door, noted windows, exits, room use, the balcony and beyond, who could see in, and what buildings overlooked the apartment.

Although the swelling around his eyes had reduced, his vision wasn't great. Moving his head quickly resulted in him seeing double. He was relying on surprise, Barb being female, and Matt coming up the rear. He pulled on his ski mask and gloves and took up his position in the hallway out of sight of the front door.

* * * * *

'Are you missing him?' Rob wound up Barb.

'Sometimes Rob, you act like a five year old.' She wasn't having any of it. 'If you must know, I've decided to spoil myself tonight. You know, a bubble bath, good book, chocolates and some champers. Just cause he's not here, why should I mope around?'

'I could wash your back!' He saw the look in her eyes. 'That's a no then, I guess.' Rob dropped his head and focused back on his work.

'Right, that's me done for the day.' She cleared her desk. 'See you tomorrow—oh, no I won't. I'm on that MSA product course, so Monday. Have a great weekend. Bye.' The back of her head disappeared from sight as she ran down the office stairs.

* * * * *

Matt slipped through the gap in the hoarding surrounding the building site opposite Zylog. From his vantage point, he could see who came and went. A woman left the building, he checked the photograph of Barbara—*yes, there she was. Right Miss Cooke,* he thought, *I don't know what you've planned for this evening but you're now spending it with me.* He set off in pursuit, keeping a discreet distance. Since he knew where she lived, he felt confident he was in control. When she walked straight past the turn to her flat, panic set in. He hadn't given any thought to the idea she might not go home. He sped up. It was the time of day when everyone heads for home after work. She entered the pedestrian zone of the High street, with all its shops and crowds of people. He needed to get closer. Too late—she'd gone.

He lost her. 'Crap, that's all I damn well need.' He didn't care who heard him. *Think, think, think ... what now?* He stood on tiptoe, hoping the extra inch would bring her back into view—it didn't. *Matt, you're a fully trained and experienced Special Agent of the CIA, now stay calm, think clearly. What does the manual say to do in these circumstances?*

He didn't need the answer; she reappeared at the entrance to Marks and Spencer holding a number of shopping bags. His heart slowed, and his breathing returned to normal.

'Gee, you just went shopping. I'm a dumb clutz,' he said. He was within touching distance of her. She caught the sound of an American accent. Curious she turned—she smiled, he returned the smile. He'd gotten too close; he slowed to a saunter. Barb was now heading in the right direction. She took the passage leading from the High Street.

He waited for her to disappear from view before entering the passage himself. Although short, it was unlit, affording him cover. He watched until she'd started climbing the stairs leading to the flats. As she turned on the half landing, he was onto the first step. He paused, checking around for any passers-by, before continuing. She made it to her front door as he reached the penultimate step. He could see her, but she couldn't see him.

Finding her key took forever. Matt knew other flat owners would be homeward bound, and any moment one could come along. She had the door open. He needed to get one foot over the threshold before she shut it. In truth, thirty feet isn't far to run under normal circumstances but with the pressure of the fast closing door, it took on a new dimension.

Brad heard her key in the deadlock. With ski mask, sunglasses and gloves on he was ready but hoping she wouldn't put up too much of a fight. He wasn't feeling fully recovered by any means. Through the open door her arm appeared. She felt for the light switch. Silhouetted in the doorway, Brad saw his chance. She didn't see him as he came out of the dark hallway. Grabbing her arm, and twisting her through 180 degrees, he held her fast. With her arm locked behind her, she screamed. He forced the gag into her mouth. Matt was now inside with the front door shut. He grabbed her free arm, pulling it behind her back. She kicked wildly at anything. In the narrow corridor, in the dark, Barbara had no idea who her attackers were. She knew only one thing—she was fighting for her life. With that single thought, she fought relentlessly.

'Barbara, hold still,' Matt's voice boomed.

Hearing her name and the American accent, stopped her dead. 'It's you,' she tried to say, but the gag ensured nothing intelligible came out.

'If we let your arms go, promise you won't try anything stupid?' Matt wanted to calm the situation down.

She managed a muffled response.

'What did she say?' Brad was hoping Matt had understood.

He shrugged. Given the half light of the hallway and his dark glasses, Brad missed the response.

'Get your ski mask and gloves on before she sees you.'

Matt scrabbled around, finally managing to do it one-handed. He switched the hall light on. Barb did her best to turn around.

'Hey, no Missy, hold still. It'll make it easier for all of us.' Brad placed his hand on the holster under his arm. She could see what he was doing. 'Now we're gonna let you go. First kick off your shoes—those heels are dangerous ... Good, now I'll let go of one arm.' In doing so he withdrew his handgun.

Barb's mind was racing. *Run, fight, get to the phone. Where's Jimmy when I need him?* Her eyes fixed on the brass statue decorating the hall table. *If I can get one, maybe I'll stand a chance against the other.* While she was thinking through her options, Matt grabbed her from behind holding her around the waist. He was able to carry her into the sitting room and onto the chair placed by the radiator. He snapped one handcuff around her right arm and the other over the water pipe.

With her free hand, she whipped the gag out. 'You bastards? Who are you, what do you want? How do you know my name?' She was hysterical.

Both men kept away.

'Sit please, Barbara.' Matt took the lead. 'Agent, put your gun away. Miss Cooke's not going anywhere. I'm afraid we cannot tell you who we are, but what we want is Jimmy Kavanagh. And we know your name from the file we have on him.' His slow, deliberate tone reduced her anxiety.

'My Jimmy's not here and won't be back tonight. Anyway, what's he done? He'd never hurt a fly.'

'That's as may be, but it's what he can do that's of interest to us.' Matt was bent down in front of her looking directly into her eyes.

'Can do—can do what?' she said, innocently.

'If you don't know that's fine. We don't need to tell you. What we do know is, he'll do anything for you. Right now the Russians are in the process of kidnapping him.' Matt checked her for a reaction.

'Russian who? What? Kidnap … I don't understand.'

'Your Jimmy has some extraordinary talents the Russians are very interested in, as are we, and we need to stop those Commie bas…, gentlemen, getting their hands on him. We have you, the Russians have Jimmy, we want him. Once he knows we have you he'll refuse to co-operate with them. After they set him free, we'll let you go.'

'Are you serious?' She sounded incredulous. 'These Russians, do you know them?'

'Not exactly know them, but we have a lot of information on them.'

'So you've seen them?' Barb had her suspicions.

'Yes, of course. Why do you ask?' Matt was now curious. 'Have you?'

'I'm sure you're familiar with Bogart.'

Matt nodded.

'Do you know Maigret?'

They swapped glances. 'Of course, the French TV detective. Why?'

'Do your Russians look like them, with their trilbies and trench coats?' She was now feeling more at ease.

'So you've seen them too. Where?' Matt had a feeling he knew the answer already.

'Here, in Maidenhead, about a week ago. They were at the Zylog offices, and again outside my flat. Jimmy thought they were journalists. They interviewed him about the incident at Microsoft's Windows Launch when he saved all those lives, including mine. So who are they?'

'KGB.' Matt said it, slow and quiet.

'What!' She was outraged. 'You mean spies! What do they want with Jimmy? You're not telling me he's a spy!'

'No we don't think so. Maybe he does work for the Brits, never thought to ask MI5.'

'Can we not be quite so casual about this? It's my Jimmy we're talking about and you say the Russians have taken him hostage. So where are they holding him?'

'Look Ms Cooke, we want him back as much as you do. We need to let them know we have you. I doubt they'll let you speak to him but the sound of your voice will be sufficient. If we make the call, all I want you to say is your name, agreed?'

'Not sure I've much choice. She decided co-operation was better than conflict. 'Okay make the call. The sooner this is over the better.'

Matt picked up her phone and dialled. It rang once, twice and again endlessly. 'They're not darn well in.' He slammed it down.

'So what now?' Barb was chancing her luck.

'We wait and try again, and again until they answer. Okay Missy?' Matt was starting to lose it.

'Hey buddy, take it easy, Ms Cooke here's done nothing.'

Barb smiled at Brad. She couldn't see if he responded since his face and eyes were fully covered.

'If we're going to wait maybe you'd like a cup of tea?' Barb sounded very calm.

'You Brits are unbelievable! Here we are in the middle of a hostage situation and you want to make tea.' Matt threw his arms in the air.

'Actually that's not a bad idea. I'm not feeling too great and a tea might be what I need,' Brad said, sitting himself down on the sofa.

Barb rattled her handcuffs. 'You'll need to let me out of these.'

Matt unhooked her from the radiator and slipped the cuff onto his wrist. 'We need to close all the curtains first.' They moved around the flat, pulling them shut. 'Now only low powered lights, we don't want to cast shadows.'

Barb's shopping lay strewn around the hall floor. 'At least let me tidy up.' She bent down to pick up the items. 'I was so looking forward to my bath.'

'We're so sorry to have spoiled your evening, Ms Cooke, but we thought protecting National Security was more important.'

'Sarcasm doesn't become you.' She busied herself making the tea. 'Here.' She thrust a mug into Matt's hand. 'Can your mate manage to get his own?'

CHAPTER 11

A BRIDGE TOO FAR

Sheila came down the stairs of 44 Lancaster Mews. As usual, the hall was in darkness and the kitchen door shut.

'Right, I want you two to close your eyes. I'm not coming in until you agree.' Standing in the hall she was like an excited child waiting to get her parent's approval.

'Of course my dear, we are in anticipation of you.' Vladimir could hardly say they'd watched the whole dressing and make-up process on the video camera. 'Come in, come in my dear.'

She pushed open the door. Both men stood at the far side of the kitchen with their eyes closed. She clicked-clacked in. 'No, don't open yet.' She wanted to be sure she had the light falling on her. She struck a Marilyn pose. 'Okay, wot'd you fink?' she cooed.

'Spectacular, my dear. I thought it was her standing zere! Just as beautiful as I remember her. No, actually more beautiful, radiant, sexy; words cannot speak for me. Sheila, you look sensational. Worth every ruble. Jimmy Kavanagh will be putty in your hands. No sensible man could resist your charms.'

'Oleg, you're very quiet. Marilyn not your type?' She studied his face for clues.

'Oh very definitely; being in presence of such beauty has left me not able to speak.' He smiled at her, but his thoughts were more animalistic.

The familiar sound of a London taxi broke the spell. Vladimir picked up his hat and coat. 'Zis is it, my dear. I am going now to make sure everything is to plan. I see you and Oleg in the foyer at seventeen fifteen.' He looked at his watch just to check.

'Where do you want me? Oo that sounds a bit saucy.' She let out a little giggle.

The sight of her, her radiance and beauty, her innocence, the smell of her perfume, their closeness, and the fact they were alone stirred in Oleg passion he'd long forgotten. His eyes followed her every move. She was electrifying. He was in danger of blowing a fuse.

'Sheila, you have no idea what you do to men. Your power over zem.' He lunged for her like a demented beast.

Working in the café, mostly alone, with customers who were more rough trade than fair, had given her years of experience in dealing with unwelcome advances. Without batting an eye, she simply stood on his foot with her stiletto. Any thoughts of sexual gratification he was harbouring were replaced instantly by a very direct, intense and overwhelming pain. He stopped dead in his tracks.

'Oh so sorry, Oleg. I didn't see your foot there. Now wot were you saying?' She played the innocent very well.

He hobbled back to the far side of the kitchen. 'Photographs …' He winced as he tried to walk. 'I put camera up in room next door.' He wanted to follow but the pain was too much. 'I sit here for minute.'

'I'm ever so sorry, really, I just didn't see your foot. These 'eels are so dangerous. Can I get you a cuppa tea or summat?'

He shook his head. 'Nyet, I be fine soon.'

'You say next door, let me take a look.' She left the kitchen. Oleg slipped off his shoe. His sock was soaked in blood. 'Sheila ...,' his call was pathetic. 'Sheila,' he said it again more forcefully.

'Oleg, wot is it?' She replied, keeping up her act.

'Could you fill washing up bowl wiz warm water, I need put my foot in.'

She came over to take a look. 'Oh that looks bad. I'm so sorry, really, it was an accident.' She filled a bowl and found a towel, placing them on the floor. 'Ere you go.' Crouched down in front of him, he had what would be, under most circumstances a very pleasurable view of her cleavage. Instead the sight reminded him of how he came to be in so much pain—it had the opposite effect.

'Zank you,' he said through gritted teeth, 'zere is first aid kit in one of zose cupboards.' He waived his arms.

'Yeah sure.' She felt it was the least she could do. Bandaged up, he was ready to take some pictures.

'We need to be quick, our taxi will be here soon.' He focussed, zoomed, directed and redirected, until he was satisfied he'd captured sufficient images.

'I look forward to seeing 'em,' she beamed. 'Maybe I'll get a poster sized print for the café wall. That'll keep my customers 'appy. Well, the lecherous ones at least.' She giggled.

*   *   *   *   *

Their photography session was brought to an end by the sound of a diesel engine throbbing in the Mews. Oleg grabbed his hat and coat off the stand and hobbled to the front door. Sheila's wrap and clutch bag were upstairs. She dashed up to the bedroom, catching sight of herself in the wardrobe mirror. One final preen: 'This is it, gal.' She pushed her bust out for good measure. 'I could fancy you myself.' As she came out of the front door the taxi driver saw her and she registered the look of admiration on his face. She felt confident, as if she could take on the world and win.

'Where to, gorgeous?'

'Grosvenor 'ouse 'otel, Park Lane.' She didn't need to say Park Lane—the driver had done The Knowledge—but it wasn't every day she got the chance to say it. She was milking the experience for all it was worth.

Before the taxi had fully stopped, the doorman had her door open. 'Madam,' he gestured for her to get out.

'I bet this is 'ow the Queen feels.' She placed one foot on the ground. Standing half in and half out of the car, she hesitated, smiling at anyone and no one, waiting for acknowledgement from a non-existent crowd of admirers. She wasn't a famous film star but that didn't stop her enjoying the moment. The doorman took her hand in his gloved hand. The joy of her smile was seen by a photographer, the sort who hang around exclusive venues to capture the comings and goings of the rich and famous. The flash gun fired once, then again. She would have stayed for more but Oleg intervened.

'Come, Sheila.' He led her into the foyer. 'Zis is meant to be covert operation, not your media debut. Now where is Vladimir?'

'Don't be such an old misery guts, it's just a bit of fun.'

Vladimir was sat in a sumptuous leather high backed wing chair. Three others of similar design were arranged about a low coffee table. They joined him and spoke in hushed tones, as was expected in such a situation where garrulous behaviour was frowned upon. The norm suited them; the last thing they wanted was eavesdroppers taking an interest.

Vladimir spoke first. 'I have ordered tea.' He observed them both; they smiled in agreement. 'From conference room, zey will pass zis way. Kavanagh will need to come zis way to get to bar. So you need to be ready.' He checked with Sheila. 'Now bar is for conference people only. I have been speaking wiz woman from Conference Creations, remember, Maggie. In process I obtained,' he drew quote marks with his fingers, 'a badge wiz name. Here.' He passed it to her.

'Miss Ann Wegner, Sphinx Software Limited,' she read out. 'You want me to wear this? But it'll spoil my outfit.'

'Nyet, keep it. You will need to show it to get into room, zat is all. When inside your attention must be full on him. You have got to do whatever it takes to get him to leave wiz you.' Vladimir threw her a look to emphasise the *whatever it takes* dictat. 'Better soon than later — we want to begin to work on our experiments.'

'Experiments,' she picked up on the word. 'You said it again. I thought you said no experiments.' She didn't like the sound of that.

'Oh it is an expression, nothing more.' Vladimir's dismissive response told her not to pursue the matter.

Sheila's eye's wandered around the room taking in the décor.

'Course I've been past loads of times but I've never been in.' She craned her neck looking at everyone and everything. 'Cor it ain't 'alf posh. Do you fink she comes 'ere?'

'Who, my dear is *she*?' Vladimir had no idea.

'You know, 'er, the Queen.' She looked around again. 'Look ... oi there he is.' She pointed.

'Be discreet my dear.' Both men followed her finger. 'Da, I see him. Right, good luck.' Vladimir squeezed her hand, before he and Oleg slid down in their chairs, try to make themselves less visible. Sheila stood, giving herself a last minute adjustment. She joined the flow of conference guests streaming through the foyer.

'Talk about being different, look at her.' Vladimir nodded in her direction.

*　*　*　*　*

Jeans and t-shirt were the order of the day amongst the mostly male throng. Strawberry blonde hair, expensive evening wear and stilettos were definitely in the minority. Unperturbed, Sheila progressed towards her prey. Jimmy passed through into the bar without stopping, as did the rest.

The security guard, visually scanning everyone for their badge, stopped her. 'Excuse me Miss.' A large burley man came up to her. 'Badge please.'

She opened her clutch bag; he peered in.

'Thank you Miss.' He stood aside.

Oleg and Vladimir breathed a sigh of relief.

The room was full, the bar queue was growing, and Jimmy wasn't visible. Sheila pushed her way to the far side of the room. She held his picture in one hand just to be sure.

'So do you think the use of the Network Capture Monitor will be useful to track IP requests?'

She turned to see who was talking. 'Sorry, miles away, wot'd you want mate?' She smiled.

'I think it'll be really useful, especially with the new GUI interface.'

She smiled again. 'Actually I'm waiting for someone.' She didn't want to appear rude.

The man stood his ground, his gaze resting on her cleavage.

'Didn't your mother tell you it was rude to stare?' She lost her tolerance.

He took the hint and moved away.

Like bees to a honeypot, another geek took his place. He went to speak but she beat him to it. 'Before you ask, no, even with a GUI interface.' She rotated on her heels, leaving a very bewildered bloke behind.

Are all computer guys tall, she thought. All she could see were the backs of T-shirts proclaiming *Reading Festival 1985,* or Wham! tour dates, or *You Can Rely on*

Cisco Routers to get you from A to B. She needed a vantage point. She found a low table surrounded by half a dozen chairs; no one was using them. Stepping gingerly onto it, she gained sufficient height to see across the crowd. Off to her right she recognised a tall, well-built figure with dark hair and a swarthy complexion. It was him, without a doubt.

'Okay I can see him, now wot?' Feeling self-conscious standing on the table talking to herself, she tried a discreet whisper: 'Jimmy.' The room was full and noisy, and he was too far away to hear. 'Jimmy,' she said it louder. This time it reached about three fellows in front. The wrong guy turned around. She waved a dismissive hand.

She had to resort to more drastic tactics; raising both hands to her mouth to form a loudhailer, she tried again.

'Jimmmyyy …' Third time lucky. He turned, as did most of the people in the room. Vladimir and Oleg slipped further down their chairs, wanting to disown her.

Judging by his frown, he didn't recognise her but given she'd been so forceful, he thought it only polite to find out what she wanted.

'Right, okay. That was …,' he tried to think of a suitable adjective, 'loud.' He checked her over. 'To whom do I owe this pleasure?' He smiled broadly; it was clear he didn't recognise her.

'A friend suggested I look you up.' She hadn't thought of a cover story. 'So 'ere I am.' Her words hung in the air.

'Do you think it would be better if you got off the

table?' He took her hand to help. Their palms met: there was a jolt. Not painful, but sufficient for them to be left bemused as to what had happened.

'Oi, wot's that?' Clearly Sheila felt it as well. 'You got one of those joke 'and shake buzzy fings? You're a bit old for stuff like that, ain't you?'

'Drink?' He didn't know how to answer her.

She fancied a pint of London Pride but remembered where she was. 'Malibu Cocktail please, oh and can I 'ave an umbrella?' She giggled. *Don't forget gal,* she told herself, *not too many now, you're working.* He left her to go to the bar.

'Here.' Jimmy passed the umbrella separately. 'Good health.' He took a long drink of Guinness as she sipped her Malibu.

'Now then, tell me who you are.' He waited expectantly — she froze.

'Umm, I'm ...'

'Okay let's make this easy. Start with your name. I assume you have one.' He chuckled.

She felt a right Charlie, 'Yes of course I 'ave. I was named after my mother.'

'And do I know your mother?'

'No, I don't fink so.' Sheila creased her brow.

'Then that's not going to be of much help. Who are you?' He said it slowly and deliberately.

'Cor blimey, you must fink I'm a right idiot!'

'Just tell me your name and that will all change.' *She's not far wrong,* he thought.

'Sheila.' She smiled.

'See, that wasn't so difficult.' He took another

swig in celebration; she let herself have another sip.

Jimmy extended his hand. 'Pleased to meet you, Sheila ...' He waited, hoping she might complete his sentence.

'Lovett,' she giggled, 'and yes I do.' She blushed.

'What?' He looked confused. He withdrew his hand.

'My name. Every time I tell anyone they always ask, so before you did, I answered.'

'Sorry?' He was none the wiser.

'It's Irish, like yours.'

'Actually, how do you know my name?'

'We have a mutual friend. I wasn't born there.' She wanted to change the subject.

'Where, Ireland?' He took another swig of Guinness, hoping it would clear up his confusion.

'Brisbane, born and bred. My dad's Irish. He emigrated there in the '30s and met my mum, Sheila.'

'You don't sound like an Aussie.'

'No, me and Mum moved to London when I was ten. Dad ran off with some shearer. I dunno much cos she won't talk about it. Listen to me prattling on.' She took a sip. 'Shall we try again?' She held out her hand. 'Sheila Lovett.'

Jimmy took it. Again as their palms came together there was a jolt, a sort of attraction, a sharing of energy. They were ready for it this time—no pulling back, no desire to break the connection. They stood transfixed, enjoying the feeling. Both embarrassed, they let go of one another.

'Right Sheila Lovett, now we've been introduced,

how can I help you?' He drained his glass. 'Another?' He'd gone before she could answer.

'Oh wot the heck.' Sheila finished her drink before he returned.

'I saw you on the telly, and I cooked breakfast for you.'

'Ahh,' the penny dropped. 'You're that Sheila — but you look so different.' He licked his lips. 'Yes, so very different.'

'Better or just different?'

'Gorgeous, stunning, sexy.' The Guinness had removed his inhibitions.

She ran her tongue around her lips. *Crass, I know,* she thought, *but it works every time.* This time was no different.

'So what are you doing tonight?' He gave her a wry smile.

She resisted saying *you.* 'Well it doesn't involve the Grosvenor.' *Being forward is so much fun,* she thought. 'I know a quiet intimate place not far from here.' She looked into his eyes, waiting to see how he'd react. There, she saw it—the flash of excitement, the dilation of his pupils. He was hers. She finished her drink; he did likewise.

'Lead on.' He followed her out into the foyer. She caught sight of Vladimir and Oleg and gave them a wink. Jimmy guided her to the street exit before climbing into a taxi.

'Where to, love?'

'44 Lancaster Mews.' She just smiled at Jimmy.

* * * * *

They sat in silence. Apart from a table lamp, the flat was in darkness. The church clock struck seven. Time was dragging. The phone rang but no one moved. *Barb, only Mum, give us a call when you can, nothing urgent.* The answer phone clicked on, then off.

'I need the loo.' Barb sounded calm and collected. The two men exchanged glances.

Matt stood. 'Key?'

Brad fished around in his pocket and tossed it over to him. In the semi-darkness he misjudged his throw. It fell, disappearing under the sofa. Barb's thoughts went into overdrive. Both Matt and Brad were down on their knees scrabbling about looking for it. Distracted, this was a chance for her to escape. Within reach was a cut glass vase. Again she was sure she might get one, but two was less certain. The seconds ticked by; her thoughts raced. *They're still both vulnerable; it was now or never.* It was never. Matt retrieved the key.

Crawling around on his hands and knees left Brad feeling dizzy. He flopped back on the sofa. Freed, Barb was able to visit the bathroom. Matt stood guard outside. Next to the cistern was a bottle of bleach toilet cleaner. She considered it. Her problem was the thought of inflicting pain or suffering on another person, albeit her captors, was alien to her. She put it back; reasoning was the answer, violence begets violence. If she co-operated they'll have no reason to be unpleasant to her. She unlocked the door.

'Are you hungry? I know I am.' She studied

300

Matt's body language, looking for any signs to help her judge his mood, his state of anxiety, how stable he was.

'Yeah, sure, great.' He gave little away.

Barb rooted around in the kitchen cupboards wondering what to give her captors. Not the sort of thing you do every day, she mused to herself. 'Spaghetti Bolognaise?' she offered.

Matt stood leaning against the doorframe watching her go calmly about the business of preparing supper for three. She took up her chef's knife to chop onions—at that he became wary. His hand went inside his jacket, reaching for the holster it hid. She saw. Any thoughts of tackling him disappeared. She smiled to herself.

'What's so funny?' Matt growled.

'Oh nothing.'

'Hey, don't treat me like a fool.' There was an edge to his voice. 'What are you laughing at?'

'I was just thinking, do you do this sort of thing often?'

'Look Ma'am, what those Russians are up to we're not sure but we know it ain't good for the US or you Brits. We need to do what we need to do to ensure our safety.' He was very matter-of-fact.

'So, not to put it politely, scaring the shit out of me, holding me against my will at gunpoint, is quite acceptable in your book?' Though calm outwardly, she was seething inside.

'As I said Ma'am, we need to do what we need to do. There is always collateral damage in any situation.' Matt tried to make light of the circumstances.

'So that's all I am, collateral damage? That makes me feel, how do you guys say it, *a whole lot better*.'

'See, I knew you'd understand.' He stood upright, folding his arms as if to say *I told you so*.

Sarcasm is lost on you brainless brutes, she thought to herself.

'Does Robin like garlic?' She nodded her head in the direction of the sitting room. Matt's brow furrowed. 'Well it seems you two think you're Batman and Robin, saving the planet singlehandedly from the jaws of a Communist onslaught.' She was past caring what they thought of her, she just wanted them out of her flat.

'Oh no Ma'am, there are thousands of us in the CIA, we couldn't do it by ourselves.'

It appeared the more flippant she became, the more seriously they took themselves. Now she knew they were CIA the threat diminished, assuming they weren't acting alone.

The front doorbell chimed. Matt had his gun drawn and Barb in an arm lock before it completed its tune.

'Shush, say nothing if you want to live.' He pressed the barrel to her temple.

The chimes went again.

'They can see the lights on, they know I'm in,' Barb whispered, the tremble evident in her voice.

'Okay but remember I'm right behind you. Just get rid of them.' He let her go.

'Coming,' she called at the front door. 'Oh Rob, hi, wasn't expecting to see you.' Her voice sounded its usual self.

'Barb, yeah hi, just finished work and noticed you left without picking up your course details for tomorrow. I was coming past so I thought I'd drop them off.'

While he was speaking, she kept mouthing, 'Have you a pen?' He took one from his inside jacket pocket. Taking the papers, she scribbled across the top sheet, *I'm a hostage here, get Jimmy—now.* He read as she wrote. He wanted to ask questions but she cut him off.

'Thanks Rob, must go. I've a nice hot bath and some champers waiting for me. Sorry I can't invite you in.' She dropped her voice, 'Do that for me now!' The look in her eyes confirmed she wasn't lying. 'Okay?' She wanted to make sure Matt wasn't suspicious.

'You expecting anyone else?'

'No, I'm expecting no one.'

*   *   *   *   *

Rob ran down the stairs, out into the passage and onto the High Street. He wandered over to the Chinese Restaurant and looked up. The faint glow of the single light gave nothing away. He paced—not knowing what to do was the worse bit. *Police, maybe. Speak to my wife? No, it would only make her hysterical. Call Mike, maybe—after all, both Barb and Jimmy work for him—but he lives in London. Right, back to the office. At least there's a telephone there and Jimmy's hotel details.* He checked his watch: *seven thirty. He'll be drinking, or eating or womanising. No, not womanising on a Support Course; anyway, he has Barb now.*

He rooted through Jimmy's desk—nothing except his desk diary. He'd taken all the paperwork with him.

Thursday 28th November, Windows Support, Grosvenor. Accomm: Crown Lancaster Gate. He dialled Directory Enquiries, getting numbers for both.

'Hello, I'm after a guest. He's on the Microsoft Windows Course. It's urgent I speak to him.' Rob waited, listened, listened and waited. He was being put through 'Hello, who is this?'

'Maggie, Conference Creations, can I help you?'

'Jimmy Kavanagh, it's very urgent, can you get a message to him?'

'They're all in dinner. I'll try, what's the message?'

'Ring me, Rob on 01628 877425. Or Barb. No, not Barb, just me, and tell him it's very urgent.'

Maggie sensed the panic in his voice. 'I'll do my best, assuming he's still here.' She hung up the phone; Rob did the same.

He made the next call: 'Hi, Crown Hotel? You've a Jimmy Kavanagh staying there tonight. I need to get an urgent message to him.' He listened. 'Okay, he's not checked in. Can I leave a message for him to ring Rob on 01628 877425. It's life and death, and it doesn't matter what time he calls.'

He put the phone down, wondered if he was doing the right thing. *Who would hold Barb hostage? Why get Jimmy to rescue her and not the police?* He mulled over the questions. *Should he be doing more? Well yes, but what,* he thought. He decided to go home in case Jimmy phoned.

* * * * *

'Can we go via the Crown Hotel, Lancaster Gate, please.' Jimmy added; the taxi driver nodded.

Sheila wondered why. She looked at him quizzically.

'I'm supposed to be staying there tonight. I was late this morning and haven't checked in. Look, you wait in the taxi, I'll only be two minutes.' He ran up the steps and in through the revolving door. Sheila could see him at Reception.

'The name's Kavanagh, initial J, just one night, no luggage.' Jimmy wanted to check in as quickly as possible.

'Just sign here.' The receptionist pushed a form at him. 'Wake-up call or newspapers?'

'No thanks.' He signed, moving to leave as he did so.

'Room 220. Oh, Mr Kavanagh.' The receptionist called after him: 'There's a message for you marked *urgent*.'

Jimmy thought to ignore it, dismissively waving his hand. He continued towards the exit but curiosity got the better of him. He read the note—he was confused. Why would Rob want to speak to me urgently. He returned to reception.

'Is there a phone I can use please?' He looked over her side of the counter.

'Is it a UK number?'

'Yeah, Maidenhead.'

The receptionist passed her phone. 'Nine for an outside line.'

'Rob, what's the panic? Has Mike gone off on one

of his rants cos sales are down?' He laughed.

'No nothing like that. It's Barb.'

Jimmy froze at the mention of her name. In pursuit of his basic instincts he'd forgotten her. 'What about her? She's alright isn't she?' He felt his stomach flip.

From the back of the taxi Sheila could see he was agitated. Deciding to find out what was wrong, she paid the driver.

'Hey Jimmy.' She put her arm through his. 'Wot's 'appening?' She was concerned.

'I'm not sure.' He needed to think about the call to Rob. 'It's Barb, he says she's being held hostage in her flat and is asking for me.' He paused, mulling over the words, trying to make sense of them. He noticed the time was eight. 'It's not too late to get back to Maidenhead tonight.'

Sheila felt her prize slipping away. She was pulled between her commitment to Vladimir, her desire for Jimmy—she knew there really was something between them—and his need to help Barb. She assumed she was his woman and in real danger as no one would make up a story like that.

'Sheila, as much as I'd love to stay, obviously things have changed. Barb needs me. I've got to go.' He took her by the shoulders and looked deep into her eyes. 'I mean it when I say I'd love to stay.'

She held his gaze. 'But she's your fiancée, you 'ave to go.'

'No nothing like that, we've only been together a week. Early days, but we do work together.' He headed back to reception. 'Emergency at home. I won't need my room tonight thanks. Right Sheila, I must be off, you do understand … don't you?' He headed for the front entrance.

'Jimmy, please, I've not been totally 'onest with you.' She had no option but to come clean. 'You know at the Grosvenor you asked me 'ow I knew your name?

He stopped in his tracks.

'Yeah.' He wondered what was coming next.

'The mutual friends are the two Russians.'

'What, the ones who bought me breakfast. So?'

'I'm sort of working for them.' She was embarrassed.

'What do you mean, sort of *working for them*? Has this whole evening been a charade?' He felt hurt.

'No, not at all. I knew from the other morning I wanted to get to know you better. I knew there was something between us. You were too busy telling them your story to notice. Then they asked me to do this.'

'What's this exactly?' He was suspicious.

'Chat you up at the Grosvenor and then take you back to their place.'

'Why?'

'Because,' she hesitated, 'they fink you're special—'ave some powers. They want to experiment on you. It sounds daft now, but they offered me loads of money to do it. Cos my bastard ex-boyfriend stole my savings, I said yes.'

'Only because you needed the money?'

'Mostly yeah, but that was before we actually met proper.'

'And now?'

'Now,' she said coyly, 'I'd love to get to know you proper, money or no money. But I've sort of made them a promise and I don't want to let them down. Not like those bloody Yanks. They kept feeling my bum or looking at my pants.'

The look on Jimmy's face said he'd lost track of the conversation. She saw.

'Oh sorry, there were two American spies, you know CAI, watching Vlad and Oleg till the other night when we 'ad loads of 'elicopters and blokes in masks and guns clear them out. I fink it's cos I rammed a broom handle in the younger one's face. Broke his nose and all sorts. You should 'ave seen the blood, it ruined 'is Chelsea shirt. I didn't care cause I'm a Spurs supporter like my Mum. She lives in Tottenham.'

Jimmy felt as if he was reading a book and accidently turning over several pages at once. 'Slow down, one thing at a time. You're working for the two Russians?'

'Yeah, Vlad and Oleg.'

'Who are journalists.'

'No, I don't fink so. They're spies, you know K ...'

'GB?' He pondered the significance of the news. 'And they want to experiment on me?'

'Yeah, but they said nuffink nasty, no torture or nuffink otherwise I wouldn't 'ave agreed to, you know.'

'Seduce me?'

'Well, more chat you up really, but you never know.' A twinkle appeared in her eye.

'And the Americans?'

'Well, they 'ired me as well to spy on the Russians to find out more about you. They're interested in you too. But then they weren't nice to me and after the broom handle thing, they disappeared, so I fought ...'

'So where are Vlad and Oleg now?'

'Probably waiting for me, wondering where I am. See, they were at the Grosvenor and going to follow us to the Mews but of course, I've not made it back. I bet they're worried sick.'

'The Mews?'

'Yeah, just up around the corner, past my café, number 44. I'll show you if you like.'

'Do you trust them?' He was being cautious.

'Well so far they've done everyfink they said they would. They seem okay, certainly better than them Yanks.'

'I'm beginning to think the Russians, Yanks and Barb's kidnapping are related. Using her to get to me.'

'Kidnapping!' She was shocked.

'Yeah, that phone call I made was to a work colleague. He'd been to Barb's flat and she passed him a message saying she was being held hostage and to get me.'

Jimmy, led by Sheila, walked up Lancaster Gate, left past her café and down the Mews. 44 appeared empty; no lights were showing. She took the key from her bag.

'I'm guessing but I fink they'll be in the kitchen, they usually are.' She slipped the key in the lock. 'Come on. They've got no bulbs, so be careful.' She walked a couple of steps. 'Vlad, Oleg, I'm here.'

The light from under the door grew to fill the hallway.

'My dear, where have you been? We worry.' He looked past her. Jimmy was hovering in the hallway. 'My dear man, come in.' Vlad greeted him like some long lost friend. 'Here, take seat.' Oleg was sitting in the half shadows, watching without commenting.

Jimmy noticed and gave a nod. Without their trilbies and trench coats they appeared different.

'I've agreed to come because I need your help.' Jimmy stared at each one in turn. 'Barb …'

'Da, we know Ms Cooke, your girlfriend.' Vladimir tried to make him feel easy.

'She's in trouble because of me, you, I'm not sure which, but we need to help her now.' His urgency was obvious.

'Trouble, what trouble?'

'It's the bloody Yanks.' Sheila clarified the situation. 'They're 'olding her 'ostage.'

'Where, when, why?' Vladimir was genuinely shocked.

'Now, in her flat in Maidenhead. I suppose they've got her as a way of getting to me. You know, a bargaining chip.'

They all fell silent thinking about what had been said.

Jimmy was first to talk. 'You got a phone here?'

'Of course, why?'

'Before we do anything, I need to know she's alright.' He stood up. 'Where is it?'

'Hold on. We need plan.' Vladimir wanted to

control the situation. 'Assuming she is being held by Americans, zey are not going to let you have cosy chat wiz her.'

Oleg nodded to show his agreement.

'What are you suggesting?' Jimmy was getting anxious.

'We have lots of, shall we say friends, we could, how do Americans say it, *liberate* her. Yes, liberate, zey are very happy when zey are liberating people, towns, countries.'

'No way, you go storming her flat and someone will get hurt. It's too confined, dangerous. No, we need to get them to take her out into the open. They want me. It's an exchange we need to agree.'

'So where you suggest, Hyde Park?'

'Vladimir, listen to Jimmy, he's right.' Sheila decided if she was to trust anyone, it would be him. 'He's got an idea, listen to 'im.'

'So in all your war films, where do prisoner exchanges take place?' Jimmy waited for an answer. 'On a river crossing, a bridge, of course.'

'We would not know. In Moscow we shoot prisoners.'

'Zat is not helpful, Oleg.' Vladimir wanted to hear more. 'So what you suggest?'

'Can you get us a car to take us to Maidenhead?'

'I could have it here in five minutes.'

'With some friends?'

'Of course.'

'Sheila, you go back to your café.' Sheila looked disappointed. 'It'll be safer for you there.' Jimmy winked at her. 'Tottenham are the best, Mum's the word ... understand?'

'Oh ... yes, of course, Mum's the word.' She stood up. 'I fink I'd better go now. Bye then.' She presented each a kiss—Oleg, Vlad and finally Jimmy. Stretching to reach he bent and whispered in her ear, 'I'll find you in a day or two.'

The sound of the front door latch confirmed she'd gone.

'Right, you ring your friends.' He checked his watch. 'Okay it's eight thirty. We'll need a quiet place for an exchange. I'm going to phone her flat and ask to speak to a Yank.

'Phone is in hall, near front door.' Both men watched intently.

The sound of ringing was clear. 'Come on, answer ...' It did: 'Hi Barb, say nothing, try not to look surprised. We've got a plan to get you out, just do as I say and trust me ...'

'Who's this?' A gruff male voice came on the phone.

'It's me, Kavanagh, the one you want.'

'Right Kavanagh, as you seem to already know, we're holding Ms Cooke and yes, we want you. So this is what I suggest ...'

'No, you listen to me. Ms Cooke is totally innocent in all this. I'm offering myself, no strings, for her release.'

'How are you proposing to do that?' Matt was interested to hear more.

'At midnight tonight, we'll do an exchange, in

Maidenhead. I'll be on the Taplow side of the Thames Bridge. You bring Ms Cooke to the Riviera hotel side. She knows exactly where it is. At the stroke of midnight, according to the church bells, I'll start to walk across … alone. You let her do the same. You'll have me and she'll go free. Agreed?' He held his breath, his heart pounded in his chest. He hoped above all hopes they'd go for it.

'I can't see a problem with that. Midnight you say, and Ms Cooke knows where to be.'

'The Riviera's less than a mile from where you are now.' Jimmy let out a sigh and punched the air.

'By the way buddy, she's a damned good cook. Cooke by name and cook by nature.' Matt put the phone down.

'So you heard that?' Jimmy looked at Vladimir and Oleg for confirmation. 'We need to be on the Taplow side of the bridge for eleven forty five at the latest. Can you and your friends organise that?'

Vladimir picked up the phone and spoke in Russian. Jimmy had to trust him.

'One thing,' Oleg said, 'before we lose you, can we have demonstration of your powers?'

Jimmy thought, *why not?* 'Get me some knives and forks and drop them in a pile on the table.'

Oleg did. 'Okay, here you are.'

Jimmy waved his hands across the pile. Like soldiers on parade, they moved into neat lines. The look on Oleg's face was reminiscent of an excited schoolboy. He got his camera out.

'Again please.'

Jimmy jumbled up the cutlery as Oleg took a

picture of the heap. He did his hand waving, and Oleg shot multiple pictures. Vladimir came back into the kitchen.

'Zey will be here soon.'

'Not too soon I hope.' Oleg wanted to test Jimmy some more. 'What else can you do?'

'Come.' Jimmy took him to the front door. They went outside and pulled the door shut. With a twist of his palm, Jimmy unlocked it. Oleg took pictures all the time.

'Anything more?' Oleg said hopefully.

'Come on, he is not performing monkey,' Vladimir intervened.

*   *   *   *   *

The sound of wheels on cobbles announced the arrival of a large black Volga. Vladimir recognised the noise of the engine.

'Mr Kavanagh, our car has arrived. Please, after you.'

The three men sat in the rear, with Jimmy the meat in the sandwich. Except for the odd Russian phrase spoken by Vladimir to the driver, the journey passed in silence.

'You want M4, Junction 7 and then the A4 towards Taplow and Maidenhead.' Jimmy was trying to be helpful. 'There's a garage forecourt on the right just before the bridge. It'll be closed this time of night. Park in there, you'll be out of sight.'

The driver nodded. Vladimir didn't need to translate. They parked up.

'Eleven forty, good. I want to walk the bridge before they get here just to check the lay of the land.'

Vladimir opened his door. 'I'll come wiz you. We do not want any heroics, after all.'

From the Taplow side, the bridge inclined up towards the centre; it was sufficiently steep to make seeing across it impossible without walking onto it. The 18th century construction consisted of a solid stone deck built over seven arches supported by pontoons. As they walked, Jimmy counted. The fourth arch marked the centre and seemed to be the area where boats passed under it. Marking the beginning and end of each arch were street lamps mounted on the balustrade in pairs. The centre arch was between pair four and five.

If they make their way to the Riviera, Barb will come over the bridge on my left side, Jimmy thought. I need to get her to cross to the right side of the road before she reaches the centre.

'Have you seen enough?' Vladimir didn't like being exposed. He thought the bridge provided the Americans too good an opportunity to double-cross them. They returned to the warmth of the car. Confirming Jimmy's assumptions, there was virtually no traffic nor pedestrians at that time of night. They wound down the window and listened for the church bell.

* * * * *

For Barb time was dragging. The kitchen clock said 8:25.

'Gee Ms Cooke, you're some cook.' Matt smiled at his own joke again; with his ski mask pulled down over his mouth, she couldn't tell.

Barb cleared away. 'I suppose you won't be doing the washing up?' She said, trying to lighten the mood.

'You suppose right; in my book that's women's work.' The matter of fact way in which he said it caused her hackles to rise. She bit her tongue. *No don't lose it, wait it out. Jimmy will be here soon.*

Matt and Brad went into a huddle. She couldn't make out what they were saying. They both looked at her before returning to their conversation.

'Okay Ms Cooke, we're going to try calling those Russians one more time.' Before Matt had chance to pick up the phone it started ringing. Barb was nearest and instinctively picked it up.

'Hello.' She heard Jimmy's voice: *Hi Barb say nothing, try not to look surprised. We've got a plan to get you out, just do as I say and trust me.* Matt snatched the handset off her.

'Who is it?' He put his hand over the mouthpiece, mouthing to Brad, 'It's Kavanagh.'

Matt returned to his phone conversation. 'Right Kavanagh, as you already seem to know we are holding Ms Cooke and yes, we want you, so this is what I suggest.' Matt was interrupted. He listened as Jimmy told him of the exchange on Maidenhead Bridge at midnight. He relayed Jimmy's words to Brad—Barb also heard.

'So Ms Cooke. Do you know the bridge and the Riviera Hotel?'

'Absolutely, it's a quarter of an hour's walk past our offices and straight down. At this time of night there'll be no one around.' She was unsure what to think.

She mulled over Jimmy's words. He obviously had some plan. She really had no choice but to do as he said and trust him.

Matt slid open the patio windows leading onto the balcony. A burst of cold air swirled around the room, 'It's cold out, you'll need a coat.' He sounded quite concerned.

Barb had trouble reconciling her kidnapper with a caring individual. *I suppose he isn't all bad,* she thought.

'Brad, come on, stay with us, it's time we moved.' Matt shook him. He'd fallen asleep behind his sunglasses. 'Now Ms Cooke, the way we're going to play this is you're going out first. We'll be right behind you with a gun trained on your back, so no funny business. I want you to walk to The Riviera. We'll follow at a discreet distance. One thing: never look back. Wait at the hotel. We've agreed midnight. Once the bell starts chiming, you start walking nice and slow. If I say stop, then do, and come back. Have I made myself clear?' The kidnapper in him had taken over.

'Yes, fine, I've no choice.' She sounded matter of fact.

'You do as I say and we'll all live happily ever after.' He checked his watch. 'Let's make a move.'

She was glad something was happening, even if she didn't really know what. Composed, she was certain Jimmy wouldn't put her in danger. From the coat peg, she chose her least favourite just in case it got lost, damaged or whatever.

'Now?' She wanted confirmation from them. Matt motioned to her. Opening the front door and stepping over the threshold hit her in a way she hadn't expected; the smell of the air, feeling its freshness brush her cheeks; tiny but significant. From the landing there was a wide, expansive view, not a great one, but there was distance between her and other objects, buildings, cars or whatever. It didn't matter. The walls of her flat were oppressive, almost claustrophobic. Now she was surrounded by space. She descended the steps, moving through the passage to the High Street. Her hearing was in overdrive, listening for any sound to tell her where they were; nothing was forthcoming. The urge to turn around was difficult to fight. Were they, weren't they? She hadn't heard her front door close. Now a new horror entered her thoughts. *What if they left the flat without locking the door?* All her things, her precious, sentimental things would be stolen. She started to list the items one by one. These thoughts were more upsetting than being held captive.

She progressed down the High Street. It was deserted — even The Bear was closed. All the stragglers had gone, and only a single car passed by. The drumbeat from the speakers at full volume announced its presence long before it came into view. Barb kept her focus forward, not daring to look. The driver might take it as a signal to stop, talk or worse, he might be cruising. *No, be sensible — not with speakers so loud!* Her imagination was running away with her. Passing the Zylog offices, she stared up at the windows hoping there might be someone working very late who might just be looking out of the window as she walked past. Remote but possible.

Reaching the A4 the bridge was clearly visible

with its distinctive Victorian street lamps. She focussed on it, desperate to see something, anything to give her hope. Nothing stirred, not even an urban fox. Alone, vulnerable and frightened, the Riviera's neon blue sign loomed up. *Okay, now I just wait,* Barb thought. Jimmy's words — *Just do as I say and trust me*—were her only comfort in this stressful time.

'Bong,' the clock chimed for the first of twelve times. Barb set off. Her heart was beating louder than the church bell. The first step became two, then three. *Not too fast.* Advancing, more of the bridge came into view. On the other side of the road she saw Jimmy. Her pace quickened. She was now in the middle of the road. He was getting larger as he came towards her. She completely crossed the road. They were heading directly towards each other. Only a couple of lamp-posts separated them.

They touched. There was no hugging nor speaking. In a single movement he'd ripped her coat off letting it fall to the ground. Without hesitation, in a deft move he lifted her onto the balustrade, and pushed her over the edge. He jumped with her. Instinctively she took a gulp of air, clamping her nose shut with her hand. The cold river water engulfed them both. Everything went black, she felt numb. Her feet hit the river bed; she pushed hard, as if fighting for her life. When she broke the surface, she was in Jimmy's arms; he kept her head above water. Swimming under the arch, the swift current added impetus. Struggling against the flow Jimmy dragged them into the shallows. He wanted to stay in the shadow of the bridge.

Nestled between the bridge structure and the Riviera hotel was the ramshackle wooden construction of the Rowing Club. It was built close to the bridge façade but far enough away to allow someone who was desperate to hide; to crawl into the gap created. Conscious, confused and oh so cold, Barb tried not to let the sound of her shivering give their position away.

Unable to see much, their listening sense was heightened. Neither spoke. Their breathing was shallow; they strained at every sound. The Thames flowed past, unhindered by lock or weir. Sitting rigid with fear late at night with the KGB and CIA lurking nearby, the sounds of little bubbles and eddies thrown up by the current, which would normally go un-noticed, took on massive proportions. The Church bell sounded again. Chiming only once; it gave them a sense of time. Some half-hour had passed, and Jimmy felt it was now safe to speak.

'Yeah, sorry about that. I know if I'd told you to jump you'd have refused. Forgive me but I did it to save us.'

'Where do you think they are?' Barb's whisper was barely audible.

'Given the KGB on one side and the CIA on the other and on British soil, I shouldn't be surprised if they backed off. A shoot-out on Maidenhead Bridge wouldn't go down too well in the news. I didn't want to take any chances. Rob lives at Bray, it's only twenty minutes walk. If we go to your flat or my house someone's bound to be watching. The road down by the hotel's a dead end. It turns into a footpath under the railway bridge. We'll go through there and pick up the Bray Road, well away from here.'

'Ah shit.' Barb tried to stand—she was less than ladylike. 'My leg's gone to sleep.' She managed a crouching position. 'Just wait a minute till I get some feeling back.'

'Better now?' Jimmy was keen to get moving. 'When we're out of here, I'll be able to support you more easily.'

Progress was slow. Behind them the bridge was getting smaller, more distant with each step. Soon it was out of sight.

At Rob's no lights were. Not wanting to wake the whole house, Jimmy took a handful of gravel and threw it up at the bedroom window. A curtain drew back. Rob pressed his face to the glass. It disappeared only to reappear when the front door opened.

'Quick, get in here.' They didn't need a second invitation. 'Quiet, the kids are asleep. Look at you, you're soaked. Barb, up to the en-suite, Claire's up there, she'll sort you out. Jimmy, at the top of the stairs is the bathroom. You shower, I'll find you something to wear. I'll make you up the sofa bed in the lounge. We'll talk in the morning.

*   *   *   *   *

Vladimir and Oleg watched Jimmy go. With each chime he went further onto the bridge.

'Why we cannot see her?' Oleg was sure something was wrong.

'It is bridge. It rises up in curve in middle so you cannot see across ... zere, look, here she comes.' Vladimir felt happier now.

'She is crossing road towards him. Zat is not supposed to happen.'

'Where is your heart? Zey are lovers. Of course she wants to feel his embrace.' Watching them took Vladimir to some romantic place where all was well with the world. He was lost in his thoughts.

'So what he doing?' Oleg was pointing. 'Look, he has taken her coat off.' Before he'd finished speaking, Oleg had flung the car door open and was off running towards them.

'Leave zem.' Vladimir witnessed their performance. Before Oleg had taken a dozen steps, the pair had disappeared over the side of the bridge. The inky black waters swallowed them up. Oleg ran across the carriageway oblivious to the oncoming car. The driver's swift reaction saved him. He couldn't see them in the river. He moved further onto the bridge to get a better view. Instead he saw two men watching him. They were on the Maidenhead side, not moving — their fixed expressions and intense glares told him to go no further. He returned their stare. Instinctively his hand went for his shoulder holster. Before his fingers closed around the stock both Americans had their weapons trained on him. Vladimir caught up; he could see all three.

'Oleg, do not think about it. Zis is England, zey are Americans, we are Russians, come back towards me, slow, no sudden movements.'

Oleg retreated — the Americans did the same. The bridge, devoid of spies, returned to its purpose; to carrying people and traffic. With a last look over his shoulder, Oleg saw the Americans heading in the direction of the town centre.

On the drive back to London, Vladimir radioed in to get number 44 cleared, cleaned, swept of bugs and returned to what it normally was; a home, a sanctuary from the hustle and bustle of living in a major city.

'Do not despair, Oleg. Jimmy Kavanagh will, I am sure, reappear at some point or some place. You listen to my words.' He closed his eyes, letting the events of the last few days play out in his head.

*   *   *   *   *

Claire's Friday started at six thirty, with two very energetic children wanting her undivided attention. She tried her best to keep them entertained. Inevitably, Jimmy and Barb were woken.

Turning a sofa into a bed and the sitting room into a bedroom didn't ascribe them the usual norms of privacy or restricted access. It was a free for all; Claire with tea, the children bouncing everywhere, and Rob trying to get to the bottom of the events of the previous night.

'Jimmy, what's going on? Who are these people? Why did Barb get taken hostage?' Rob couldn't contain himself.

Jimmy took the next hour answering his questions as best he could or wanted to.

'So is that it? Is that the last of them? Should you go to the police or MI5 or whomever?' Rob thought more could be done.

'Rob, what would be really helpful,' Barb sounded forlorn, 'is if you'd go to my flat and check the front door. If my place has been burgled then without doubt, I'm going to the police.'

'Why don't all three of us go? That way you can see for yourself.'

'And collect some things. I'm going to spend a few days at my parents'. I'm not feeling great about sleeping there with those two lurking about, or ever again if the truth be told,' She sounded sad at the prospect.

The door to Flat 2, 32 High Street was firmly locked. Apart from a table lamp glowing pointlessly, everything was as it should be. Barb was very relieved.

'Rob, tell Mike I'll ring him after the weekend. Just say I had an emergency at home. He'll understand.' Barb busied herself packing. 'What about you, Jimmy?' She sounded diffident.

He checked his watch. 'I'm still on my course. If I go now I'll be there for morning coffee.'

'Do you think that's wise? Won't they be watching the place?' Rob was looking out for him.

'Yeah, maybe, but Spurs are playing Chelsea Saturday. I quite fancy going.'

'Damn football! I don't know what grown men see in that game. A load of fellas chasing a leather ball around a grass field watched by others wasters in freezing conditions.' Barb expressed her feelings in no uncertain terms.

'You got somewhere to stay?' Rob sounded envious.

'Think so, a B&B, of sorts. The landlady does a great breakfast.' Jimmy smiled from ear to ear. 'I've a feeling she'll have a room for me ...'

EPILOGUE

Barb never lived back in her flat. She couldn't bring herself to stay in a place with such memories. Zylog, or more precisely Mike Wiley, created a post of a North West Regional Sales Director, based in Chester. The proceeds from the flat's sale provided her with the funds to purchase a significant property in Alderley Edge, Cheshire. She and Jimmy remain friends but only via telephone or email, although they did see each other at monthly sales meetings in Maidenhead. Barb still has John's phone number but as of yet, has not rung it. She doesn't have a current boyfriend.

Rob and Claire took their cruise. They spent quality time together. Jessica, already three years old, is a constant reminder of their Caribbean trip.

After an internal investigation, Special Agent Brad Mason was reassigned duties. He now edits the Belgian section of the CIA World Fact Book from a small office North of Washington, Virginia. Matt Serrano, on the other hand, took early retirement to devote his time to the Paranormal Research Society of North America (PRSNA). He's recently been credited by the Society for sightings at the Manor in Vicksburg, Mississippi. During the American Civil War, the house was used as a hospital for both Union and Confederate soldiers. Many died there, and haunt the place today.

Oleg's interest in the paranormal waned in favour of technology, or more precisely emerging digital gadgetry. The latter opened up new opportunities to listen, see, record, transport, track and store information far faster, more reliably and with greater accuracy than any *human* power. He still works for the KGB.

Vladimir on the other hand, can be found at the Café de Flore on Boulevard Saint-Germain, Paris, talking to anyone who'll listen, regaling them with stories of his exploits in the KGB, without naming names of course. If their concentration lapses, he makes a cigarette butt jump from the ashtray, or a teaspoon fall from the saucer. He says the look on their face is worth a thousand words.

Jimmy was right in his assumption. Both bed and breakfast were on offer. Sheila felt the same, and he moved in permanently. They now have season tickets for Tottenham Hotspurs, never missing a match when their hero Stevie Hodge plays.

As most of Jimmy's customers were London based Government Departments, Zylog were extremely happy to let him relocate to Lancaster Mews.

*   *   *   *   *

'Jimmy,' Sheila called up the stairs. 'Ave you seen Stevie-'odge? He ain't with me.'

'How far can a baby crawl? He must be close by. Is he in the back yard?'

'The only way he can get out there is frough the cat flap. He'd need the cat's magnetic collar to do that and he ain't got one of those.'

Jimmy went over to the window. 'Well he's out there. Take a look for yourself ...'

'I guess being magnetic runs in the family.' Jimmy smiled to himself.

ABOUT THE AUTHOR

James is a full time fiction author. Prior, he spent 35 years in the IT industry and wrote on a wide range of non-fiction IT subjects including many hundreds of training manuals.

Born 1952 in Oxfordshire, UK, James draws on his local knowledge to provide inspiration and settings for his characters and locations for his plots.

He turned his attention to fiction during the summer of 2009. Writing with unbridled passion was new to him. The excitement of not knowing where a story was going but having an evolving host of characters spurred him on. Written for the inner child in all of us, **The Hole Opportunity** was the first product of his imagination. **A Tunnel is Only a Hole on its Side,** book II of the Hole Trilogy was published in 2013. Book III of the Hole Trilogy—**Marmite Makes a Sandwich, Dynamite Makes a Hole,** is due for release in 2017.

This book, **The Unexpected Consequences of Iron Overload** was written specifically to raise awareness of Haemochromatosis

Currently James is focused on the importance of values in child development. To this end he's written the **Billy Books** series for children and parents.

Websites:www.jamesminter.com www.thebillybooks.co.uk
E-Mail: james@jamesminter.com
Amazon Author Page: amazon.com/author/jamesminter
Goodreads: www.goodreads.com/james_minter
Twitter: @james_minter;
Facebook: www.facebook.com/author.james.minter

OTHER WORKS BY JAMES MINTER

The Hole Opportunity, Book I of the Hole Trilogy

Colin and Izzy Griggs' traditional farming way of life is under threat by red tape from Brussels and Whitehall. Wanting a new way to earn a living Colin takes inspiration from a doughnut, and sets up a "Hole Farming Business". His first job is to supply 18 holes for the newly refurbished golf course. Colin's ineptness leads to a number of incidents surrounding the grand opening, creating an arch enemy of the Club's Captain: Major Woods.

His business is given a much needed boost by the arrival of Lady Wills into the Manor House. She requires holes for her ornate ponds but before awarding the contract needs a reference from Colin's previous employer: Major Woods.

How will Colin manage to get the reference he needs to save his business? How exactly can you farm holes? And who is really wearing the stockings in the Griggs household?

Set in the rural village of Henslow, this book is a true English farce with miscommunication, double-entendres, humorous plot lines and a host of memorable characters. PG Wodehouse would be proud.

A Tunnel is Only a Hole on its Side, Book II of the Hole Trilogy

Book II and sequel to the well-received *The Hole Opportunity*, sees Colin striving to build on his business success by turning his attention to supplying even larger holes.

The town of Harpsden is to get a bypass; the proposed route cuts directly across the golf course. After much local objection led by the Golf Club Captain, Major Woods, a compromise route is drawn up involving a half-mile tunnel section under the fairways. The contract for the tunnel is, in Colin's eyes, a perfect way to grow his hole business since a tunnel is only a hole on its side!

With no love lost between the Major and Colin, the ensuing debacle spawns a host of hilarious situations, scrapes and misunderstandings including the resurgence of stocking wearing but this time not by Colin.

Marmite Makes a Sandwich, Dynamite Makes a Hole,
Book III of the Hole Trilogy

The news story of 15 previously unknown Constable drawings hits the national media. The news is picked up by the leader of a London gang with a reputation for bank jobs. He decides a trip to the country to liberate them is an easy earner.

Having found Griggs Hole Farming on the internet, he seeks the help of Colin's hole making skills to break into the local branch of Lloyds bank. However, Colin's loyalty to his community versus his love and affection of his wife, Izzy, puts him to the test. Stocking wearing appears again but this time not on legs ...

The Billy Books,
An Eight Book Series for 7 to 11 year olds.

Billy and his friends are children entering young adulthood, trying to make sense of the world around them. Like all children, they are confronted by a complex, diverse, fast-changing, exciting world full of opportunities, contradictions, and dangers through which they must navigate on their way to becoming responsible adults.

What underlies their journey are the values they gain through their experiences. In early childhood, children acquire their values by watching the behaviour of their parents. From around eight years old onwards, children are driven by exploration, and seeking independence; they are more outward looking. It is at this age they begin to think for themselves, and are capable of putting their own meaning to feelings, and the events and experiences they live through. They are developing their own identity.

The Billy Books series supports an initiative championing Values-based Education, (VbE) founded by Dr Neil Hawkes. The VbE objective is to influence a child's capacity to succeed in life by encouraging them to adopt positive values that will serve them during their early lives, and sustain them throughout their adulthood. Building on the VbE objective, each Billy book uses the power of traditional storytelling to contrast negative behaviours with positive outcomes to illustrate, guide, and shape a child's understanding of the importance of values.

This series of books helps parents, guardians and teachers (PSHE Key Stage 2) to deal with the issues that challenge children who are coming of age. Dealt with in a gentle way through storytelling, children begin to understand the challenges they face, and the importance of introducing positive values into their everyday lives. Setting the issues in a meaningful context helps a child to see things from a different perspective. These books also act as icebreakers, allowing easier communication between parents, or other significant adults and children, when it comes to discussing difficult subjects.

INTERNATIONAL HAEMOCHROMATOSIS ORGANISATIONS

Hemochromatosis Society Australia Inc	www.haemochromatosis.org.au
Canadian Hemochromatosis Society	www.toomuchiron.ca
Association Hemochromatose France	www.hemochromatose.fr
Hemochromatose Vereniging Nederland (Holland)	www.hemochromatose.nl
Irish Haemochromatosis Association	www.haemochromatosis-ir.com
New Zealand Haemochromatosis Support & Awareness Group	www.ironz.org.nz
Haemochromatosis Society of South Africa	www.haemochromatosisza.org
Iron Disorders Institute (USA)	www.irondisorders.org
L'Associazione per lo Studio dell'Emocromatosi e delle Malattie da Savraccarico di Ferro	http://www.emocromatosi.it/